COMRADE COWGIRL

What Reviewers Say About Yolanda Wallace's Work

24/7

"This story is intense, exciting, a bit erotic, romantic and very, very good!!"—*Prism Book Alliance*

"Ms. Wallace as always delivers an entertaining read that is fun and well researched. Thrill seekers this is your book."—*The Romantic Reader Blog*

Break Point

"I adored this book. I'm not big into tennis but I cared about both of the main characters. I like that they both basically stuck to their morals to do the right thing rather than the thing that people were trying to make them do instead."—*Blow Pop's Book Reviews*

"Wallace captures the spirit of the time, from the changing attitudes of the Great Depression, to the terrifying oppression of the Third Reich, working in real events and people to construct a vibrant setting. The romance is strong..."—*Publishers Weekly*

"[*Break Point*] is so full of suspense, gads I nearly bit my fingernails to the quick! The characters are so easy to care about. The near constant anxiety as I worried endlessly for Meike's life was almost too intense. It was interesting to see Helen grow and so painful to see what Meike was put through but when they were together it was such a relief!"—*Prism Book Alliance*

"*Break Point* is a heart wrenching story set at the height of WWII with a refreshing perspective—of Germans who do not endorse of the actions of Hitler and his henchmen and of an American being manipulated by an FBI agent for government purposes. This is countered with the love story of two people, who might be destined to find completion together, but first, they must overcome obstacles that sometimes seem impossible—a compelling tale of history and compassion, destiny and enduring love."—*Lambda Literary Review*

"If you are a sports fan this book will definitely appeal to you. …[A] well written tale."—*The Romantic Reader Blog*

Divided Nation, United Hearts

"I found myself totally immersed in the story of Wil Fredericks, a woman who runs away to join the Union army disguised as a man and meets the woman of her dreams. …Yolanda Wallace has managed to write a wonderful love story set against the worst of times. I loved it and highly recommend this book. Five stars!"—*Kitty Kat's Book Review Blog*

"*Divided Nations, United Hearts* delivers on its promise."—*Just Love Reviews*

Tailor-Made

"An enjoyable romance that hit several harder-to-find demographics in the lesbian romance market: a religiously observant protagonist, an interracial relationship, and a gender-nonconforming protagonist."
—Veronica Koven-Matasy, Librarian, Boston Public Library

"Wallace has proven to be a varied writer who crafts diverse characters in a wide range of settings, and this take on a simple, sweet, butch/femme love story really showcases her soft writing style and firm grasp of lesbian romance. This story reads easily and flows smoothly. It had me smiling from the first page"—*Love Bytes Reviews*

True Colors

"[In *True Colors*], Robby has three jobs, none of which is likely to endear her to the President or his advisors. As well as working in her friend's shop, she also writes a pseudonymous political blog and performs as a go-go dancer in a popular lesbian bar. When [the President's daughter] Taylor asks her on a date, Robby at first thinks only of the gossip she might pick up for her blog. As the two grow closer, however, Robby—as well as Taylor—has to work out how much, if any, of her life she is prepared to sacrifice for love. I really enjoyed this book. ...I definitely want to investigate this author's back catalogue as soon as I get some spare reading time."—*The Good, The Bad and The Unread*

The War Within

"*The War Within* has a masterpiece quality to it. It's a story of the heart told with heart—a story to be savored—and proof that you're never too old to find (or rediscover) true love."—*Lambda Literary Review*

Rum Spring

"The writing was possibly the best I've seen for the modern lesfic genre, and the premise and setting was intriguing. I would recommend this one."—*The Lesbrary*

Murphy's Law

"Prepare to be thrilled by a love story filled with high adventure as they move toward an ending as turbulent as the weather on a Himalayan peak."—*Lambda Literary Review*

Lucky Loser

"Yolanda Wallace is a great writer. Her character work is strong, the story is compelling, and the pacing is so good that I found myself tearing through the book within a day and a half."—*The Lesbian Review*

Visit us at www.boldstrokesbooks.com

By the Author

In Medias Res

Rum Spring

Lucky Loser

Month of Sundays

Murphy's Law

The War Within

Love's Bounty

Break Point

24/7

Divided Nation, United Hearts

True Colors

Tailor-Made

Pleasure Cruise

Comrade Cowgirl

Writing as Mason Dixon:

Date with Destiny

Charm City

21 Questions

COMRADE COWGIRL

by
Yolanda Wallace

2019

ISBN 13: 978-1-63555-375-8

This Trade Paperback Original Is Published By
Bold Strokes Books, Inc.
P.O. Box 249
Valley Falls, NY 12185

First Edition: March 2019

CREDITS
EDITOR: CINDY CRESAP
PRODUCTION DESIGN: SUSAN RAMUNDO
COVER DESIGN BY JEANINE HENNING

Acknowledgments

I always empathize with my characters when I'm working on a manuscript. Since this book is set on a Russian cattle ranch, I alternately found myself freezing from nonexistent frigid temperatures and craving cheeseburgers that were all too real. Note to self: pick a warmer (and less fattening) locale next time.

Writing is hard work, whether you're working on your first book or your twentieth. Though it doesn't get any easier over time, it does get to be more fun. I had a blast writing *Comrade Cowgirl*, and I hope you enjoy spending time with the characters as much as I did.

I would like to extend my usual thanks to Radclyffe, Sandy, Cindy, and the rest of the Bold Strokes Books team for providing the incredible support system that allows me to continue indulging my favorite hobby.

I would also like to thank the readers for their continued support. You. Are. Awesome.

As always, I would like to thank Dita for continuing to put up with me and all the characters in my head. Ride 'em, cowgirl!

Dedication

To Dita,

Your love of Westerns finally rubbed off on me.

CHAPTER ONE

Laramie Bowman hated hospitals. She hadn't been inside one since she was born. Leave it to Trey to break her streak. Then again, breaking things was something her big brother was especially good at.

There were two hundred six bones in the human body and Trey had broken at least a dozen of his over the years, some more than once. And that was before he had decided to leave the family ranch behind in order to pursue his dream of finding fame and fortune on the rodeo circuit.

Trey was an excellent roper and he could wrestle steer with the best of them, but he was only a fair bull rider, the rodeo event that garnered the most attention from fans and media alike. Thanks to his skills in the timed events, he had been able to rack up enough points to win several competitions. He had the requisite collection of gaudy trophies and even gaudier belt buckles to show for it. More often than not, though, he finished well off the podium but inside the top eight, earning him just enough money to keep fueling his dreams.

His goal was to win one of the major events on the circuit so he could sign a lucrative endorsement deal and save some of the money he spent keeping himself and his horse fed and his piece of crap truck on the road. The sturdy pony was fairly young, but the ancient Ford was on its last legs. Depending on what the doctor said when he got out of surgery, Trey's rodeo career might be, too.

Laramie held her hat in her hands as she paced the halls of Broken Branch General Hospital. Trey had been hurt before, but never this bad. She closed her eyes while images of Trey's accident played through her mind.

Trey had lasted the full eight seconds on the bull he had been riding, a fifteen-hundred-pound Brahman with a bad disposition and an even worse reputation. When he had jumped off the bull and attempted to clear the ring so he could see how the judges had scored his ride, the bucking, spinning bull had made an unexpected turn.

The animal's huge haunches had caught Trey in the side, sending him flying through the air. The crowd, Laramie included, had watched in horror as Trey had slammed into the unforgiving fence surrounding the ring. The bullfighters, once known as rodeo clowns, had prevented the bull from charging Trey's broken body as he lay unconscious in the dirt. Now Laramie and her parents were waiting to see how much damage had been done.

Laramie fingered the bib number pinned to her denim shirt. She had entered the women's barrel racing event so she could test her skills against Sherry Sampson, the sixty-year-old living legend who was favored to win the world championship for the umpteenth time, but she hadn't had a chance to tackle the cloverleaf-shaped course before she had rushed out of the stands to kneel by Trey's side. She had wasted her entry fee and a chance to earn a semi-decent prize check, but no matter. For her, family was more important than monetary rewards.

Rodeo was something she occasionally did for fun. It wasn't a way of life. Ranching was. All she had ever wanted to do was follow in her father's footsteps. To carry on the family legacy. She wished Trey felt the same. If he did, chances were he wouldn't be in the mess he was in now—busted up and out of commission for the foreseeable future.

"Trey's been into worse scrapes than this and came out smiling," Laramie's mother, Nancy, said. "He'll be fine this time, too."

Laramie didn't know who her mother was trying to convince, the friends and family members crowded into the small waiting room, or herself.

Laramie's father, Thaddeus Bowman Jr., was the quintessential cowboy. Hardworking, honorable, and economical with both his affection and his words.

"Yep." He patted Laramie's mother's knee. "He's a tough one, all right."

"He gets it from you, Thad." Shorty Johnson, one of the hands on Laramie's family's ranch, chuckled as he scratched his stubbled chin. The creases in the deep lines etched around his mouth were stained with tobacco juice. He was one of the wisest men Laramie had ever met, but he obviously hadn't learned not to spit into the wind. "I remember the time you worked all day with a busted leg because you was too stubborn to admit it was broke."

Laramie's father's mustache twitched as he tried not to smile. "I reckon that might have smarted some."

"Hell, it hurt me, and I ain't the one who was stuck in a cast for two months."

Chuck Kelsey and Grant Mills, two other ranch hands, joined in the fun.

"That's 'cause the docs can't make casts small enough to fit your skinny frame," Chuck said. "Anything they tried to put on you would probably slide down your leg like a stretched-out sock."

"I 'spect they'd have to try the kids' size," Grant said.

"Sounds about right."

Chuck and Grant, whose combined age was nearly a decade less than Shorty's, shared a laugh at the older man's expense.

Shorty's ears turned red like they always did whenever someone got his goat. He stretched himself to his full five feet six inches and puffed out his scrawny chest. "I might be small, but I still pack a punch. Do either of you cocky bastards want to try me on for size?"

"You boys settle down now," Laramie's mother said. She treated all the ranch hands like family, whether they were related to her or not. They gladly returned the favor. Some hadn't been home in so long she was practically the only mother they had. "This isn't the time or place for all that foolishness."

Chuck and Grant stared at their worn boots as they mumbled words of contrition.

"Sorry, Miss Nancy."

"You're right, Miss Nancy. Apologies."

Shorty and Laramie's mother were about the same age, but he looked chastened, too. "Is there anything you need us to do for you while we wait?"

"You can say a prayer or two in the chapel if you're of a mind."

Shorty looked like he was willing to do anything in the world except that. He ran a work-roughened hand through his thinning salt-and-pepper hair. "I've never been on what you might call a first-name basis with the man upstairs, but I'll give it a try if you think it might help. Come on, boys. Let's go take a knee."

Chuck and Grant followed behind Shorty like a couple of calves trying to keep up with the herd. They had been doing that since the day they were hired. Even though he'd say otherwise if asked, Shorty liked their attention. They teased him sometimes, as young men were known to do, but when it came time to work, they didn't hesitate to follow his orders. Shorty was their mentor and they, like the rest of the ranch hands, were willing to work themselves into the ground in order to earn his respect.

After Shorty, Chuck, and Grant left, Laramie's mother turned her attention in Laramie's direction. "Sit down before you wear a path in the floor."

Laramie didn't like sitting still. After countless years of twelve-to fourteen-hour days, she was used to being on the move. To always having something to do besides sit and wait and imagine the worst. But she dutifully did as she was told.

"Are you worried about Trey?" her mother asked.

Laramie shook her head as the clock on the wall silently marked the passing of another hour. "He's too stubborn to go out like this."

"Then what's on your mind?"

Laramie didn't want to say, but her parents had taught her to be unfailingly honest.

"I'm worried about how we're going to pay for all this. Insurance covers only so much, and the ranch's finances are tight as it is without adding Trey's medical bills to the mix. If he gets out of—" Seeing her mother's stricken expression, she quickly corrected herself. "*When* he gets out of here, he's probably going to be in rehab for a while. Physical therapy isn't cheap."

Her father regarded her through narrowed eyes. "Are you thinking about accepting that job offer?"

Laramie nodded. "I don't see any other way."

A few months before, the ranch was one of many in the area that had received an email from Sergei Ivanov, a Russian businessman whose fortunes had taken a hit after the bottom fell out of the oil market. To recoup his losses, he had decided to join the recently reinvigorated Russian agricultural industry. He bought thousands of acres of pastureland in the central part of the country, stocked it with cattle, and hired a bunch of locals to feed and care for them.

According to Sergei's email, the locals didn't have any idea how to do the jobs they had been hired to do, and he was on the lookout for two experienced ranchers to show them the ropes. Preferably American and preferably from Wyoming since the state's climate was so similar to central Russia's—relatively mild in the summer and nearly desolate in the winter.

Laramie's father had taken one look at the amount of money Ivanov said he was willing to pay and laughed off the email as too good to be true. Laramie, however, hadn't been able to dismiss the offer so easily. If Sergei was true to his word, he could provide her and her family a much-needed lifeline.

"Are you sure?" Laramie's mother asked. "You've always been a homebody, and that place is an awful long way from home."

"It typically takes two to three years to take a herd from ranch to market," Laramie said. "If the hands are fast learners, I'll be back in no time."

"And what if they take a while to catch on? Their winters are just as long and cold as ours. What will you do if you get lonely? You can't spend every night taking potshots at starving predators trying to make a meal out of the cattle. When it's twenty degrees below outside, it feels pretty good having a warm body to snuggle up to."

Laramie knew what her mother was getting at. Homosexuality was illegal in Russia. Even though Laramie didn't wrap herself in the rainbow flag or march in pride parades, she had always been honest about her sexuality. Doing so in Godoroye, the small town where Sergei Ivanov's ranch was located, could result in a much more serious rebuke than the occasional frown of disapproval she and a girlfriend received when they sat too close to each other in the bleachers at a college football game or slow danced in a cowboy bar.

"His company's offering four times what I can make here. For that amount of money, I can stand a few lonely nights."

"Three years' worth?" Her mother turned to her father for backup. "Are you really going to let her do this, Thad?"

Laramie's father started to say something, but he clammed up when Lloyd Whitaker, Trey's surgeon, walked into the waiting room. Dr. Whitaker's paper cap was soaked with sweat, and his scrubs were stained with blood. Trey's blood.

Fearing the worst, Laramie swallowed hard. "How is he, Doc?" she asked as her parents clung to each other for support.

Shorty, Chuck, and Grant returned from the chapel just in time to hear the prognosis.

Dr. Whitaker removed his surgical cap and took a deep breath before he began to speak.

"When Trey was brought in, he looked like he'd been in a car crash. He had a ruptured spleen, four cracked ribs, a broken clavicle, and a dislocated hip, but we managed to repair the damage. He has a long road ahead of him, and he might need to have his hip replaced one day if arthritis sets in, but he's going to be fine."

"Oh, praise Jesus." Laramie's mother dabbed her eyes with a tissue. "When can we see him?"

"He's in recovery now. I plan to keep him sedated a while longer. His body needs time to heal. I'll fetch you as soon as he starts to come around."

"Thanks, Doc." Laramie's father pumped Dr. Whitaker's hand. "I appreciate what you did for my boy. The next time you need a case of steaks, just say the word."

Dr. Whitaker squeezed Laramie's father's shoulder. "Let me get him back on his feet first, Thad, and I'll be sure to take you up on that."

"Tell it to me straight, Lloyd." Shorty asked the question that was on everyone's mind. "Will he ride again?"

Dr. Whitaker chuckled as he tried in vain to smooth his tousled hair. "Based on the extent of his injuries, I wouldn't recommend it.

But he's a Bowman, so I know better than to tell him no. That will just motivate him to try even harder to prove me wrong."

"Like father, like son," Shorty said as he, Chuck, and Grant exchanged jubilant slaps on the back. "I told you he'd pull through."

"Yes, sir, you sure did," Chuck said. "If you'll excuse us, Mr. and Mrs. Bowman, we'll be getting back to the ranch now. It's still light out and we've got work to do."

"Thanks for coming, boys," Laramie's mother said. "Make sure you get something to eat before you work yourselves into the ground."

"Yes, ma'am. We sure will," Grant said. "Pearl isn't as good a cook as you are, but she won't be getting any complaints from me tonight, that's for sure."

After everyone cleared out of the waiting room, Laramie's father took her by the arm and turned her to face him.

"If you're taking that job just for the money, don't. We'll make a way somehow. We always do. But if you look me in the eye and tell me you're doing it for the adventure, I will drive you to the airport myself."

Laramie was daunted by the idea of spending three years in a foreign country with no idea how to speak the language or what the local customs were, but she was thrilled by the challenge. She had been in Trey's shadow since they were kids. She had never minded it before, but maybe this was her chance to shine.

"Ranching's my life," she said, "but I always dreamed I would see more than the backside of a steer one day."

"So did I," her father said with a faraway look in his eyes, "but I guess my kids will have to do it for me."

He draped his arm across her mother's shoulder, signaling the matter had been settled. Her mother didn't look happy, but Laramie knew she could count on her to support her decision. Whether her mother agreed with her or not, she trusted Laramie's judgment.

"Watch out for yourself over there." Her mother's grip was firm, but her hands trembled as she held Laramie's hand in both of hers. "Don't forget where you came from. And, most importantly, don't forget who you are."

Laramie returned the pressure. "Never."

She was a Bowman. It might not mean much where she was going, but it meant everything to her.

Anastasia Petrova ordered a *kvas* and turned her back to the bar. Even though she was in what was supposed to be a safe space, she couldn't afford to let her guard down. Lyubov was the most popular gay club in Moscow, which made it a target for everyone who wanted to see the club shut down and its regulars thrown in jail for daring to frequent an establishment that catered to queers. That could be anyone from government officials to private citizens.

The fight for gay rights in Russia was an uphill struggle. It had been for years. None of the various organizations Anastasia had joined had been able to gain much traction in the seemingly hopeless battle to have some of their country's more provincial laws overturned, namely the ones that labeled her and her friends as criminals simply for being who they were.

The current regime's propaganda machine was much more effective at getting the word out than Anastasia and her cohorts were, but she refused to admit defeat. She spent her mornings organizing protest marches that yielded little to no results, she spent her afternoons trying to hand out flyers to disinterested or downright hostile passersby, and she preferred to spend her nights gleefully breaking most of the laws she hoped to eventually abolish.

"Would you like to open a tab?" a bartender in a black mesh tank top and gold hot pants asked as he filled a chilled mug with a fermented beverage made from rye bread.

"No, thanks."

Anastasia slid a few rubles toward him. The cover charge had taken a large bite out of her limited budget. She needed to go easy tonight if she wanted to have enough money to pay her half of this month's rent. One drink, perhaps two if she met someone she wanted to impress, but certainly no more than that. Otherwise, Mischa would be on the hunt for a new roommate, and she would be looking for a generous friend or sympathetic ex-lover who would allow her to sleep on their couch until she saved enough money to get a place of her own.

Mikhail Ivanov ordered his usual *mors* and leaned forward to check out the bartender's ass as the bartender poured the drink. *Kvas* was slightly sweet, but *mors* wasn't nearly as subtle.

"How do you drink that stuff?" Anastasia asked as Mischa gave the bartender a generous tip, along with his phone number. The non-carbonated fruit drink he favored was made from berries, fruit juice, water, and enough sugar syrup to send her into a diabetic coma.

"The same way I do everything else: with style." He took a sip of his drink and checked out their surroundings. "This place is usually packed on Fridays. The crowd's so thin tonight everyone will be going after the same people."

"You're not afraid of a little competition, are you?"

"No, having to work for it makes the conquest that much sweeter."

"Not as sweet as that drink you're guzzling."

"You're just jealous because I can drink as many of these as I want without having to worry about losing my girlish figure." Mischa struck a pose like a supermodel on the cover of a fashion magazine. "But seriously. Where is everyone?"

"Didn't you hear? There was another crackdown last week. A marriage equality meeting I was attending was broken up by a group of anti-gay vigilantes who chose to practice their own version of conversion therapy using crowbars instead of psychobabble. They cracked a few heads, but no one was seriously hurt."

Mischa's mascara-accented eyes widened. "Are you okay?"

"I escaped out the back door before they managed to surround the place. That's why I always insist on meeting in venues that have more than one exit. Nothing ever happens to me. I'm bulletproof, you know that."

"You're lucky is what you are, but everyone's luck runs out eventually. I'm worried about you, Ana. You're starting to make a name for yourself. You need to be more careful."

"I need to be less out, you mean?"

"You need to learn to play the game. How many jobs have you lost because you insisted on telling your bosses and co-workers that you're a lesbian?"

Anastasia lowered her eyes. "Too many to count."

"And what will you do if the next employer decides that firing you isn't good enough and reports you to the authorities instead? You could be labeled an enemy of the state. No one talks about it, but everyone knows what happens to those people. Do you want to be the next person who dies or disappears under mysterious circumstances?"

"If I didn't know any better, I'd think you actually cared about me."

Anastasia tried to muss his perfect hair, but Mischa grabbed her hand before she could.

"I need you to stop joking around and listen to me for once."

Anastasia was rendered mute by the seriousness in Mischa's tone. She often teased him about sounding like a nagging aunt. Tonight, he was even worse than usual. She knew he meant well, but she wasn't accustomed to having people worry about her. To having someone care. She wasn't sure if she liked it.

She had been forced to fend for herself almost from the minute she was born. Her parents, whoever they were, had left her on the steps of an orphanage in Drezna when she was a few days old. She and dozens of other kids had grown up in that accursed place. Some had eventually gotten adopted. Others, like her, hadn't been so fortunate. She had run away when she was seventeen and had been on her own ever since.

An armchair psychologist would probably tell her she fought so hard to update the definition of family because she didn't have one of her own. Their arguments might have merit, but she wasn't in the habit of self-examination. She had more important things to do than sit around navel-gazing. Like changing the world, for starters. Tonight, though, she'd settle for a drink, a few laughs, and a beautiful woman to share both. After, that was, she listened to Mischa's latest lecture.

"I'm not asking you to go back in the closet," Mischa said. "I know the very idea is anathema to you."

"Then what are you asking me to do? Be one person by day and another by night like you?"

In the mornings, Mischa dressed as conservatively as the other cubicle-dwelling drones in the accounting firm he worked for. When the workday was done, out came the makeup and more daring fashions.

"I'm the same no matter where I am or who I'm with," she said. "Anything else is too much work."

"We both know you're allergic to that, right? Is that the real reason you can't keep a job? Because you're too lazy to make the effort?"

Anastasia winced. Mischa's barb had unexpected sting.

"I'm sorry. I didn't mean that. Come here." He set his drink on the bar and gave her a hug. "I admire you for not playing by society's rules. Maybe I'm a little envious, too. I want to tell my family who I really am, but they wouldn't understand."

"Then it's a good thing I don't have a family."

Anastasia took a sip of her *kvas* to help her stomach the lie. She tried not to get too attached to anyone so she wouldn't end up getting hurt, but sometimes she yearned to belong to someone so badly she couldn't stand it.

"Do your parents still think I'm your girlfriend?"

Mischa laughed. "Mama keeps asking why it's taking me so long to make an honest woman out of you."

"You should tell her that's never going to happen."

"I've tried. She just changes the subject from weddings to grandkids."

Anastasia nearly choked on her drink. "I love you, Mischa, but not like that."

"The feeling is mutual, believe me." He was quiet for a moment, then he gave her a tentative glance. "Are we okay?"

"Yeah, we're okay," Anastasia said as she locked eyes with a gorgeous redhead who was sending her all the right signals.

When the woman offered her an enticing smile, Anastasia knew she'd be taking her home tonight. She didn't want to make her move too soon, though. There was no need to rush what felt like a sure thing.

"My finances aren't okay, but we are."

"If you don't mind a change of scenery, my uncle has a job you'd be perfect for."

"Which uncle?"

"Sergei."

Anastasia frowned. "Isn't he the guy who has memorized all the lines from John Wayne's movies and asks everyone to call him Duke? The braggart who says the city of Ivanovo was named for your family but doesn't have any evidence to prove it?"

Mischa nodded. "He's a little weird, but he's a good guy."

"Is he still rich?"

"Not as rich as he used to be, but he still has more money than most."

"What's the job?"

"He recently got out of the oil business and bought a thousand acres of pastureland in Godoroye."

Anastasia frowned. "Godoroye? That's in the middle of nowhere."

"I know, but it's apparently the perfect place for a cattle ranch. Lots of room for the cows to roam and plenty of grass for them to eat while they do it."

"Who does your uncle think he is, one of the Khachanov brothers?"

Viktor and Aleksander Khachanov were the principal owners of a prominent agribusiness company. Together, they had purchased more than a million acres of property in the Russian heartland, set up over a thousand ranches, and stocked them with almost four hundred thousand head of cattle. They hired locals to work on their ranches and brought in foreigners to train their employees. Brazilians. Australians. Even a handful of Americans had answered the call. The Khachanovs supplied beef to some of Moscow's hippest restaurants, where customers were willing to endure a thirty-minute wait for a gourmet hamburger.

"Uncle Sergei says he wants to learn from the Khachanovs' example," Mischa said. "Their business model has proven successful and he plans to follow it to the letter. He's hired a couple of Americans to train his staff. Neither of them speaks Russian and none of the ranch hands speak English so he needs a full-time translator to act as a go-between. I would love to get paid to be surrounded by a bunch of cowboys in tight jeans all day and night, but your English is better than mine. Do you want the job? It's a three-year gig."

"How much does it pay?"

"More than what you're making now."

"Funny."

She didn't want to spend three years dodging cow patties on a cattle farm several hundred kilometers from real civilization. And anti-gay sentiment was even worse in small towns than it was in vast metropolises like Moscow and Saint Petersburg. But a paycheck was a paycheck and she desperately needed one.

"I'll think about it and let you know tomorrow."

"Tomorrow? Why not tonight?"

Anastasia finished her drink and set her empty mug on the bar. "Because I see someone who needs my company more than you do."

Mischa followed her line of sight. "She's pretty."

"I know."

"I think I've seen her somewhere before."

"That's supposed to be my line."

"No, I mean it." Mischa grabbed her arm. "I've seen her and the two guys she's with."

The redhead was standing between two nervous-looking men who were chugging bottles of beer. They were acting like it was their first time in a gay bar and they were trying to work up enough courage to make a move on someone.

"Did you see them here?"

"No."

"Then where?"

"I'm not sure, but something doesn't feel right." Mischa set his half-finished soda down and pulled her toward the door. "Let's go."

"We just got here."

"Trust me, okay?"

Anastasia didn't protest. Mischa had a nose for danger. She had faith in his instincts. If he sensed something was off with the trio, she chose to believe him. Even if it meant she would be sleeping alone tonight instead of with the beautiful stranger she had her eye on.

The redhead sidled in front of her before she and Mischa reached the door. "Leaving so soon?"

The woman was even more enticing up close than she was from a distance. Ignoring the voice in the back of her mind trying to convince her that Mischa might be wrong for once, she tried to find a polite way to blow the woman off.

"We have a party to get to. Our friends are waiting."

"I would like to be your friend tonight," the redhead said. "Where's the party?"

The way the redhead looked in her white lace blouse and black miniskirt, Anastasia wished she had a party to take her to, then steal her away from.

"On Nikolskaya," she said quickly, naming one of Moscow's most upscale streets.

"I know where that is," the redhead said. "We will walk with you."

"That's okay," Mischa said forcefully. "We can manage."

"Are you sure?" one of the toughs with the redhead said. "You look like you need a strong man to protect you."

When the guy made a clumsy attempt to stroke Mischa's face, Anastasia spotted the gun stuck in the waistband of his pants. Mischa must have spotted it, too, because he tightened his grip on her arm.

"Maybe next time."

They walked out of the club and onto the street. As they walked, they constantly looked over their shoulders to make sure they weren't being followed. Anastasia doubted the trio would try anything on a crowded sidewalk, but she didn't want to take any chances.

"Now I know where I've seen them before," Mischa said once they were a safe distance away. He touched her arm, signaling her to slow her pace. "It was in a selfie in my friend Marat's phone. Those three must have been who he crossed paths with the night he was bashed."

Three weeks before, Marat's neighbors had made repeated calls to the police to report a disturbance. When the cops had broken down the door to Marat's apartment, they had found him beaten and bloodied on his bedroom floor. The official investigation had chalked it up as a sexual encounter that had turned violent. Everyone except the police knew better, even though Marat had been in a coma ever since and had been unable to identify his attackers.

"We should go to the police," Anastasia said.

"And do what?"

"Describe what those three look like so the cops can arrest them before they attack someone else."

Mischa lit a cigarette and blew out an angry plume of smoke. "The police don't care about people like us, Ana. Most of the cops I've come across would rather reward people like that than arrest them. They can do anything they want to us. *We're* the criminals, remember?"

Anastasia hated the helpless feeling that washed over her when she realized Mischa was right. She looked back at Lyubov. How could a place whose very name meant love be the target of such hate?

She had moved to Moscow in search of a better life. Perhaps one day she could finally find it. If not here, then somewhere she could truly be free. Getting there took money. Money she didn't have.

"Tell your uncle I'll take the job."

CHAPTER TWO

"If I had known I'd have to spend three whole days catching planes in three different countries," Shorty said as he and Laramie headed to the baggage claim area after their plane landed in Moscow, "I never would have let your mama talk me into following you all the way to Russia to keep an eye on you."

Laramie tried to determine which of the many luggage carousels corresponded to their flight. As she and Shorty traveled farther and farther east, she spotted fewer and fewer signs that were written in English. She had gotten real good real fast at figuring out what various illustrations were supposed to represent, but she couldn't make heads or tails out of Cyrillic. The alphabet was filled with so many strange symbols it reminded her of a physics equation, and math had never been one of her strong suits.

"Save the tough talk for Chuck and Grant," she said as she searched for someone who might be able to lead them in the right direction. "I've known you longer than they have so I know all about the tender heart you're hiding underneath all that bluster."

Shorty slapped his sweat-stained Stetson against his leg. "Just make sure that's a secret you keep between me and you, hear? There ain't no reason for you to run around telling everybody else about it."

"I'll keep your secrets if you keep mine."

"That's a promise I doubt either one of us will come close to breaking. Not here, anyway." He resettled his hat. "I don't know where the hell we are now, but it ain't Wyoming, that's for sure."

"Welcome to Moscow, Shorty. Tonight, it's our home away from home."

He took a wary glance around the bustling airport as hundreds of passengers speaking what sounded like nearly as many languages hustled to and fro.

"Given a choice, I'd rather sleep in my own bunk. At least I'd know what I'm in for."

"I know what you mean."

Shorty looked as uncomfortable as Laramie felt. She couldn't blame him. They had flown from Denver to Chicago yesterday, followed by an overnight flight that had taken them to Frankfurt, Germany. Today's first leg had taken them from Frankfurt to Saint Petersburg, their second from Saint Petersburg to Moscow. Their final destination was Godoroye, a town nearly three hundred miles away, but the airport that serviced it was so tiny it received flights from Moscow only three days a week. The next available flight wasn't until Wednesday morning, which meant they would have to check into a hotel for the night after they met with Sergei Ivanov, their new boss.

She was tempted to hop a train to get the final part of the journey over with, but she had heard the Russian transportation system was notoriously finicky and she was too worn out to deal with the added stress. At that moment, all she wanted to do was find someone who spoke English.

After she spotted a uniformed airport employee, she walked over to him and held out her boarding pass. "Can you tell me—"

"*Nyet*," he said sternly before she could finish her sentence.

"Do you speak—"

"*Nyet*," he said again before he abruptly turned and walked away.

"I take it *nyet* means *no*," Shorty said sarcastically.

"And you thought you weren't going to be able to understand what anyone was saying over here."

"If we stay long enough, I'm sure I'll pick up a few other choice words along the way."

"Just make sure you don't teach any. We came to train these boys, not corrupt them."

Shorty grinned, a welcome sight to see among so many grim faces.

"I've got to leave my mark somehow, don't I? These next three years will seem a lot longer if I have to worry about holding my tongue. If these fellas are real cowboys, they'll be able to take a good dressing-down without running home crying to their mamas."

"As long as nothing gets lost in translation."

"Speaking of which, how can we be sure the translator Ivanov hired is saying what we want him to instead of making stuff up?"

That was one of many unpleasant scenarios running through Laramie's mind. She hadn't had a good night's sleep since they'd left Wyoming, her thoughts preoccupied by everything that could possibly go wrong. She was used to taking orders, not giving them. She was starting to wonder if she was ready for the increased responsibility. She had felt certain she could handle the challenge when she left Broken Branch, but more and more, doubts crept in the farther she found herself from home.

It's too late to second-guess yourself. You've already jumped out of the frying pan into the fire.

And she was starting to feel the heat.

At thirty-one, she was too old to need looking after, but she was glad Shorty had decided to make the trip with her. It would be nice having someone familiar to lean on when she felt like she was about to fall flat on her face.

"I guess we'll just have to lead by example," she said, trying to allay Shorty's concerns as well as her own. "Most of what we do can't be taught. It has to be learned from experience."

"Sounds like we're going to be spending most of our time playing charades," Shorty mumbled under his breath.

"Let's hope we have better luck in the future than we are today."

"Are you American?" someone asked after a second employee walked away without giving Laramie the information she needed.

"Yes, I am."

Laramie was so grateful to hear someone besides her and Shorty speaking English she barely noticed the thick accent in which the words were delivered. What she couldn't miss was the beauty of the woman who had sought her out.

The woman's dark hair was styled for comfort rather than fashion. She was wearing jeans, sneakers, and a T-shirt with a picture of a defunct boy band on the front. Laramie wasn't too keen on the woman's taste in music, but she liked what she saw.

The woman's eyes were so blue they reminded Laramie of the sky back home. One of them, at least. Her left eye had an imperfection similar to the one sported by an actress on one of Laramie's favorite TV shows. A birthmark that made it appear that her pupil had blown. The image was arresting.

"This is you?"

The woman pointed to the sign she was holding, a laminated piece of paper with Laramie's and Shorty's names printed on it.

"Yes, it is," Laramie said with a sigh of relief. She felt like she and Shorty were finally starting to make progress.

"I am Anastasia Petrova," the woman said. "I am translator. After you get luggage, I take you to office of Mr. Ivanov so he can discuss job with you."

Laramie was anxious to get the meeting behind her so she and Shorty could do what they had come here to do: work.

"Laramie Bowman. Pleased to meet you."

Laramie held out her hand. Anastasia regarded it for a moment before giving it a tentative shake. She did the same when Shorty removed his hat and extended his hand.

"You are Pernell Johnson?"

"You can call me Shorty, ma'am."

"Shorty?"

Anastasia said the word as if trying it on for size. She must have liked the fit because she flashed a shy smile as she released Shorty's hand.

"Don't be fooled by my small stature," Shorty said with a wink. "I make up for it in other ways."

"I will...how you say?" Anastasia scrunched her face into an adorable frown as she tried to come up with the appropriate phrase. "Ah." Her face lit up when she finally found the phrase she had been searching for. "I will take your word for it."

"Well, all right then." Shorty leaned to whisper in Laramie's ear. "I don't know how good of a translator she is, but she's got spunk, I give you that."

Anastasia certainly had something, though spunk wasn't the word Laramie would have used to describe it. She had been told she and Shorty would be provided with a translator, but she had no idea who that person would be. She had been expecting someone who looked as rough-and-tumble as the land she and Shorty would be ranching, not someone who seemed so slight she would probably blow away in a stiff breeze.

Anastasia looked like she was in her mid to late twenties, but her eyes belonged to someone several decades older. Laramie wondered what sights had left her with such a haunted look. She quickly banished the thought from her mind. She hadn't flown halfway around the world to chase after a woman, no matter how intriguing. She was here to make enough money to keep her family's ranch going and earn enough leadership experience to be able to run it one day. She couldn't allow anyone to get in the way of her goals. Her family's future depended on it.

"May I?" Anastasia reached for Laramie's boarding pass. She examined it for a minute or two, then said, "You will follow me, yes?"

"You bet your sweet ass—" Shorty quickly turned apologetic after Laramie shot him a look. "I mean, yes, ma'am, we sure will. Lead the way."

"You never told me your real name was Pernell," Laramie said as they trailed Anastasia through the maze of carousels.

Shorty screwed his Stetson back in place. "What did we say about keeping secrets?"

"You will find bags here."

Anastasia pointed to a carousel that had already started ferrying luggage from the plane to the terminal. Laramie recognized a few of the people surrounding it as passengers from her flight. The middle-aged man wearing white knee-high socks and black sandals had been seated in front of her. He had inclined so far he had practically slept in her lap the last two hours of the trip.

She relaxed a little, knowing she and her belongings would soon be reunited. Having tangible reminders of home made her feel less like a stranger in a strange land. She didn't care about her clothes. She had brought jeans and work shirts. Nothing fancy. She could buy more if she had to. But she would be lost without her saddle. She'd had the same one since she learned to ride, and she longed to put it to use now. To strap it to a decent mount and spend hours tending to the herd.

Did the men she would be training even know how to ride a horse? Lord, she hoped so. Because if they didn't, she and Shorty would have to teach them how to do that, too. One more thing to add to her growing list of duties.

"Have you been working for Mr. Ivanov long?" she asked as Anastasia returned her boarding pass.

"No, today is…how do you say? My first day."

"So I guess we're both still learning the ropes, aren't we?"

Anastasia frowned as she considered the question. "I am sorry. I do not understand. What are you meaning by ropes?"

"Huh?"

Laramie felt like they were talking in two different languages even though they were allegedly speaking the same one.

Looks like the ranch hands aren't the only ones who've got a lot to learn.

Anastasia didn't know what to make of the Americans. Shorty's gruff exterior provided a stark contrast to his impish sense of humor. He lacked sophistication, but she liked the fact that he was unpretentious. He seemed to have nothing to hide, which meant she would always know where she stood with him. She definitely couldn't say the same as far as Laramie was concerned. Shorty made his feelings and intentions clear. Laramie's thoughts were harder to discern.

Try impossible.

At least Shorty allowed his true personality to shine through. Laramie seemed so caught up in making a good first impression she couldn't relax and be herself.

After their initial meeting, Anastasia was left wondering if Laramie ever thought about anything other than work. Did she ever go dancing, have a drink, make love, or do anything remotely resembling fun? She was so dedicated to her job she probably never did anything that didn't involve the care, feeding, or marketing of cattle.

Anastasia could be single-minded, too, when the cause was dear to her heart, but she wasn't immune to succumbing to an attractive distraction every now and then.

Laramie might consider herding cows an enjoyable diversion, but Anastasia could think of much better ways to pass the time. She could be doing several of them right now. Instead, she was being forced to shepherd two complete strangers through the streets of Moscow so they could spend the afternoon meeting with Mischa's eccentric uncle. Hopefully, she wouldn't have to babysit them tonight, too. Mischa had planned a surprise going-away party she wasn't supposed to know about, and she wanted to enjoy every second. It was her last night in a real town for the foreseeable future, and she wanted to make it a night to remember.

After Laramie and Shorty located their possessions, Anastasia grabbed a luggage cart so they could pile their suitcases and saddles onto it. She couldn't believe they had dragged the bulky saddles all the way from America. The well-oiled leather certainly smelled good—like a mixture of sweat and sunshine—but the only horse she had ever ridden was on a merry-go-round, and she intended to keep it that way. If she wanted to risk life and limb, she didn't have to travel all the way to Godoroye for that. She could stay in Moscow and do it for free.

Chances were she would be working for free, too, since no company she knew wanted to be associated with an out lesbian, and the gay rights organizations she did volunteer work for couldn't afford to pay her a decent salary.

She would have been lost without Mischa. She was grateful he had put in a good word for her with his uncle. Sergei had been more than happy to hire his favorite nephew's "girlfriend." Would he have been so generous if he knew the truth about their relationship? Probably not.

Now she had to find a way to be true to herself without betraying Mischa in the process. She couldn't out herself without casting suspicion on him, too. Her family had already turned their backs on her. She would never wish the same fate on her friends.

Shorty pushed the heavily laden cart through the crowded airport as Anastasia led the way to ground transportation. For such a small man, he was stronger than he looked. Was there also more to Laramie than met the eye? While Laramie's attention was diverted by a group of Lithuanian tourists in tie-dye T-shirts squabbling over which sight to see first, Anastasia give her a once-over.

Laramie was at least a head taller than Shorty. The tips of her shoulder-length blond hair were bleached nearly white from constant exposure to the sun. She wasn't wearing a hat today, but she must wear one when she worked because the top half of her forehead was bone white and the rest was as tanned as her handsome face. She had broad shoulders and the thick thighs of a footballer, though Anastasia suspected the well-developed muscles had come from hours spent gripping a horse's sides while riding at full gallop rather than running after a soccer ball for ninety minutes at a time.

The mental image of Laramie astride a horse like a Valkyrie from Norse mythology gave Anastasia an unexpected rush of pleasure. Powerful women always got her going, and Laramie exuded strength from every pore. Anastasia was wildly attracted to her, but she knew nothing could possibly come of it.

If she and Laramie slept together even once, they would have to keep the encounter a secret from everyone in the company they both worked for. If they made it a common occurrence and successfully managed not to draw attention to themselves, that didn't change the fact that Laramie would be returning to Wyoming after she imparted the knowledge she had been hired to share.

Why should Anastasia literally risk her life on something that wasn't meant to last? On someone who would walk out of her life as easily as she had sauntered into it?

She hoped Mischa had invited more women than men to tonight's party. She wanted a pleasant memory to hold on to while she spent the next three years silencing her own voice in order to act as someone else's.

When she, Laramie, and Shorty reached the sidewalk, she hailed a cab and gave the driver the address to Sergei Ivanov's office, which was located in a skyscraper in Moscow's commercial district. Laramie and Shorty climbed in the back seat of the cab. She took the front. She would be sharing quarters with them soon enough. Until then, she needed some space.

"Take the long way around," she said in Russian as the taxi driver started the meter. "Show them a little of what the city has to offer."

"Gorky Park and the Kremlin?" he asked.

"Red Square, too. Try to get as close as you can to Saint Basil's Cathedral."

She had never been inside Moscow's most famous church, but visitors couldn't seem to get enough of the fanciful architecture.

"Who's paying for this tour, you or them?"

He looked at her as if he didn't think she could afford the fare.

"Don't worry about it. You'll get what's coming to you."

She flashed some of the money Mischa's uncle had fronted her for cab fare. Even with the impromptu detour, the bills in her hand were way more than she needed for the drive from the airport to the office and the short jaunt from the office to the hotel. Perhaps she could conveniently forget to return what was left at the end of the day. No, being considered a thief would not only reflect badly on her but Mischa as well.

She wasn't used to taking someone else's feelings besides her own into account. No wonder she couldn't manage to keep a girlfriend. She had thought it was because she was too open, but perhaps it was because she was too selfish.

Something to work on while I'm stuck in Godoroye.

Even though she couldn't speak the language, Laramie seemed to sense something was amiss.

"Is there a problem?"

Anastasia turned to look at her.

"We have time before your meeting with Mr. Ivanov so I asked driver to show you some popular attractions," she said in English. "Would you like to take tour now or see city on your own?"

Laramie and Shorty conferred with each other. He seemed keen on exploring Moscow after the meeting so he would have time to take it all in, but she said something about having to be at the airport at the butt crack of dawn and he changed his mind.

Anastasia made a mental note to do some research on common American colloquial expressions so she could figure out what they meant. If she couldn't understand what Laramie was saying, how was she supposed to explain it to someone else?

"Now's fine," Laramie said.

Anastasia relayed the information to the taxi driver, who put the car in gear and pulled into traffic.

"Your friends have strange accents," he said. "Where are they from?"

"Wyoming."

The word was so exotic she said it slowly so she would be sure to pronounce it correctly.

"Where is that?"

"The American West."

She hadn't known anything about Wyoming until she'd gone on the internet and performed some research. The images she had come across were breathtaking. Wide grasslands with snow-capped mountains looming in the distance. Gorgeous waterfalls spilling into crystal clear rivers. And shaggy buffaloes roaming everywhere. The huge animals looked like yaks but were twice the size. She wondered if they looked as big in person as they did in the photographs she had seen. If so, what a sight they must be.

"Americans, huh?" The taxi driver switched to English as he looked back at his passengers. "Uncle Sam. Yankee Doodle Dandy." He flashed a thumbs-up sign. "Yippee ki-yay, motherfucker."

Laramie's mouth fell open in shock. Her expression was so comical Anastasia had to force herself not to laugh. She knew doing so would make the situation worse instead of better.

Shorty certainly didn't find the situation as amusing as she did. He looked so mad she thought he was about to climb over the seat.

"Do you care to repeat yourself, bub?" he asked.

The taxi driver shrugged.

"What did I say?" he asked in Russian. "Bruce Willis is an American movie star, no? The little man has never seen *Die Hard*? Ask him if he wants to watch my copy. I have a DVD he can borrow."

"What's he going on about?" Shorty asked. "If he's trying to get smart, tell him to pull the car over so we can settle this man-to-man."

"There's no call for that," Laramie said. "Calm down, Shorty. He didn't mean any harm."

"Could've fooled me."

"He's like a chicken with wet feathers," the taxi driver said. "They should call him Rooster instead of Shorty."

Anastasia shook her head at the absurdity of both men. She couldn't decide the best way for them to settle their differences: resorting to their fists or splitting a bottle of vodka. Unfortunately, they didn't have time for either.

"Forget the tour," Laramie said. "We've got a meeting to get to. Just take us to the office."

"As you wish."

Anastasia wasn't surprised to discover Shorty had a quick temper. Most men who were small in stature tried to use every means at their disposal to make themselves seem bigger than they actually were. Some bought fancy cars. Others, like Shorty, picked fights for no reason.

Laramie was evidently used to dealing with Shorty's moods, though, because she had taken his outburst in stride. Her voice was soothing as she calmed him down. Like a mother soothing a restless child. Anastasia could have listened to her all day.

What did it take to make the stoic American's pulse quicken, she wondered, and why was she so eager to find out?

CHAPTER THREE

When the cab stopped in front of an office building in downtown Moscow, Laramie couldn't get out of the car fast enough. The ride had been one of the most awkward journeys she had ever taken, and she was relieved it was over. While Anastasia paid the fare, she and Shorty retrieved their belongings from the trunk of the car.

"I thought you were supposed to be looking after me, not the other way around," she said as she hefted her saddle onto her shoulder. Thankfully, her suitcase had wheels so she didn't have to carry it, too. "This isn't Broken Branch. There's no Sheriff Billingsley willing to let you off with one night in the pokey when you get caught committing a minor offense. If you get in trouble here, no matter what the charge, you could spend the rest of your days in a gulag somewhere. If you think Wyoming's cold, try Siberia."

"I know."

Shorty looked abashed, but Laramie wanted to make sure he truly got the point and wasn't simply saying what she wanted to hear until she decided to let the matter drop. He was worse than a kid when it came to being reprimanded. He didn't want to listen to the lecture. He just wanted it to be over.

"That man wasn't trying to disrespect you. He was trying to make conversation. He barely speaks English and you don't speak any Russian. There's a language barrier, remember?"

"Yes, I do. And I slammed right into the obstacle. I don't know what got into me. I guess I'm just tired and ornery from all this traveling. I'm gonna shake hands and make things right. I don't want us to part ways with him thinking ill of me." He set his saddle on his suitcase and hitched up his jeans. "If you're still worried about whether you can do the job, don't be. You're as good as your mama when it comes to telling people what for."

Shorty's playful wink took some of the sting out of his words. Despite the manner in which it was delivered, Laramie was grateful for the vote of confidence he had given her. She had been questioning herself practically since she had accepted Sergei Ivanov's job offer. She couldn't let her doubts show, however. If she didn't believe in herself, neither would the men she and Shorty had been hired to train.

She remembered how nervous she had been before her first barrel racing competition. How she had felt like throwing up when she tried to mount her horse. The stakes were higher this time—her family's livelihood was on the line instead of a fancy blue ribbon and a tiny prize check—so the nausea she felt now was ten times worse than it was then.

"Mr. Ivanov is waiting," Anastasia said after she helped Shorty make amends with the cab driver. "We go inside?"

"Yes, please."

Laramie took a deep breath and followed Anastasia into the building. The gorgeous view of Anastasia's jeans hugging her hips and thighs helped settle her nerves. It also helped spike her libido, which was something she hadn't planned on happening.

She dragged her eyes away from the tantalizing sight. She was here to work, not make friends. And taking a lover was definitely out of the question. But three years was a long time to go completely without. Fueling a few fantasies couldn't hurt anyone. She took another look. This time, Anastasia caught her staring.

Anastasia's eyes betrayed a flicker of interest, but her expression hardened into a frown. Anastasia shook her head, but Laramie couldn't tell if she was shutting her down completely or cautioning her to be more careful. Sometimes it was harder to read a woman's mind than it was to rope a steer. Missing her mark with Anastasia could prove to be much more than a minor annoyance.

Laramie's first impulse was to apologize, but she didn't want to draw unwanted attention to the incident. If she did, she could be the one who ended up cooling her heels in jail tonight instead of Shorty.

Anastasia led them to an elevator that allowed them to see outside the building as they slowly ascended. They were in the car so long Laramie felt like they were making a trip to heaven instead of the building's top floor. She admired the panoramic view of the city, taking in some of the sights she and Shorty had missed out on when they had been forced to pass up the tour Anastasia had proposed.

She spotted Red Square in the distance. She had seen it in an old Sean Connery movie, but it was even more breathtaking in person than it was on the TV screen. Colorful Saint Basil's Cathedral looked like a large-scale gingerbread house. She was tempted to pinch herself to make sure she wasn't trapped in a contemporary fairy tale.

"I haven't been up this high since I took a trip to Jackson Hole a hundred years ago," Shorty said.

"I didn't know you liked to ski."

"I don't, but I like spending time with snow bunnies, if you catch my drift. When I retire, I'm thinking of buying a cabin and settling there. I can go hiking or whitewater rafting in the summer, and watch city folk try not to break their fool necks on the slopes in the winter."

"I've never heard you talk about the future before." His favorite subjects had always been the past and the present, not what was to come. "I always thought you'd be glued to your saddle until it was time to put you in the ground."

"So did I."

"What changed your mind?"

"You proved me right."

"How did I do that?"

"I always knew Trey would never be level-headed enough to run the ranch when Thad finally decides he's had enough, but I suspected you might be. Trey was born a dreamer. He still is. He's a good man, he's as tough as they come, and I love him like he was my own son, but he doesn't have a head for business. He would rather play cowboy than be one. He spends his time competing on the rodeo circuit and chasing tail instead of putting in a hard day's work. He's not like you. You chase tail on occasion, too," he said, his voice barely above a whisper, "but you're smart enough to know that there's a time and a place for such things. Even when you were a little girl, you never got too worked up whenever something went wrong. When the time comes for you to take over the day-to-day operations, you'll be fine on your own. You won't need me to wipe your ass for you."

Laramie smiled to herself. Shorty had been treating her like one of the boys for so long he often forgot she wasn't one. Coming from him, there was no greater compliment.

"If Chuck and Grant stay dedicated to the task of learning how things work," Shorty continued, "they'll be there to back you up."

"What if they've moved on by then?"

"There'll be someone else to take their place. There always is. We'll get them trained up, too, just like we're gonna do with these boys."

Good ranch hands were hard to find. And even harder to keep. If the competition didn't offer them more money to draw them away, they sometimes went into business for themselves. Laramie never held it against them when employees put in their notice. She liked when people showed ambition. When they reached for something more instead of settling for what they already had.

Were the hands on Sergei Ivanov's ranch equally ambitious, or were they simply happy to have a job? She wanted workers with fire in their bellies, not clock-watchers who did as little as possible while they counted the minutes until they collected their next paycheck.

The elevator bounced to a stop and the doors slid open, revealing a large room filled with dozens of cubicles and an equal number of bustling employees. Sergei Ivanov's empire encompassed many business interests besides ranching, and he apparently housed each of his various companies in the same building. The shared space cut down on each company's operating costs, but how was anyone supposed to know who was responsible for what?

Laramie preferred organization, not chaos. She had spent some time in the ranch office the summer her mother had taught her how to keep the books, but she had never worked in a space like this one. A space filled with ringing phones, overlapping conversations, and so much background noise she was surprised anyone ever got anything done. Give her the mooing of cows, the neighing of horses, and the occasional distant howl of a wolf any day.

Anastasia walked up to what Laramie assumed was the receptionist's desk and addressed the woman sitting behind it. As they conversed in their native tongue, Anastasia pointed to Laramie and Shorty. The receptionist nodded, picked up the phone on her desk, and spoke into the receiver. She listened for a moment, then ended the call.

"Mr. Ivanov will see you now," Anastasia said.

She had barely gotten the words out before a portly middle-aged man wearing a tracksuit, designer cowboy boots, and a bad toupee came barreling out of the main office.

"Welcome, my friends." He shook Laramie's and Shorty's hands with more enthusiasm than was probably warranted. "I am Sergei Ivanov. You must be Laramie Bowman and Pernell Johnson, yes?"

"Call me Shorty."

When Ivanov smiled, his capped teeth were so white it looked like he had a mouthful of candy-coated chewing gum. "Call me Duke. I am big John Wayne fan. You?"

"I've always been more partial to Gary Cooper," Shorty said.

Laramie didn't have a dog in the fight. To her, a good movie was a good movie, no matter whose name appeared above the title.

"*High Noon* was great picture, pilgrim," Duke said, "but *The Man Who Shot Liberty Valance* is better, no?"

Duke's belly shook as he laughed, reminding Laramie of Santa Claus. In this case, though, the proverbial sack he was carrying was filled with money instead of toys.

He invited her and Shorty into his office so they could talk, but it was more of a monologue than a dialogue since he didn't give them a chance to get a word in edgewise.

"How was your flight? Would you like something to drink? Water? Beer? Vodka? I have everything. Name it and it is yours."

Laramie set her luggage in a corner of the room and took a seat at the small conference table positioned near the floor-to-ceiling window.

"Thank you, but I don't drink on the job."

"Drinking makes job more fun."

Duke poured three shots of vodka. He handed one to Shorty, one to Anastasia, and kept one for himself.

"Don't mind if I do," Shorty said before he downed the shot.

Duke laughed again and refilled Shorty's glass. "You are, as they say, man after my own heart." He emptied his glass, then reached for the bottle. "Drink up, Ana. You're falling behind."

Anastasia rushed to catch up with Shorty and Duke. Laramie was getting a buzz just watching them.

"I speak English so we won't need Ana's services during our meeting," Duke said. "Is shame, no? One less pretty thing to look at while we talk business. My nephew is lucky man, wouldn't you say?"

"Your nephew?"

Anastasia had pinged Laramie's gaydar the moment she laid eyes on her. Learning that Anastasia was romantically involved with a man instead of a woman threw her for a loop.

"Ana's lover is my brother's son Mischa. I used to think Vasily was too soft on him when he was growing up, but Mischa turned out to be good boy. A real man's man." Duke pounded his chest with his meaty fist. "He and Ana have been dating for five years now. Is long time to spend time together with no ring to show for it, but they are right to take their time to come to a decision. Nothing ruins love faster than marriage. Trust me. I have been married four times."

"How many times have you been divorced?" Shorty asked.

"Three," Duke said, "but the fourth could happen any day now. That is why I keep good lawyer on retainer."

Shorty's eyes listed to half-mast as he and Duke cackled at the joke. He could drink beer until the cows came home, but he had never been able to handle his liquor. If he downed one more shot, he'd probably snore his way through today's meeting. If, that was, Duke ever got around to starting it.

Anastasia set her shot glass on the table and waved off Duke's offer of another drink.

"I must check on hotel reservations to make sure everything is in order."

When she turned to Laramie, her cheeks were flushed from either alcohol or embarrassment. Laramie felt for her. It couldn't be easy working for a man who insisted on making her private life a public spectacle. She hated to think she might soon be subjected to the same treatment. She liked playing her cards close to the vest, not displaying them for all the world to see.

"I take you to hotel after meeting," Anastasia said. "There is good international restaurant on first floor, but there are many other places to eat nearby if you would like to try local food."

The only Russian dish Laramie was familiar with was borscht, and she wasn't in the mood for beet soup.

"Will you be joining us for dinner?" she asked hopefully.

No matter where she decided to dine, she didn't know if she would be able to navigate a menu without help. Having a familiar face around couldn't hurt, either, even if it belonged to someone who was involved with someone else.

"No, I already have plans."

"What kind of plans?" Duke asked.

His tone suggested that, depending on Anastasia's answer, he might ask her to make some adjustments to her schedule in order to accommodate his.

"Mischa is throwing farewell party for me."

"Of course he is."

Duke wrapped a possessive arm around Anastasia's shoulders. She seemed to endure rather than enjoy the attention. Did Duke's nephew have a similarly outsized personality or did he have other qualities that attracted Anastasia's interest? Laramie couldn't help wondering what those qualities might be—and if she possessed them.

"Since I will be keeping you and Mischa apart," Duke said, "I cannot deny him a chance to give you a proper good-bye." He gave Anastasia a kiss on the top of her head before he freed her from his grip. "You two enjoy yourselves tonight. I will do my best to make sure our guests are entertained."

Anastasia caught Laramie's eye on her way to the door. "Enjoy your evening."

Once again, Laramie was struck by the depth of emotion behind Anastasia's gaze.

"You, too," she managed to stammer.

She didn't know what kind of entertainment Duke had in mind for her and Shorty, but she could easily imagine him taking them on a tour of Moscow's finest strip clubs. She didn't want to watch bored dancers gyrating for tips. She planned to spend the first part of the night sitting in her room with her feet up while she devoured a juicy steak and a nice baked potato accompanied by an ice cold beer. She planned to spend the rest of it trying to convince herself she wasn't the least bit attracted to a woman who was practically part of her new boss's family.

❖

Anastasia was disappointed by the turnout. Mischa had invited plenty of women to her farewell party, but she had already slept with most of them. The rest had either failed to spark her interest or rebuffed her advances. Either way, it was plain to see she wasn't getting laid tonight. Or any time soon, for that matter.

She told herself it was for the best. She didn't want to revisit the past and she couldn't afford to invest in something new. Not when she was only a few hours away from catching a plane that would take her far away from everything she knew and everyone she loved.

Godoroye was a beautiful town, but it was also incredibly remote. Anastasia wasn't counting on Wi-Fi, but she hoped she would at least have a cell phone signal. If not, she'd be stuck trying to hold a meaningful conversation with a bunch of cows whenever she got bored or lonely.

Unless they were trying to get into your pants, most Russian men only talked to other men. The Americans, thousands of miles away from home with only each other to lean on, would probably stick to themselves, leaving Anastasia where she had always been: on her own. She had never minded it in the past. Now it didn't hold the same appeal. What she had once called independence now felt like something else. Something she couldn't define. Something she didn't want to claim.

The kitchen sink had been filled with ice and converted into a makeshift cooler. As she grabbed another bottle of beer from the dwindling supply, Anastasia found herself wondering what Laramie and Shorty were doing tonight. Was Sergei dragging them to all the businesses he owned to show off some of his vast wealth?

She smiled at the thought of the Americans being subjected to one of Sergei's infamous nights on the town. She hoped he wouldn't pull any of his usual tricks. If he did, Laramie might never be the same again. Though she was hard to figure out, Anastasia liked her just the way she was. Liked her perhaps a little too much. If they had met under different circumstances, maybe they could have—

"None of that."

Anastasia stopped her imagination from running wild. She had no place in her life for what-ifs. Only what truly was. Still, she couldn't help wondering if she should have offered to accompany Laramie and Shorty tonight. Not to translate but to run interference between them and Sergei. Perhaps Laramie had refused his invitation and decided to venture off on her own. A far more likely scenario, in Anastasia's opinion.

Would Laramie and Shorty be able to communicate, or would they be lucky enough to find someone who spoke English? Restaurants that served international cuisine had English translations on their menus. Most menus in establishments featuring Russian cuisine, however, were printed solely in Cyrillic.

Anastasia imagined Laramie and Shorty wandering into a local restaurant, blindly pointing to something on the menu, then being presented with some exotic dish they had never seen before. She laughed at the thought of Laramie holding her nose while she tried to eat a bowl of sour *shchi*, cabbage soup made with sauerkraut.

"Lucky for them, burger and pizza sound the same in any language."

She doubted Laramie would become fluent in Russian while she was here, but Anastasia hoped she would pick up a few words and phrases. Doing so would make Laramie's job considerably easier. Her attempt to learn the language would alleviate some of the communication issues she would have to face, but the men she had been hired to train would also view it as a sign of respect. Would they, in turn, give Laramie the respect she deserved? Would they be willing to take orders from a woman? Anastasia had her doubts. She had a feeling Laramie might have a few of her own, both about the job and about her.

She still remembered the look on Laramie's face when Sergei had said Mischa was her boyfriend. A look that was simultaneously shocked, relieved, and disappointed. She had sensed Laramie's interest in her even before she had caught her checking out her ass, but

Laramie's forlorn expression after Sergei made his big announcement had confirmed her suspicions.

At the time, she had longed to correct Sergei's statement. She still did, but she was unable to do so. Revealing the truth about her relationship with Mischa—revealing the truth about her—would result in negative ramifications for both of them. She would lose the job she so desperately needed and he, just as certainly, would lose his family.

Mischa was her best friend. More than that. He was like a brother to her. She knew how important each member of his family was to him. His parents. His sister. His aunts, uncles, nieces, nephews, and cousins. Even though he complained about them from time to time, he loved them all. She could hear it in his voice when he told one of his famously long-winded stories about them. She could see it in his face when he talked to them on the phone.

She couldn't willingly cost him something he held so dear. No matter what price she had to pay, she would continue to keep his secret—and hers.

She wandered through the apartment she and Mischa shared, stopping every now and then to make small talk with friends she hadn't seen in a while. Even though she hadn't officially moved out yet, she felt disconnected. Like she didn't belong. The feeling was heightened when she discovered two different couples having sex in her bed.

"Great party, huh?" Mischa asked when she returned to the living room and flopped next to him on the couch.

Anastasia felt like the excuse that had brought everyone together, not the reason they were here.

"I should leave every week."

Mischa visibly brightened at the idea.

"We could make that happen. You can catch the train home every Friday and we'll throw a party every Sunday before you head back."

"If it wouldn't end up costing me a fortune in train fare, I'd do it." She leaned her head on his shoulder. "I'm going to miss you."

"Stop. Don't make me cry." He fanned his hands in front of his face. "I'll ruin my makeup."

"We can't have that."

"Tell me about the Americans."

"I already told you."

"I know, but tell me again. The only Americans I've ever come across are tourists asking for directions to some landmark or another. Some were nice. Others were rude to me because my English isn't that great. They thought speaking louder and slower would help me understand them better. Are Shorty and Laramie nice? Are they like the cowboys in the movies Uncle Sergei's always watching?"

"Shorty is. He reminds me of the guys who end up playing the sidekick. He knows how to do the job, and he knows what it takes to be a leader, but he prefers to have a secondary role."

"And Laramie?"

Anastasia considered the question.

"She's not like anyone I've ever seen. The women in those movies always need a man to save them. She doesn't seem like she needs anyone."

"Wrong. She needs you."

"For what? I've never ridden to anyone's rescue."

"That doesn't stop you from trying."

He glanced at one of the marriage equality flyers on the coffee table. Flyers she had helped create and disseminate. She would miss being on the front line of the movement. Perhaps she could continue the fight a different way. And from a distance.

"Laramie already has the right to get married. She doesn't need me to help her do that."

"She needs you to help her get her point across. She might know everything there is to know about ranching, but it won't matter if she can't find the right words to pass on that knowledge to someone else. That's where you come in."

"You're making my role seem much more important than it is."

"Am I? Or are you choosing to downplay it because you don't want to recognize the responsibility you've been given?"

The enormity of the situation had started to become clearer to her over the past few hours. As each minute ticked by, she felt the weight on her shoulders grow heavier. The job she had agreed to perform wasn't the lark she had initially considered it to be. It wasn't just a chance to make some easy money while she stood around and watched the grass grow. Sergei's ranch was part of a multimillion-dollar corporation. Laramie would play a vital role in ensuring its success. So, by extension, would she. Any mistake she made could prove costly in more ways than one.

She took a sip of her beer as she weighed her options. It was too late to back out, but did she have what it took to move forward?

"I've never been important to anyone except you. I'm not used to having people depend on me. I don't want to let you down, Mischa. I don't want to let myself down."

"You won't."

"How do you know?"

"Because I've never seen you want anything as much as you want this. You've been waiting for a chance to prove yourself and this is it. Take it."

He pressed a gentle kiss to the top of her head. His gesture of affection was identical to his uncle's, but her reaction to it was vastly different. She welcomed Mischa's touch, but she had wanted to squirm away from Sergei's. Like most of the things he did, the kiss had seemed more like an attempt to impress his audience rather than express a genuine emotion. Had Laramie bought the act, or had she seen right through it? Laramie's expression hadn't betrayed her inner thoughts. Anastasia wished she knew what they were. What did Laramie think of her? Of the whole situation?

I've got three years to find out.

Mischa's words of encouragement made Anastasia feel better. She lifted her head as her spirits followed suit.

"I grew up not knowing who I was. Maybe it's time for me to find out who I am."

❖

As Laramie had expected, the multiple shots of vodka he had downed before the meeting put Shorty down for the count. He passed out as soon as they checked into their respective rooms. Grateful he had saved them from being subjected to what Duke considered "entertainment," she pulled off his boots, tossed the covers over him, and left a bottle of water by the bed in case he woke up parched during the night.

Once she got Shorty squared away, she set out to find something to eat. The peanuts she'd had on the flight from Frankfurt were long gone. She could use some serious protein. A few carbs wouldn't hurt either.

Her spirits flagged when she tried to place an order with room service. The employee she spoke with said the kitchen was out of steak due to "supply problems." Laramie didn't recognize any of the other dishes on the menu so she decided to visit the concierge desk to see if there were any good restaurants close by that served something she wouldn't have to venture out of her comfort zone to eat.

"There is a good burger place a short distance from here," the concierge said. "It isn't a very long walk, but I could call a taxi for you if you like."

Laramie flashed back to the testy encounter Shorty had experienced with a cab driver that afternoon. They hadn't gotten stuck with the same one during the drive from Duke's office to their hotel, but she didn't want to risk having recent history repeat itself.

"No need to call a cab. I'd like to stretch my legs, and tonight seems like the perfect night for a stroll. What's the name of the restaurant?"

"It's called Beef. *Govyadina* in Russian. Take a right after you exit the hotel and keep going straight until you see this sign." He wrote the restaurant's name in Cyrillic on a piece of hotel stationery and slid it toward her. "If you get confused, look for the line out front. There's usually a thirty-minute wait."

"Is the food that good?"

"Until recently, most of the meat served in local restaurants was imported from other countries. The restaurants that serve Russian beef are very popular. We can never keep enough of it in stock."

An unfortunate fact Laramie had discovered firsthand.

"I guess that explains why I'm here."

"And we're happy to have you. Enjoy your meal."

"Thank you."

Laramie tipped her hat and headed outside. The night air was cool but pleasurably so.

"Not bad for mid June."

The temperature was somewhere between fifty-five and sixty degrees Fahrenheit, if she had to hazard a guess. In that respect, it was just like being at home. Except home was nothing like this.

She took in all the strange sights, sounds, and odors as she slowly walked along the crowded sidewalk. Shops and restaurants lined both sides of the street. Anything she could possibly want was on sale. Storefronts were filled with everything from jewelry to high-end electronics to samples of various exotic-looking dishes. She walked past crispy Peking ducks, pungent cabbage rolls, and fragrant stews. Her stomach growled louder and louder with every step.

Finally, she came across a restaurant with a sign whose lettering seemed to match the note in her hand. The line to get inside was about ten deep.

"Good thing I've got plenty of time on my hands."

The flight to Bryansk International Airport wasn't scheduled to take off until tomorrow morning. The trip itself was supposed to last a shade over ninety minutes, the car ride to the ranch another thirty. Three days of traveling had almost come to an end. Laramie couldn't wait for the "getting there" to be over so the real journey could begin.

As she waited her turn in line, she tried to remember the most important parts of the meeting she and Shorty had had with Duke that afternoon. The logistics appeared to be the same, despite the change in locale. The personnel, however, couldn't have been more different.

Except for the trainers, none of the men Duke had hired had any previous ranching experience. All had toiled at various jobs in Moscow until they had seized a chance to earn a steady paycheck in their hometown. One had been a butcher, one a history teacher, and one a plumber. The rest of the employees in the personnel files had similar stories: no prior experience and no proven ability to do the work.

When she finally got inside, the greeter showed her to a table and handed her a menu. A black-clad waitress whose bright pink hair was pulled back into a ponytail approached her a few minutes later.

"My name is Natalia. What would you like?"

Anastasia ordered a burger and fries and a bottle of beer.

"What kind of beer?"

Natalia's eyes never left the note pad in her hands. She seemed more interested in taking orders than in the people placing them.

"Whatever's coldest."

Natalia flashed a wry smile, then shook her head as if she had heard the line a million times before. "Do you like light or dark beer?"

"I like it all."

The comment finally elicited a flicker of interest. When Natalia looked up from her notepad and met Laramie's eye, her smile soon changed from wry to knowing. Her shoulders relaxed and she nodded to acknowledge their unspoken kinship. When she spoke again, her voice was considerably less frosty.

"We have many brands of beer. Which one is your favorite?"

Laramie was glad to find someone she could be herself with, even if she couldn't completely let down her guard. "Just bring me the one you think is the best."

"You are American, yes?"

Laramie nodded.

Natalia jotted something down on her note pad. "I will bring you Stary Melnik."

Laramie's favorite bar back home had added a few craft beers and imports to its list of staples, but she had never heard of the brand Natalia had suggested. She didn't want to be rude, but she didn't want to waste her money on something she didn't like.

Natalia must have read her expression because she smiled warmly and said, "I am told it tastes like Budweiser. The king of beers, yes?"

When Laramie took a sip, she didn't think the beer tasted like Bud, but it did remind her of everything she had left behind. She closed her eyes as a wave of homesickness washed over her.

"Is good?" Natalia asked.

Laramie opened her eyes. "It's the best thing I've had all day."

Unfortunately, the food wasn't nearly as good as the beer. The burger wasn't terrible, but it wasn't exactly memorable either. She took another bite and chewed slowly as she tried to figure out the mystery. All the flavors were there, but something was missing. It finally came to her as she reached for another French fry. Though the meat was supposedly fresh-ground, it tasted more like the frozen dreck that ended up in most fast food restaurants.

She removed the top bun and took a closer look at what was inside. The cow from which the burger had been derived had been well fed, which was reflected in the quality of the meat, but she could tell the animal hadn't been cared for. It had simply been treated as a commodity.

Laramie finished her meal and pushed her empty plate away from her. She tried not to get too emotionally attached to the cattle in her herds because of the nature of the business she was in, but she made sure each of her charges knew they were valued for more than their market price. She needed to instill that philosophy in the men she had been hired to train so the people of Moscow could discover how a real burger was supposed to taste.

"This job is going to be even harder than I thought," she said to herself as she sipped her beer. "Hopefully, the experience will be worth it."

Now that her hunger pangs had been sated, she leaned back in her seat and indulged herself in a little people watching. Though the locale was different, the dynamic was the same. The tables were filled with friends enjoying each other's company and couples trying to decide if tonight's date would be their first or their last.

Laramie hadn't been gone long and she already missed the give-and-take of going out with someone. Talking to her. Getting to know her. Trying to determine if the attraction she felt was purely physical or could develop into something more.

She stared at a woman seated alone at a table meant for two. Unlike her, the woman seemed to be waiting for someone, if her frequent glances at her watch were any indication. Her dark brown hair was worn up and away from her face. Her makeup was perfect, highlighting rather than obscuring her features. Her dark blue dress was low-cut and clung to her curves. Whoever had stood her up was an idiot who obviously didn't know what he—or she—was missing.

"Careful," Natalia said when she came to clear the table. "Bad things can happen to you if you were to get caught staring at another woman like that in public."

Laramie dutifully dragged her eyes away from the gorgeous brunette across the room.

"That's the second time I've been caught staring today," she said under her breath. "I must be losing my touch."

Natalia indicated Laramie's glass. "Would you like another beer?"

"I'd love one, but you'd better bring me the bill instead. I have an early day tomorrow."

Her flight to Bryansk was supposed to depart at seven, which meant she needed to be at the airport no later than five. She had asked the concierge to give her a wake-up call at three thirty in case the batteries in her travel alarm clock decided to give up the ghost overnight. If she wanted to get more than a few hours' sleep, she needed to head back to her hotel sooner rather than later.

"Is too bad," Natalia said. "My ex is having a party tonight. I planned on going after my shift, but I would rather not go alone. Would you like to come?"

Laramie hesitated. She wasn't in the habit of following strange women home—or accompanying them to parties thrown by their ex-girlfriends. But everything else was different here. Why shouldn't the sentiment apply to her, too?

"When does your shift end?"

"In thirty minutes."

Laramie leaned forward and rested her forearms on the table. "In that case, you'd better bring me another beer to tide me over while I wait."

CHAPTER FOUR

Anastasia wasn't surprised to see Natalia Pavlyuchenkova walk into her apartment. After the party began in earnest, Mischa had warned her that he had invited Natalia so she wouldn't be blindsided if Natalia actually decided to attend. Anastasia was prepared for the shock of seeing her ex again just a few short weeks after their breakup. What she wasn't prepared for was the sight of the woman at Natalia's side.

Laramie was dressed in the same clothes she had been wearing that afternoon, but she looked different somehow. More confident. More relaxed. Damn if both didn't look good on her. The hat must have been responsible for the change in her demeanor. She was wearing a battered gray Stetson pulled low over her eyes. She looked like a gunslinger checking out the competition as she slowly surveyed the crowded room.

"Who's that with Natalia?" Mischa asked.

Anastasia took a beat and tried to regain her bearings. Even though she hadn't left home yet, she already felt like she was in a different world.

"One of the Americans I'm supposed to provide translation services for."

"*That's* Laramie? What is she doing here?" Mischa's mascaraed eyes narrowed. "Do you think she'll tell my uncle about us?"

Laramie struck Anastasia as the kind of person who could be counted on to keep a secret rather than spilling it, but leave it to Mischa to automatically assume the worst.

"She can't tell him about us without revealing the truth about herself, too. No matter how good a trainer she is, the law is the law, and Sergei would be forced to abide by it. I doubt Laramie flew three thousand miles just to get fired on her first day."

"She isn't a citizen. Technically, Uncle Sergei wouldn't *have* to turn her in."

"When money is involved, technicalities don't matter."

Mischa sighed. "You're probably right."

"Aren't I always?"

Mischa rolled his eyes. "Don't get me started."

Anastasia's breath caught when Laramie's roving gaze settled on her face. She stood frozen, uncertain whether she should acknowledge Laramie's presence or ignore it.

"Let's go say hello," Mischa said after Laramie raised a hand in greeting.

"Okay."

Anastasia fought down a pang of jealousy as Natalia wrapped her arm around Laramie's. She couldn't tell if she was upset because she was seeing Natalia with someone else or because that someone else was Laramie. Surely, it had to be the former because the latter could prove to be her undoing.

"Natalia, I'm glad you could make it." Mischa kissed her on both cheeks, then took a step back. "Who's your friend?"

Laramie extended her hand. "I'm Laramie Bowman. You must be Mischa. I've heard a great deal about you."

Mischa glanced at Anastasia before he shook Laramie's hand. "Such as?"

"All good things, I assure you. Your uncle sings your praises."

Mischa's cheeks colored under his foundation. "My uncle has tendency to exaggerate."

"So I've been told."

Laramie shoved her hands in the back pockets of her jeans. The pose caused the opening in the front of her denim shirt to widen. Not far enough to give Anastasia a peek at her cleavage, but enough to offer her a good look at the smooth skin of her chest. Anastasia's mouth watered at the sight.

"It's good to see you again, Anastasia," Laramie said. "You look nice tonight."

Anastasia hadn't put much thought into her outfit—a purple button-down shirt and a pair of white jeans—but it gave her a thrill to know the ensemble had earned Laramie's seal of approval.

"*Spasibo.*"

"You're welcome. I think that's what I'm supposed to say. *Spasibo* does mean 'thank you,' doesn't it?"

Anastasia was impressed that Laramie had already managed to pick up a few phrases—even if her Western accent gave the words a twang Anastasia had never heard before.

"You learn fast."

"I have a good teacher."

Laramie's broad smile made Anastasia wish she could see it more often.

Natalia looked back and forth between them. "You two know each other?"

"Yes," Anastasia said. "Laramie and I both work for Mischa's uncle Sergei."

Natalia snorted a laugh. "That should be interesting." She tightened her grip on Laramie's arm. "Did Ana tell you she is the ex I mentioned to you earlier, or did she try to convince you that Mischa is her boyfriend? He's not, you know. He's simply her roommate."

"Actually, *she* didn't say anything. Duke did all the talking."

Natalia laughed with even less mirth than before. "He usually does. He is the kind of person who likes hearing the sound of his own voice."

"Something the two of you have in common," Anastasia said in Russian.

Natalia stared at her silently for a moment, then took a deep breath and said, "I came here tonight to wish you well, have a few drinks, and share some laughs for old times' sake. I didn't come to trade insults with you, Ana. We've already wasted more than enough time doing that, don't you think?"

Anastasia couldn't help but agree with her. She didn't know if their relationship had failed because they were too different or too similar. Either way, there was no denying what they had was over.

"Thank you for coming," she said, switching back to English so Laramie wouldn't feel too out of place. "Both of you."

"Have a good time in Godoroye," Natalia said as she pulled Anastasia into a brief but warm embrace.

Anastasia breathed in her scent. The perfume she favored mixed with the lingering aroma of the food she had served tonight. Anastasia missed the feel of her body. The tenderness of her touch. Being in Natalia's arms again reminded her how good they had made each other feel in bed. And how miserable they had been out of it.

By most accounts, the end had almost been a blessing in disguise, though Anastasia wasn't quite ready to see it that way. At times, their relationship felt like a mistake. One she never should have made and had no intention of making again. She was done with trying to find love. After all, what had it ever brought her but heartache?

Natalia pulled away.

"Don't do anyone I wouldn't do." This time, her laugh finally had a hint of humor in it. She tugged on Laramie's arm. "Let's see if I can find some more beers you might like. I did good job last time, didn't I?"

"Yep," Laramie said, "you did just fine." She tipped her hat to Mischa. "It was nice meeting you."

"You, too," Mischa said.

He and Anastasia watched Natalia sift through the dwindling collection of drinks. Their search must not have proved to be fruitful because Natalia quickly gave up on the beers and led Laramie to the liquor stash instead.

"Do you think they've slept together?"

Anastasia pursed her lips at the absurdity of the idea. "Laramie's flight landed only a few hours ago. Not even Natalia works that fast."

Mischa arched an eyebrow. "Are you sure?"

Across the room, Natalia giggled flirtatiously while she poured two liberal shots of Stoli. Laramie seemed taken aback by the potency of the vodka after she downed the shot, but she was obviously basking in Natalia's attention. The kind of attention Anastasia couldn't give her.

Anastasia drained the rest of her beer. "At least someone's getting laid tonight."

Mischa gave her a consoling pat on the back. "Too bad it isn't you."

❖

Laramie's mind was reeling. The three vodka shots she and Natalia had downed in quick succession had a great deal to do with it, but her main problem was the vast amount of new information her pickled brain was being asked to process.

Anastasia was Natalia's ex. Mischa wasn't Anastasia's boyfriend but her BFF. According to Natalia, Mischa hadn't asked Anastasia to become his beard. She had willingly assumed the role. They were out to their friends, but his family didn't know he was gay so they had spent the last five years pretending to be an item. Quite well, apparently, since Duke obviously had no clue about the true nature of their relationship.

What would he do if he did? Disown Mischa? Fire Anastasia? If society was as conservative here as everyone claimed, both options were possible.

Laramie was left wondering what it all meant. She took another shot of vodka as she desperately tried to connect all the dots. The picture that ended up taking shape in her mind was clear but complex.

Technically, Anastasia was single and free to pursue a relationship with the woman of her dreams. In actuality, though, she was caught in a trap of her own making because she couldn't allow herself to find happiness without costing Mischa some of his. Though they weren't romantically involved, their fates were hopelessly intertwined.

Natalia, thankfully, was far less complicated. She was attractive, fun, and easy to be with. Exactly what Laramie was in the mood for. Natalia was sending plenty of signals that she would be amenable to bailing on the party in favor of a more private celebration. Though the idea had considerable appeal, Laramie preferred to remain where they were rather than follow Natalia to her apartment or invite her back to her hotel.

She had never been averse to one-night stands before. Why was she balking now? Three reasons came immediately to mind: the past, the present, and the future.

Anastasia and Natalia had a history that didn't seem to be completely resolved. Fate, in the form of Sergei Ivanov, had brought Laramie and Anastasia together for the moment, but they weren't guaranteed to remain part of each other's lives once their respective contracts expired.

Laramie had way too much going on in her professional life. If she intended to keep her sanity, she needed her personal life to remain as uneventful as possible. She didn't do drama, and this situation was growing messier by the minute.

"Thanks for inviting me, but I think I'd better be going."

Natalia moved closer until their bodies were touching up and down. A song Laramie had never heard before, something slow and sensual, was playing in the background.

"Can't you stay a little longer?" Natalia asked, grinding her hips to the music. "You haven't danced with me yet."

Laramie felt like she was getting a lap dance standing up, though it wasn't nearly as sexy as she would have expected it to be. She placed her hands on Natalia's waist to still the movement of her hips. Natalia's gyrations weren't having the desired effect. They were making her nauseous rather than turning her on. Or perhaps the vodka was to blame. She gently pushed Natalia away and pressed both hands against her churning stomach.

"I think I'm going to be sick."

Natalia recoiled in horror as Laramie broke into a sweat and puffed out her cheeks. She pointed frantically behind her. "Bathroom is over there."

Laramie made a mad dash for the door Natalia had indicated. She barely made it into the bathroom before the contents of her stomach came spilling out. The vodka came first, followed by the cheeseburger, fries, and beers she'd had at Beef. All had tasted better the first time around.

After her stomach muscles finally stopped heaving, she flushed the toilet, turned on the faucet, and gathered water in her cupped hands. She rinsed out her mouth, then splashed water on her face. Her arms shook as she leaned against the sink. Anastasia's face swam into view while she regarded her reflection in the mirror.

"Are you okay?" Anastasia asked.

"Yes, I feel much—"

Another wave of nausea hit her before she could finish her sentence. She dropped to her knees in front of the commode as she puked again.

Anastasia came inside and closed the door behind her. "This is my fault."

Laramie flushed the toilet again, then sat with her back against the wall. The cold tile felt good pressing against her overheated skin.

"How is this your fault?"

"I should have warned you Natalia has hollow leg. No one can outdrink her. Not even Sergei."

Laramie smiled despite her embarrassment. "Now you tell me."

"Would you like me to take you back to hotel? I can stay with you tonight and make sure you do not miss your flight tomorrow. I will not need to share bed. I can sleep in chair."

Laramie was touched by the offer, though part of her wondered if Anastasia was looking out for her interests or Duke's.

"You don't have to do that. I've set my alarm clock and I have a wake-up call scheduled with the front desk in case something goes wrong. I'll be fine on my own. Besides, I wouldn't want to drag you away from your party."

Anastasia shook her head. "Party is not for me. Is for everyone else. You need me more than they do." She picked up Laramie's hat from where it had fallen and held out her hand. "Come. We go."

Laramie was a proud woman, but she wasn't too proud to accept help when she knew she needed it. She gripped Anastasia's hand and allowed her to pull her to her feet. She swayed a little before she steadied herself. She hadn't been this drunk since she had attended a kegger in college. She had tossed her cookies that night, too, though she had managed to avoid doing it in front of someone on which she hoped to make a favorable impression.

"I'm sorry you had to see me this way."

Anastasia wrapped an arm around her waist to provide support as she led her out of the bathroom. Mischa took a step toward them, but Anastasia waved him away.

"Believe me, I've seen worse."

Laramie could tell by the look in Anastasia's expressive eyes that her statement was more than a figure of speech.

"You'll have to tell me about it sometime," she said as Anastasia led her to her bedroom.

"I don't want to bore you."

"I doubt anything about you could ever be considered boring."

Laramie held Anastasia's gaze so Anastasia wouldn't doubt her sincerity. Anastasia was the first to look away.

"You are entitled to your opinion," she said with a shrug.

Anastasia stuffed a change of clothes into a carry-on bag and slung the bag over her shoulder. Then she retrieved the large suitcase standing sentry in the open—and empty—closet. The walls were bare. If not for the rumpled sheets on the bed, the room would have appeared unoccupied.

"We go now," Anastasia said briskly as she charged toward the door.

Laramie had no choice but to follow. As Anastasia and Mischa said their good-byes, she took one last look at the Spartan room. Anastasia seemed to live life without leaving much of a trail behind, but she was certainly starting to make a mark on her.

CHAPTER FIVE

Outside, Anastasia hailed a cab and helped Laramie crawl into the back seat while the cab driver deposited her bags in the trunk. Their abrupt departure from the party had been somewhat embarrassing, but it did have one upside. Having to leave early had prevented her and Mischa from weeping in each other's arms while they engaged in a long, drawn-out good-bye. When it came to bidding farewell to someone she cared about, short and sweet was always best.

The cabbie eyed her and Laramie after he climbed into the driver's seat of the dented Lada, the much-ridiculed car brand that was currently undergoing yet another attempted image makeover in an effort to boost the company's lackluster sales.

"Where to?" he asked.

Anastasia gave him the address of Laramie's hotel and leaned back against the cracked leather seat that reeked of fresh sweat and stale cigarettes.

The cab driver started the meter and used the rearview mirror to peer at her reflection. "It looks like your friend has had a little too much fun tonight. If she gets sick before we reach the hotel, I'm charging you a cleanup fee."

Anastasia tried to remember how much cash she had on hand. Enough to pay the fare, but not enough to cover any ridiculous surcharges the driver decided to tack on the final bill. She thanked her lucky stars Sergei had made arrangements to send a company car to ferry Shorty and Laramie to the airport tomorrow. One less expense she would have to worry about.

"She'll be fine. Just drive."

Despite her assurances, she could tell Laramie's energy was starting to fade. Her eyes were half-lidded and her breathing was growing shallower by the minute.

Unsurprisingly, Laramie fell asleep almost as soon as the car pulled away from the curb. Her snores were so loud they drowned out the sound of the Philipp Kirkorov song playing on the radio. Not that Anastasia minded. She liked Kirkorov's gender-bending style, and the Bulgarian-born musician had been named the best-selling Russian artist five times during his storied career, but she had never been much of a fan of his music. She preferred One Direction.

Music critics might beg to differ, but she thought 1D's first four albums were on par with the Beatles' early releases. Pure pop that made you feel good and didn't try to manipulate your emotions or ask you to think. Then Zayn had to screw things up by deciding to go solo. The group's fifth album—their first as a quartet—was okay, but it didn't have the same spark. Neither did their solo work. Now the group was on hiatus, code speak for taking a break from recording and performing with each other until some promoter threw enough money at them to pique their interest in a lucrative reunion tour. Anastasia wasn't holding her breath. Neither, by the sound of it, was Laramie.

Anastasia tilted Laramie's hat forward until it covered most of her face. The thick felt served as an effective dampener, muffling Laramie's snores so they sounded more like a blender than a pneumatic drill.

"Her husband must not get much sleep," the cab driver said.

Anastasia almost corrected his assumption about Laramie's sexuality like she always did when someone made the same assumption about her, but she managed to catch herself in time. Though she frequently outed herself, she would never do it to someone else.

"She doesn't have a husband," she said instead.

"It's easy to see why."

As the cab driver laughed at his own joke, Anastasia regarded Laramie out of the corner of her eye. Laramie didn't have a husband, true enough, but did she have someone to call her own? Was there someone besides her family waiting for her to return to Wyoming when her time in Godoroye came to an end? Anastasia wouldn't doubt it. Even though a line of drool was starting to form in a corner of Laramie's mouth, the passed-out cowgirl was quite a catch.

Laramie's long legs were stretched as far as they could reach in the cramped space. Her work-roughened hands rested in her lap. Anastasia was tempted to run a finger across the thick calluses on Laramie's upraised palms, but she didn't dare. Not here. The cabbie seemed to sense something was different about them. It wouldn't do for him to assume that they were a couple. He was a big man. Almost twice her size. If he figured out they were lesbians and decided to express his disapproval, the situation could turn dangerous. Laramie was in no condition to defend herself and she couldn't fight him off on her own.

She moved closer to the passenger's side door to put some distance between herself and Laramie, then waited for the seemingly endless ride to be over.

"We're here," the cab driver said after he braked to a stop in front of Laramie's hotel.

Despite its pretty trappings and exorbitant price tag, the hotel wasn't quite as grand as it seemed. Par for the course in modern-day Moscow. The rooms were small, the beds were hard, and the food in the restaurant was only a level or two above what was served in most school cafeterias. Which mattered more, Anastasia mused as she climbed out of the taxi, the trappings of success or success itself?

The cab driver retrieved her luggage and deposited it on the sidewalk. "One hundred rubles," he said, holding out his hand.

Anastasia balked at the price. The meter had stopped far short of the amount the cabbie had just demanded, but she was in no position to argue. Not when she needed his help. She opened the driver's side door and tried to pull Laramie out of the car, but Laramie wouldn't budge. She looked at the cabbie, who was still holding out his hand for his fare.

"Grab an arm and help me take her upstairs."

The cab driver wagged his finger. "I will drag her out of my car to make room for my next fare, but carrying her inside will cost you extra."

"Forget it." She looked around for someone more willing to help her, but the doorman didn't volunteer to offer his services either. "Do you mind if I borrow one of those?" she asked, pointing to one of the luggage carts lined up in the lobby.

The doorman glanced at her clothes—an off-brand shirt and knockoff designer jeans—with obvious disapproval. "Those are for guests who pay by the night, not by the hour."

Anastasia gritted her teeth in frustration. "Sergei Ivanov is the principal owner of this hotel. The woman in the taxi and I both work for him. She is a registered guest. Her room is being paid for by Mr. Ivanov, and I would very much like to take her to it." She could hear her voice rising in anger, but she didn't try to reel in her temper. "Would you like to call Mr. Ivanov so he can confirm who we are, or do you want to keep standing here wasting everyone's time?"

"No," the doorman said contritely. His attitude changed as soon as she mentioned Sergei's name. If she had known it would have such a profound effect, Anastasia would have dropped it sooner. "That won't be necessary. Wait here."

He ran inside like wolves were on his tail. He returned a few minutes later with a porter in tow. The porter dragged Laramie out of the back seat and loaded her on the cart. Laramie's hat managed to stay on, even though her head lolled back and forth like she was a rag doll.

Anastasia turned to the cab driver. "Here's your money."

"This is only eighty-seven rubles," he said after he counted the bills she had given him.

"Exactly." She pointed at the meter, which had stopped just short of eighty-seven rubles. "And I'll need a receipt for my expense report." Someone was going to pay for all the torment he and the doorman had put her through, and it wasn't going to be her.

He mumbled a few curses under his breath but did as she asked.

"Is there anything else you need?" the doorman asked after the porter placed her luggage between Laramie's splayed legs.

"No," she said, enjoying the unexpected taste of power, "I can take it from here."

She followed the porter inside as he steered the luggage cart across the lobby and into the elevator. The porter didn't say much as they rode the elevator upstairs. She liked the fact that he did his job without looking down on her or trying to suck up to her.

Upstairs, she fished Laramie's key card out of her pocket and used it to access the room Sergei had booked. She gave the porter a generous tip after he set her bags inside the door and placed Laramie on the bed.

"Do you need a receipt for this, too?"

"No," she said as they shared a laugh. "Why don't we keep it between us?"

He slipped the bills into his pocket and darted his eyes toward Laramie. "Good luck."

"Thanks. I think I'll need it."

After the porter pushed the luggage cart out of the room, she locked the door behind him and took a look around. The room was listed as a suite, but it was probably less than thirty-seven square meters. It had all the basic necessities, though. A bed, a desk, a couch, and a bathroom with a walk-in shower. The minibar was well stocked, though Laramie wouldn't have much use for it tonight.

Laramie.

Anastasia walked over to the bed and looked down at her. Her features, tense and guarded while she was awake, were placid as she slept. Anastasia used the tip of one finger to brush a stray lock of hair off Laramie's cheek. Laramie stirred but didn't rouse from her slumber.

Anastasia backed away from the bed. How was she supposed to handle this situation? She had watched out for drunk friends before while they slept it off, but Laramie was a stranger, not a friend.

Even though the couch was so small Anastasia doubted she would be able to find a comfortable sleeping position, sharing a bed with Laramie was out of the question. She couldn't shake her suspicion that most hotel rooms were rife with hidden cameras, and she didn't want to be spied on while she slept next to a woman she thought she might be attracted to.

She removed Laramie's boots, turned her on her side, and placed a trash can next to the bed in case she got sick again. She headed to the bathroom to change into the sleepwear she had brought, then grabbed an extra blanket and pillow from the closet. She set the alarm on her phone after she texted Mischa to let him know she had arrived safely. He didn't respond right away so she assumed he must have been hooking up with the guy he'd had his eye on all night.

She took one last look at Laramie before she turned off the light. "At least I'm not the only one sleeping alone tonight."

Her legs were too long for the couch so she curled into the fetal position. She suspected most of the muscles in her back and legs would be cramping by the morning, but it was still better than sleeping on the floor or on a worn-out cot like she'd had to do in the orphanage she grew up in.

One thought came to mind as she drifted off to sleep. *I could get used to this.*

❖

The tinny sound of electronic chimes cut through Laramie's head like a buzz saw. She blindly reached for the alarm clock next to her bed and pressed the snooze button. The sound lessened but didn't die.

"What the hell?"

She groaned as she lifted her head, the movement sending shock waves of pain throughout her body. Her head felt like it was about to explode, her mouth tasted like something had crawled into it and died, and the rest of her didn't feel too good either.

"Sorry," an apologetic voice said in the dark.

A cell phone's glowing display lit up Anastasia's face as she opened an app and disabled the alarm.

Laramie squinted as she turned on the light next to the bed. "How did I get here?" She tried to think, but gave up when the effort proved too painful. "I remember hailing a cab and I have a vague recollection of riding in a luggage cart, though that doesn't make any sense."

"If you do not remember what happened, I will not tell you. I need this job."

Anastasia tossed her covers aside, swung her legs off the sofa, and stood as if she didn't expect her legs to be able to bear her weight. Laramie tried not to admire the glorious sight of Anastasia in the tight tank top and boy shorts she had slept in the night before.

"Did you have as much to drink as I did?"

Anastasia's enigmatic smile was all the answer Laramie needed. "Not quite."

"Good. First Shorty, then me. I'm glad someone managed to show a modicum of responsibility last night."

Anastasia's tank top rode up as she stretched, revealing an enticing expanse of skin. Laramie licked her lips and turned away.

"How is head?"

"Pardon?"

"Head." Anastasia tapped her temple. "How is head? Does it hurt?"

"Like you wouldn't believe."

"And stomach?"

"It's mercifully empty."

"You will feel better after you have food. Something greasy to soak up alcohol. We get *butterbrods* and fried eggs after we check in at airport, yes?"

Laramie didn't know what *butterbrods* were and wasn't sure she wanted to find out, but she didn't seem to have much choice. She flinched at the shrill sound the telephone emitted when it rang. The concierge making the wake-up call she had requested.

After Laramie hung up the phone, Anastasia shook two pills out of a bottle in her carry-on bag and handed them to her, along with a bottle of water from the minibar. "Take these for headache."

"Thank you." Laramie downed the pills and hoped it wouldn't take long for them to start working their magic.

"Would you like to shower first, or shall I?"

Laramie drank the rest of the water and pushed herself to her feet. She didn't feel dizzy like she had when she first woke up, but her head was still in a fog. "You go. I need to check on Shorty to make sure he's none the worse for wear."

Anastasia laughed as she headed to the bathroom. "If he looks as bad as you, we are in for long day."

If Laramie didn't stop thinking about how good Anastasia's ass looked in those boy shorts, she would be in for a long night. Several, in fact. She grabbed her key card off the counter and avoided looking at her reflection in the mirror. She didn't need visual evidence that she looked even worse than she felt. She needed to sober up before she got to Godoroye because this certainly wasn't the first impression she had hoped to make on her new trainees. She wanted to earn their respect, not their scorn.

She crossed the hall and knocked on Shorty's door. She thought she would have to bang on it for a while before she received a response, but Shorty answered right away. When he opened the door, he looked as fresh as a daisy. He was showered, shaved, and already dressed. His bed was made, his bags were packed, and he was ready to roll.

"I came to wake you up," she said, "but it looks like I'm too late."

"I might get knocked down a time or two, but I always get back up. Right now, I don't know if I can say the same about you. What did you get into last night?"

"I might have had one too many at Anastasia's going-away party."

"One or a dozen?"

He poured her a cup of coffee from the carafe he had made. It was black and so thick a spoon would have stood straight up. Just like she liked it.

"I lost count after four."

"No wonder you look like shit. Did you have fun at least?"

"Let's just say our translator has some rather interesting friends."

"Did you meet her boyfriend?"

"I met her roommate, if that's what you're asking."

Shorty's eyebrows knitted in confusion, then arched in recognition. "Oh. So the two of you have something in common. Did you..." He waved his hand to indicate Laramie should finish the sentence for him.

"No, but we did spend the night together."

"Yeah?"

Shorty arched his eyebrows again. Though he was reluctant to reveal his own secrets, he seemed to take immense pleasure in hearing other people spill theirs. He wasn't one to gossip, but he could listen to it all day. Laramie explained what had happened before he could start speculating.

"After I puked my guts out at the party, she brought me back here and slept on the couch while I sawed logs in the bed."

"Where is she now?"

"Taking a shower while I check on you."

"I'm fine. Don't worry about me." He pulled the cup of coffee from her hands and pushed her toward the door. "Get back where you can do some good."

She retrieved her mug so she could finish every caffeine-soaked ounce of coffee that remained. Her nerves would probably be jangling for the rest of the day, but at least she would feel more alert than she did now. She needed her wits about her in order to avoid a repeat of last night's unfortunate behavior.

"Stop your matchmaking, Shorty. Nothing's going to happen between me and Anastasia. Homosexuality is illegal here, remember?"

"According to our federal government, smoking marijuana is against the law, too, but that doesn't stop people from lighting up, does it?"

"I've never seen you light anything other than the occasional celebratory cigar whenever someone gets married or has a baby. What do you know about smoking weed?"

"Let's just say the Rocky Mountains aren't the only things in Colorado that are high."

"I'm going to have to start following you when you go on vacation, old man. You have way more adventures than I do."

"If you want to catch up, you can start by going back to your room. A pretty filly and a hot shower? Fifteen minutes is all you need to have the adventure of a lifetime."

Laramie wished life was as simple as Shorty often made it out to be. In her experience, though, matters of the heart had always proven to be anything but simple.

CHAPTER SIX

After she, Laramie, and Shorty checked in at Domodedovo Moscow Airport, Anastasia found a restaurant that was open and placed three orders for *butterbrods*, fried eggs, and coffee.

"What's this now?" Shorty asked after the waitress brought their food to their table.

Not many people were taking early flights today so the wait wasn't very long. The food was piping hot and smelled amazing.

Anastasia sprinkled salt and pepper on her eggs. "*Butterbrod* is sandwich topped with butter or ham."

"Like an open-faced ham and cheese sandwich without the cheese?" Anastasia nodded in response since her mouth was full. "Sounds good to me."

Shorty shoveled food into his mouth as if he hadn't eaten in days. Laramie, meanwhile, approached hers with more caution.

"Is good," Anastasia assured her. "Try. You will like."

After Laramie took a tentative bite of her sandwich, the frown lines on her forehead slowly faded from view. "Thank you," she said when she was done. "I needed that."

"This is typical Russian breakfast. I am sure ranch cook will include it on menu."

"Well, all right then," Shorty said. "Something to look forward to."

They located their gate and waited for their flight to be called. Anastasia had thought she could control her nerves, but they started to get the best of her after she and the other passengers boarded the plane and settled into their seats.

Shorty was seated closest to the aisle, Laramie was in the middle, and she was next to the window. She turned to Laramie while the flight attendants made their final checks prior to departure.

"Would you like to switch seats with me?"

"Enjoy the view." Laramie jerked a thumb toward Shorty, who appeared to be dozing. "I'm going to follow his example and try to get forty winks in before we land. I had a hard night last night, remember?"

Anastasia remembered all too well. She hadn't felt that much stress since the local police had broken up a gay rights rally in Gorky Park by swinging their batons at attendees' heads. She had escaped injury that day, though some of her friends hadn't been so lucky. One had ended up with a concussion, another a broken arm.

All the fear and uncertainty she had felt that day returned in droves. When the captain announced they were ready for takeoff, she took a deep breath and tried to slow the rapid beating of her heart.

Laramie took a long look at her. "Is something wrong?"

The plane jerked as the pilot backed it away from the terminal. Anastasia gripped Laramie's forearm in abject terror. "I have confession to make," she said as the plane slowly crossed the tarmac.

"Are you afraid to fly?"

"I do not know. I have never been on plane before."

"Ever? How do you know your way around the airport if you've never flown before?"

"I have been here many times with friends. I bring them to airport or pick them up when they return. I keep their cars so they can spend their money on drinks instead of parking fees."

"Do your friends do the same for you?"

"I have no car and cannot afford to travel by air. I must borrow Mischa's car or take train."

Laramie looked doubtful, but Anastasia's expression must have convinced her that she was telling the truth. "I was a bundle of nerves on my first flight, too," she said gently. "I didn't know what to expect. I thought every bump and bang I heard meant the plane was about to crash. I've gotten over that, but I still hate flying through turbulence. It's like being stuck on the world's worst roller coaster."

Anastasia's heart sank. She had always liked roller coasters. Until now. "So the fear never goes away?"

"A little bit of fear is a good thing to have. As long as you don't let it overwhelm you, it keeps you from taking things for granted. How can you truly appreciate what you have until you face the possibility that you might lose it?" Laramie grimaced. "Sorry. That was an unfortunate analogy." She squeezed Anastasia's hand. "The pilots are seasoned professionals. Sit back, relax, and let them do their jobs."

It wasn't the pilots that Anastasia was worried about. Aside from the copilot who had intentionally flown his plane into a mountain several years ago, the members of the flight crew often weren't at fault when disaster struck. Equipment failure was usually to blame. In this part of the world, outside forces were occasionally the cause.

She couldn't stop thinking about the still unsolved disappearance of the airliner that had mysteriously vanished off the radar in 2014, the plane that had been shot down over Ukraine two years later, or the cargo jet that had stalled shortly after takeoff and exploded in a giant ball of flames after it crashed to the ground. That viral video had haunted her for weeks. Were the passengers onboard this flight about to become another unfortunate statistic?

"Would it help if I closed the shade?" Laramie asked.

"No," Anastasia said more sharply than she had intended.

If something went wrong, she wanted to be able to see what was coming. Whatever her imagination concocted would probably be far worse than reality. She gripped the narrow armrests with both hands as the plane shook and rattled down the runway.

"Are the engines always this loud?" she asked.

"Yes, that's normal. The pilot needs to build up enough speed to take flight. When he really hits the gas, you'll feel like you're on a rocket ship launching into orbit."

Anastasia swallowed hard. "I have never thought of myself as cosmonaut."

"There's a first time for everything," Laramie said with a disarming grin. "Hold on. Here it comes."

The plane lurched forward, and gravitational forces pinned Anastasia against her seat. Her adrenaline surged as the plane moved faster and faster down the runway. She started to fear the pilot was going to run out of room before he managed to get the heavy craft into the air. Then the nose of the plane tilted toward the sky and the tail soon followed.

Anastasia's stomach turned somersaults like she was on a thrill ride at a carnival. The sensation was almost pleasurable.

She sneaked a peek out the window, staring in amazement as the earth slowly fell away. Were they really up that high? The buildings on the ground looked as small as pieces in a board game. She nearly jumped out of her seat when she heard a loud bump.

"What was that?"

"Nothing to worry about," Laramie said. "The landing gear retracts during the flight to make the plane more aerodynamic. The pilot will put it down again when we start to descend."

When the plane reached cruising altitude a few minutes later, Anastasia finally released her death grip on the armrests. All around her, people were conversing, sleeping, or reading like they were riding the train to work rather than flying thirty thousand feet in the air. They had ignored the flight attendant's safety demonstration as well, while she had hung on to every word.

"How could anyone ever take this for granted?"

"Some people take flying too seriously. Others don't take it seriously enough." Laramie folded her arms across her chest, sank down in her seat, and closed her eyes. "Everyone has different coping mechanisms," she said with a yawn. "In time, I'm sure you'll find the one that works best for you."

Perhaps, Anastasia thought, she already had. And her name was Laramie Bowman.

Laramie felt refreshed after she woke from her nap. The extra sleep, combined with the hearty breakfast she had eaten before the flight, had her feeling like herself again. She vowed not to repeat last night's mistakes. From now on, she would be drowning her sorrows in something other than alcohol. By the time her contract ended, she would not only be wealthier than she had ever been, she would also be healthier. Not to mention hornier, but that went without saying.

The plane had started to descend, bringing about a change in the cabin's air pressure. She opened her mouth wide to get her ears to pop, then checked her watch. It had taken almost three full days for her to get to Bryansk. Provided the flight was on time, she was a little more than thirty minutes from finally reaching her destination. Yevgeny Makarov, the ranch foreman, was supposed to pick them up at the airport and drive them to Godoroye. After he introduced them to the ranch hands, he planned to take them on a tour of the property.

Laramie wanted to see the land she would be living and working on for the next three years, but she was more interested in inspecting the cattle. They were the reason she was here, and she was anxious to see if she would be tending to quality stock. If not, she might have to suggest selling their current herd and starting over. Starting from scratch would make her job more difficult but not impossible. Good thing she hadn't expected the gig to be easy.

She straightened in her seat and looked over at Anastasia. Anastasia's panic attack, if that's what it had been, appeared to have taken the wind out of her sails. As she flipped through the in-flight magazine, she seemed quiet and distant. Almost brooding. Laramie was tempted to ask her what was wrong, but she decided to give her some space.

She tried to see things through Anastasia's eyes. She wasn't the only person who had made sacrifices to be here. Anastasia had made sacrifices as well. Moving three hundred miles away from her family and friends in order to take on a job she had never performed couldn't have been easy for her.

Perhaps she and I have more than one thing in common. Too bad we can't do anything about it except commiserate over a campfire.

Trying not to imagine how beautiful Anastasia would be with the flickering flames of firelight dancing in her eyes, Laramie stared out the window. The view wasn't much to look at, but the acres and acres of rolling pastureland offered a refreshing change from the skyscrapers and drab scenery she had been surrounded by for the past few days. Even though she hadn't landed yet, it felt good being out of the city and back in the country again. She couldn't wait to feel the grass under her feet.

As the plane's rate of descent increased, Anastasia looked up from her magazine and glanced out the window. "This is what your home looks like?"

Laramie leaned closer to get a better look at a series of crystal clear lakes. "We're missing a few mountains, but yes."

"Have you never wanted to live anywhere else?"

"I like visiting other places, but when it comes to putting down roots, I would rather do that in Wyoming."

Evidently finding the discussion they were having more interesting than the article she was reading, Anastasia closed the magazine. "Wyoming is that beautiful?"

"More than that. It's home. Each time I leave, I can't wait to return. My family is there. My life is there. My heart is there. Don't you feel that way about your hometown?"

Laramie realized she hadn't asked Anastasia if she had been born in Moscow or if, like most inhabitants of big cities, she had moved there from somewhere else.

Anastasia's expression darkened. "I do not have home, which means I do not have roots."

Laramie felt like she had been offered a hint to the turmoil behind Anastasia's gaze, though she was still searching for the true cause. Would Anastasia eventually feel comfortable enough to confide in her, or would she leave Russia knowing as little about her as she did now? Knowing they wouldn't be confined to the same small space for much longer, she took a chance.

"But you do have roots. You have Mischa."

"Yes," Anastasia said with a small smile, "I will always have him. He has been good friend."

"So have you, by all accounts."

Anastasia turned to face her. "You have been talking about me?"

"I've been *listening* to Natalia."

"What did she say about me?"

Laramie thought about some of the comments Natalia had made about Anastasia's relationship with Mischa and the one Anastasia had once shared with her. "Nothing of consequence. I would rather hear that from you."

Anastasia yelped in surprise when the plane's wheels thumped against the tarmac. She looked out the window, then turned back to Laramie. "Did you carry on conversation to distract me while plane was landing?"

"No, but did it work?"

Anastasia reached for her carry-on bag instead of providing an answer. "Gather your things. We have much work to do."

Laramie smacked Shorty's leg to rouse him from his slumber, then heeded Anastasia's advice. She was here to work, she reminded herself, not make friends. If Anastasia wanted to keep her at arm's length, that was exactly where she would remain. Whether she liked it or not.

CHAPTER SEVEN

Anastasia could tell Yevgeny Makarov was going to pose a problem as soon as she laid eyes on him. She had seen his type too many times before: a middle manager who acted as if he possessed more power than he had actually been granted. As he stood in the ground transportation area holding up a placard with the name of Sergei's ranch printed on it in both Cyrillic and English, he looked like he wished he had assigned the job to someone else.

After she raised her hand to get his attention, he tossed the cigarette he had been smoking and ground the butt under the heel of his designer shoes. He worked on a start-up ranch in the middle of the Russian heartland. How could he afford five thousand dollar shoes on his salary?

"How was your flight?" he asked in Estonian-accented Russian.

"Blessedly uneventful."

"These are the Americans Sergei hired?"

"Yes, their names are Laramie Bowman and Pernell Johnson, though he prefers to be called Shorty."

Yevgeny reached to shake Shorty's hand first. "Yevgeny Makarov."

"Pleased to meet you," Shorty said, "but let's get something straight from the jump. I'm not running this here show. She is."

"What did he say?" Yevgeny looked stunned after she told him he had directed his attention to the wrong person. "Sergei hired a woman to train the men? I hope he knows what he's doing."

"He must," she said. "Unless they receive an inheritance from a dead relative, not many people become billionaires by accident."

"You're quick to defend him. Is that why he hired you, or because you're screwing his nephew?"

Anastasia's temper flared, but she didn't take the bait. The encounter felt like a test of some kind. A test she couldn't afford to fail.

"He hired me because he thought I could do the job. Why are you here?"

Yevgeny smiled, revealing two uneven rows of nicotine-stained teeth.

"The locals who applied for my position didn't have any experience managing a business this large. I did. I used to be in charge of one of the biggest chocolate factories in Moscow. At its peak, more than two hundred people reported to me."

Anastasia thought he looked vaguely familiar. Now she knew why.

"Didn't I read about you in the paper? Weren't you fired after rat droppings were found in one of your company's orders?"

"Quality control was someone else's responsibility, not mine," Yevgeny was quick to point out.

"If that's true, why wasn't that person terminated instead of you?"

Caught in a web of lies, Yevgeny abruptly changed the subject. "The van is parked not too far from here. Do you have everything you need?"

"Yes."

The luggage cart Shorty was pushing was laden with all their belongings, and Anastasia made a mental note to tell Laramie about all the professional baggage Yevgeny was carrying. Laramie needed to know the kind of man she was dealing with so he couldn't try to shift the blame to her if he proved to be as inept at his current job as he had been at his previous one.

"Then wait here until I come back to get you." He looked Laramie and Shorty up and down. "Talk about a waste of money. They had better be worth the price Sergei is paying them."

"They're not," she said. "They're worth more."

"For your sake as well as mine, I hope your loyalty isn't misguided."

"Is it me he doesn't like," Laramie asked after Yevgeny left, "or Americans in general?"

"He sees you as threat." Anastasia told them about the scandal that had tarnished Yevgeny's reputation. "If he fails at this job, he might not get another."

"I never judge a man by his mistakes," Shorty said. "I judge him by how he recovers from them."

"I'll keep an open mind, too," Laramie said. "Please make sure he knows we're here to help him, not replace him."

"I will try my best," Anastasia said, "but I do not think he will believe me, no matter what I say. You need to make effort, too. Flatter him. Make him feel important. Make him feel like his opinion matters."

Shorty pulled a package from his pocket and pressed a wad of tobacco into his cheek. "We raise cattle, little lady. We don't stroke egos."

"In Russia, that is how things work," Anastasia said. "If you wish to accomplish task, you need two things: money and influence."

"Then that puts us in a bit of a bind," Laramie said. "Because I'm running short on both."

Laramie couldn't decide which the van needed more—a thorough cleaning or a new set of shocks. The outside of the dented vehicle was so caked with mud she couldn't tell what color metal lurked underneath the grime. Thanks to the half-empty fifty-pound bag of fertilizer taking up room in the cargo hold, the interior was even more fragrant than a hog pen in mid August. The ride itself wasn't anything to write home about either. Yevgeny didn't miss a single pothole as he traversed the thirty-five miles from Bryansk to Godoroye. After he turned onto a deeply rutted dirt road and drove through the gates of Sergei Ivanov's ranch, Laramie knew how Trey must have felt when that whirling dervish of a bull slammed into him a few weeks ago.

She wished she could talk to Trey and ask him how he was doing, but she knew it wouldn't do any good. He was worse than their father when it came to admitting he was hurting. He could be carrying a severed limb in his hands like one of those unfortunate creatures on *The Walking Dead* and he would still swear he was as right as rain. If she wanted honest answers to her questions about his health, she would have to ask her mother about him the next time she called home.

Because of the nine-hour time difference between Godoroye and Broken Branch, she and her family would probably spend more time reading each other's text messages than having an actual conversation. After she completed her chores, her family would just be starting theirs. And vice versa. She would find the time somehow. She didn't want to lose the bonds she had spent her whole life trying to forge.

"Family comes first," her mother was always saying. "Everything else comes a distant second."

She had never been so far from her family before, but she had never felt closer to them. In a way, they were all in this together. Because she wasn't here for herself. She was here for them. Her chance to prove herself coincided with an opportunity to help her family when they needed it most. Now all she had to do was make sure she didn't blow it for everyone with a vested interest in the outcome of what could turn out to be an epic success or a colossal failure.

"Tarnation." Shorty's voice snapped Laramie out of her reverie. "That was some ride." He slid the door open and gingerly stepped out of the van. He looked like he was tempted to sink to his knees and kiss the ground like the Pope did each time his plane landed in a country he was visiting, but he remained upright. "I think I swallowed half my chaw when we hit that last bump." He dug out what was left of his chewing tobacco and tossed the diminished wad on the ground.

Yevgeny said something in Russian and Anastasia provided the translation. "Roads could use improvement."

"No shit, Sherlock. I hate to break it to you, but the roads ain't the only things around here that could stand to be improved." Shorty turned in a slow circle as he took in their new surroundings. "The barn could use a new roof, the fence is so rickety a stiff breeze could knock it over, and if that's supposed to be the bunkhouse, don't get me started on that there shoddy piece of craftsmanship. It don't look fit to house neither man nor beast. The main house don't look too bad. Then again, I ain't seen the inside yet. I thought this was supposed to be a multimillion-dollar operation, but what I'm seeing looks like chump change. Does the whole place look this ramshackle, or are these the best bits?"

Yevgeny's face colored after Anastasia told him what Shorty had said. "If ranch does not meet your exacting standards," Anastasia said on his behalf, "you can return to America anytime you wish, cowboy."

"Don't tempt me, comrade."

Laramie stepped between Shorty and Yevgeny to prevent them from continuing to hurl insults at each other. Though she agreed with Shorty's observations, she wished he had taken more care in choosing his words.

"It's safe to say we've all got our work cut out for us," she said diplomatically. "Mr. Makarov, why don't you show us where we'll be bunking so we can get settled in, meet the men, and take a look around?"

"You and I will sleep in main house," Anastasia said after Yevgeny barked a terse reply. "Shorty will sleep in bunkhouse with ranch hands. Elena, the cook, will show us to rooms and tell us about schedule. When she is done, Yevgeny will take you on tour of ranch."

"On horseback and not in that godawful van, I hope," Shorty said.

"Not on horse. He says ATV is much faster."

"Great," Laramie said. "Just when I thought this day couldn't get any worse."

CHAPTER EIGHT

Anastasia wasn't a betting woman. If she were, she might have been tempted to research the odds on who was most likely to win the burgeoning turf war between Yevgeny and the Americans. Yevgeny and Shorty's first battle had ended in a draw, each man having bluster on his side. Laramie could turn out to be the deciding factor. Because she had something Yevgeny and Shorty didn't: a quiet confidence that seemed to be growing more resolute by the moment.

Anastasia continued to be impressed by her. If some of her colleagues in the gay rights movement had even a modicum of Laramie's courage, they might finally start making progress instead of covering the same ground over and over again. She could accomplish every possible goal she had set for herself if she had Laramie fighting alongside her. Instead, she would have to settle for having her across the hall.

Elena Savchenko, the ranch cook, met them on the porch of the main house and led them inside.

"Yevgeny sleeps in the master bedroom on the second floor," she said as she took them on a tour of the three-story structure. Anastasia translated as she continued to talk. "The attic is mainly used for storage. The kitchen, dining room, and three guest rooms are located here on the first floor. My room is closest to the kitchen and has its own bathroom. The rooms on this end of the house have to share facilities. Both rooms are the same size. You can decide which one you would like to claim." She opened the doors to both rooms so they could see inside. "Maria, the bookkeeper, used to sleep in this room."

Laramie peered inside the room facing the front of the property. "Where is she now?"

"She married an electrician she met online and moved to Minsk last November. Yevgeny takes care of the accounting duties now. He has an office upstairs. He spends more time there than he does anywhere else. He's either very good at math or very, very bad."

"I'll need to see the ledgers and all the documentation on the animals so I can make sure all the records are in order."

"Yevgeny keeps them locked in a safe in the office. He doesn't let anyone touch them since Maria left, but I'm sure he will provide them to you if you ask."

"So it's just you and Yevgeny rattling around this big house?" Shorty asked after he and Laramie shared a look.

Neither seemed to like Elena's comment about Yevgeny being the only person allowed to handle the ranch's business affairs. Anastasia agreed with them. That was too much power for one man to have. Especially a man like Yevgeny, who was quick to take credit and even quicker to avoid accepting blame.

Elena, who appeared to be in her mid to late forties, tucked a stray lock of dark blond hair behind her ear, then placed her hands on her hips. She was tall and big-boned. The skin on her oversized hands was dry and cracked, as if it was constantly exposed to water or harsh chemicals. Anastasia could tell Elena was no stranger to hard work. She seemed happy to have a purpose, though. Despite the frown lines etched between her eyebrows, the corners of her mouth were turned up into a smile.

"In case Yevgeny gets any ideas he shouldn't, I keep my door locked and a Taser next to my bed. Do I need to keep another one on hand for you, too?"

"That won't be necessary, ma'am," Shorty said after Anastasia translated what Elena had said. "I never go anywhere I ain't invited."

While Anastasia relayed Shorty's words, Elena looked at him curiously. The top of his head barely came to her shoulder, yet they seemed to be standing on equal ground.

"Are you married, Mr. Johnson?"

"No, I've never had the pleasure, ma'am."

"A little man like you?" Elena said with a grin. "How much pleasure could you provide?"

Shorty bowed as if he were greeting a member of royalty. "You'd be surprised, ma'am. You'd be surprised."

Elena laughed good-naturedly and waved her hands to shoo him away. "Wait on the porch while the girls get settled. I will send them out to you when they're done."

"Yes, ma'am. I sure will." As he walked away, Anastasia heard him say, "That tall drink of water is making me a mite thirsty."

Even though she didn't know exactly what he meant, she thought she had a pretty good idea. Shorty was smitten. Despite her protestations, Elena seemed intrigued by him, too. Anastasia didn't know if anything would come of their flirtation, but it might be fun to watch. There wasn't much else to do around here. She had to keep herself occupied somehow. Watching a soap opera play out right in front of her might be a good place to start.

"Which room would you like?" Laramie asked. "I'll be up before dawn and in bed with the chickens, so it doesn't matter to me."

Anastasia shrugged. Neither room had a jaw-dropping view, so she would have to take other factors into consideration. "That room faces east and this one faces west. I would rather watch the sun set than hide from the glare while it rises."

"Then it's settled."

Laramie placed her luggage and saddle in the room facing the rear of the property and began making herself at home. Anastasia deposited her belongings in the room Laramie hadn't chosen. The furnishings were spare, limited to a bed, dresser, nightstand, and small table lamp. The mattress had been stripped, but a comforter and a set of freshly laundered sheets were folded on top of the storage bench at the foot of the bed.

Elena leaned against the doorjamb while Anastasia set her bags on the floor. "Your accent sounds familiar. Where are you from?"

"I live in Moscow, but I grew up in Drezna."

"I knew it!" Elena clapped her hands in delight, then gave Anastasia a crushing hug. "Drezna is my hometown, too. When did you move away?"

"Twelve years ago. How about you?"

"Close to twenty years ago now. No, almost thirty. Time certainly does fly when you're not paying attention. That explains why you and I have never met. Then again, I'm probably old enough to be your mother. It's not likely we would have the same set of friends."

Elena's mention of her mother reminded Anastasia that she had never had one. She tried to remain positive, but she felt her mood begin to sour.

"Your family must be so proud that you speak English well enough to earn such a good job," Elena said. "I have always wanted to learn English, but I never had a chance. Will you teach me?"

Elena sounded almost bashful as she made the request. Anastasia found it hard to believe that a woman who looked so strong could seem so vulnerable.

"I'm not much of a teacher, but I would be happy to share what I know."

"Excellent." Elena's bright smile banished some of the dark clouds that had started to form on the edges of Anastasia's psyche. "Where is your family? Are they in Moscow or are they back in Drezna?"

Anastasia focused on the task at hand as she made the bed. "I never had a family."

"Nonsense." Elena helped Anastasia fit the sheets onto the lumpy mattress. "Everyone has a family. Just because you're not close to yours doesn't mean they're not your family."

Anastasia straightened. She could tell Elena meant well, but she was tired of people making assumptions about her life.

"If you're from Drezna, you know about the orphanage there. The one on Petrov Street. That's where I grew up. That's the place I ran away from when I was old enough to support myself. Not only do I not have a family, I have nothing to call my own. Not even my name. The janitor who discovered me thought I bore a faint resemblance to the daughter of Tsar Nicholas II, so he named me Anastasia. My last name isn't my family name. It's courtesy of the street where I was found. Where my parents dumped me because they were too busy living their lives to raise a kid. Do you want to stand here and reminisce about the town both of us abandoned long ago, or do you want to do your job and finish telling us how things work around here?"

Elena's smile vanished as she absorbed Anastasia's verbal assault. She looked pained. Anastasia recognized that look: pity. She longed for the day when she wouldn't have to see it directed at her.

"I heard shouting," Laramie said after Elena turned and fled from the room. "Is something wrong?"

"Elena and I had argument over proper way to tuck corners on sheets. It is my bed so I prefer to make it my way."

Laramie looked skeptical. Anastasia felt awful about lying to her, and she felt even worse about upsetting Elena, but she was too stubborn to say it out loud. In time, when her emotions weren't quite so close to the surface, perhaps she would have a chance to make it up to both of them.

"Disagreement was personal. It had nothing to do with work."

"I don't care what started it," Laramie said firmly. "If you're in the wrong, do what you need to do to make things right."

Anastasia hated being told what to do, even if—as she suspected was the case now—the person delivering the orders was well-meaning.

"You are not my boss. I report to Sergei, not you."

She enjoyed the sense of freedom that gave her in an environment that could prove constricting.

"I'm not trying to be your boss," Laramie said. "I'm trying to be your friend. Whether you follow my counsel or not is up to you. It don't make no nevermind to me."

Anastasia started to say she had enough friends, but she held her tongue. In a place as lonely as this, she could use all the friends she could get.

Laramie didn't know what had transpired between Anastasia and Elena, but she could tell the encounter had left both women shaken. Neither seemed herself as Elena stood in the middle of the kitchen and discussed the ranch's schedule. Elena's arms were folded across her chest in a classic defensive posture, and Anastasia looked glum as she paraphrased what Elena was saying.

"She serves breakfast at seven, lunch at noon, and dinner at eight," Anastasia said. "She stands on porch and rings bell to let everyone know when food is ready. They eat all meals together. Like—Like a family."

Laramie glanced behind her at the long wooden table that could provide seating for up to a dozen people. Her family had a communal table back home, too. Depending on the hour, the conversations around it could be muted or spirited. Even though the primary language spoken would be different, she suspected it would be the same way here.

"If she doesn't serve breakfast until seven," she asked, "what time do the men begin their chores?"

Anastasia relayed Laramie's question and waited for a response. "Most days, they get started at eight. If they have had too much to drink the night before, it can be later. Maybe nine or ten."

"That will never do. Shorty and I need to change that mentality first off. At home, the ranch hands and I are out of bed by four a.m. and in the fields by five. We grab a bite to eat at noon if we can spare the time. If not, we keep working. We sit down for supper each night at seven and we're in bed by nine. Sometimes eight. And there's absolutely no drinking on a work night."

She didn't feel the need to point out that on a ranch or a farm, every night was a work night.

Elena laughed uproariously when Anastasia told her what Laramie had said. "She says you can try to implement changes you speak of, but men are too set in ways to adapt to something new. And they will sooner give up breathing than they would nightly glasses of vodka."

"They'll change their tunes if I add the language into their contracts. Once they sign on the dotted line, they'll be obligated to abide by the rules."

"You can do that?" Anastasia asked.

"We'll see."

Duke had hired her to improve operational efficiencies and help bring the ranch up to speed before the first batch of cattle went to market. He had granted her tremendous leeway, but he hadn't given her complete free rein. She could make suggestions, but it was up to

Yevgeny to accept or reject her recommendations. As ranch foreman, he could overrule her whenever he chose. Based on her and Shorty's initial encounter with him, she doubted he would be too willing to see things their way.

"Unless you have more questions, Elena says she has work to do. Yevgeny is waiting to show you around ranch."

"Sounds good to me." Laramie put her hat on and began to head out of the kitchen. She stopped walking when she noticed Anastasia hadn't moved from her spot at Elena's side. "Aren't you coming? Shorty and I can't do this without you, you know."

"I will be there in one moment. I need to make amends first."

On the porch, Laramie watched through the screen door as Anastasia said something to Elena in Russian. Elena's face and body language were hard at first, then she slowly started to soften. The change began with her eyes, which turned from icy to glowing. Almost maternal. Elena nodded, whispered a reply, then accepted Anastasia's offer of a hug.

"What's going on?" Shorty asked as he tried to see what had so thoroughly captured her attention.

Laramie turned her back to give Anastasia and Elena some privacy, then directed Shorty to do the same.

"You might want to mark this day in the history books."

"Yeah? Why?"

"Someone took my advice and it didn't blow up in my face for once."

"The day's still young. You've got time to muck things up."

"Thanks for nothing."

She turned at the faint sound of an engine. In the distance, she could see a large all-terrain vehicle heading their way, a thick cloud of dust trailing in its wake.

"Here comes our ride."

"Yep. Let's go make sure he and his friends haven't mucked up this ranch so badly that we can't fix it."

"You don't sound too confident in his abilities."

"Do you?"

"I wouldn't trust him as far as I can throw him."

"My sentiments exactly. If the books are in as bad a shape as the rest of the place, we'll have even more work to do."

"You said a mouthful." Shorty scratched his chin, a tactic he used whenever he needed time to think. "You have a better head for numbers than I do. I'll leave that part of the patch job up to you. Give me a set of tools and some building supplies, and I'll take care of the rest. A little touching up, and this place might turn out to be something to write home about. Provided the men are worth their salt and the cattle looks halfway decent, that is."

"You sound like Russia is starting to grow on you."

Shorty smiled as Elena and Anastasia slowly walked toward them. "It has its charms."

"Yes, sir, it certainly does."

CHAPTER NINE

The all-terrain vehicle Yevgeny was driving had two rows of seats, a roof to protect him and his passengers from the elements, and a large storage area in the back. It was in much better shape than the van he had driven to the airport, and smelled a whole lot nicer, too. He pounded the steering wheel with the heels of his hands after he braked to a stop in front of the main house.

"Who needs a horse when I have this?" he asked.

"I know he's right proud of his little toy car," Shorty said after he descended the porch steps and set his suitcase and saddle in the back of the ATV, "but tell him nothing beats a good horse. Unless this thing has an outboard motor hidden underneath the chassis, it can't cross a swollen river. A horse can swim. This thing would sink like a stone."

Laramie and Shorty slid into the back seat, leaving Anastasia no choice but to sit next to Yevgeny. She made sure she was out of striking distance when she told him what Shorty had said.

Yevgeny's eyes glinted mischievously as he absorbed Shorty's words. "In the stables, there are six horses for him to choose from. But can any of them do this?"

He shoved the ATV into gear and stomped on the gas. Anastasia hurriedly fastened her seat belt to prevent herself from flying out. Laramie did the same, but Shorty refused to take the extra precaution. Instead, he braced his arms against the back of Yevgeny's seat as Yevgeny drove in a tight circle.

Anastasia closed her eyes as dust, dirt, and debris began to make its way into the seating area of the ATV. "I think you've made your point," she said, but Yevgeny kept driving in tighter and tighter circles.

"I want to hear him say it."

She didn't have to tell Shorty what Yevgeny had said in order to provide an answer. "He is too proud—and too stubborn—to give you the satisfaction. Now stop this madness before someone gets hurt."

Yevgeny made one more lap, then eased off the gas as he turned the steering wheel toward the bunkhouse. Anastasia felt two of the oversized wheels lift off the ground. She held her breath, fearful the vehicle was about to tip over.

"I was just having a little fun with our new friends," Yevgeny said. He stopped the ATV and let the engine idle. "Tell him he has five minutes to put his things inside. If he isn't back by then, I will start the tour without him."

Anastasia chose to deliver a different message. "He says he will wait here until you return."

"Uh-huh. Sure he did." Shorty climbed out of the back seat and grabbed his belongings. "I didn't come all this way to get into a pissing contest," he muttered as he strode toward the bunkhouse.

"Since you're already in it," Laramie called after him, "make sure you don't lose."

"Roger that."

After Shorty pulled the door open, Anastasia peered inside the bunkhouse. The interior looked like a dormitory. Eight cots were lined up along the walls of the narrow structure, four on each side. A metal storage locker stood sentry next to each cot. A combination lock kept the possessions inside safe from prying eyes.

Anastasia had grown up in a room like that. She shuddered as she remembered the lack of privacy and the sliver of hope in her chest that grew smaller and smaller each time one of her dorm mates was adopted. Each time they were chosen to have homes and families of their own and she was left behind, waiting in vain for her turn to be picked. To be wanted.

"Okay, let's get this show on the road." Shorty returned carrying a thick pair of work gloves. Laramie had a similar pair tucked in the back pocket of her jeans.

"Are you planning on getting your hands dirty?" Anastasia asked.

"It never hurts to be prepared," Laramie said. "As we say in America, it's better to have something and not need it than need it and not have it."

"We have saying in Russia, too: man is born to live and not to prepare for life. Americans prepare for the unexpected and Russians take life as it comes. That explains difference between our countries, no?"

"Not all of them, but that's certainly a good place to start."

The soil, Laramie noticed, was black and rich, perfect for pastureland. The land was dry now, but when the fall and winter rains came, there would be plenty of water for the cows to drink and plenty of grass for them to graze on, lessening the need for store-bought food.

"They're skinny," Shorty said as Yevgeny slowly drove through the herd, "but they'll do."

Though Laramie was glad the cattle seemed to be in good physical shape, she still had some concerns.

"I need to see their immunization records to make sure they've had all their shots. I don't see ear tags or brands on them. How do you tell them apart?"

"He says they're cows, not people," Anastasia said. "Why would he need to tell them apart?"

Laramie pinched the bridge of her nose between two fingers. She couldn't tell if Yevgeny was being intentionally obtuse or if he truly had no idea what his job entailed.

"Each cow in the herd needs to be fitted with an ear tag, white for bulls and yellow for heifers. The number helps us keep track of each animal and chart its progress. If you don't have any tags, you need to get your hands on some as soon as possible. We'll need one tag for each head of cattle plus an extra box or two to maintain a working supply."

"He says there is no need for him to waste Sergei's money. Andrei used to be butcher. He is able to recognize each animal by sight. He has even given each beast a name and they come to him when called."

Laramie reminded herself to let Andrei know the animals shouldn't be considered pets. If he or any of the other ranch hands got too close to the cattle, their sentimentality would make it exponentially harder if not impossible for them to be able to do their jobs when it was time to take part of the herd to market.

"That's all well and good," she said, "but if Andrei up and quit tomorrow, all the knowledge he has would walk out the door with him. No matter what the expense, we need those tags. If they're fitted with a radio frequency device, they would help us locate the cattle if any of them were to get lost."

"Yevgeny says he will place order tomorrow."

"That's not good enough. Tell him to place the order today and have the tags sent overnight."

"Why so fast?"

"We're already behind. I want to start catching up."

As Anastasia relayed the message, Laramie silently celebrated her hard-fought victory. Hopefully, the subsequent battles wouldn't prove nearly as difficult.

Yevgeny pulled out his cell phone. He spoke for a few minutes, then ended the call.

"Order has been placed," Anastasia said. "The delivery fee was double, but tags will be here before noon."

"Excellent. If we work fast, we might be able to get through most of the herd before dark. What time does the sun set around here?"

"Around eight thirty during the summer months. In winter, it gets dark before five."

"Just like home."

"Do you think Godoroye will ever feel like home for you?"

"In some ways, it already does."

"And in others?"

"Let's just say the welcoming committee hasn't been as hospitable as I'd hoped it would be."

Laramie meant the comment to be a joke, but Anastasia obviously didn't take it that way.

"I apologize if my efforts have not met your expectations. If there is anything you would like me to do differently, please make me aware what that might be and I will do my best to improve my performance."

Anastasia must have thought her job was on the line. Laramie felt like kicking herself for causing her unnecessary concern. She placed her hand on Anastasia's arm.

"You've been great. Don't change a thing."

Anastasia's expression slowly changed from panicked to relieved. "*Spasibo.*"

"How do I say, 'you're welcome'?"

"*Pozhaluysta.*"

"*Poz* what?"

Anastasia laughed and slowly repeated the word again and again until Laramie was finally able to say it correctly.

"*Gesundheit,*" Shorty said like he always did when he heard a foreign word or phrase he couldn't pronounce.

"Wrong language," Anastasia said, "but you have very good German accent, Mr. Johnson."

"Must be all the bratwurst we cook up back on the ranch."

"Must be."

Anastasia regarded Laramie's hand. Laramie pulled away, realizing she had allowed the contact to linger several moments too long. She reminded herself to be more careful with her actions so she wouldn't upset the conservative societal norms. She also vowed to be more careful with her words so she wouldn't keep tripping over the language barrier. She thought it might be best if she kept her mouth shut and her hands to herself. Unfortunately, she wouldn't be able to get much work done that way.

They rode in silence for a while. Then Laramie heard the distinctive sound of a calf in distress. She pointed to a rise off to the right.

"Tell him to head toward that ridge."

After Yevgeny topped the hill Laramie had indicated, she noticed a group of men crowded around a hole. The hole must have been filled with water at some point, but most of the water had evaporated, leaving thick black mud behind. A calf, about nine months old by the looks of him, was struggling to free himself from the mud. A cow, most likely the calf's mother, lingered nearby. The pair lowed at each other constantly, their calls sounding more plaintive by the minute.

The four men surrounding the hole seemed to be debating the best approach to free the trapped animal. Based on their gestures, one seemed to be in favor of looping a rope around the calf's neck in order to pull it free. Another indicated the animal's front legs. The other two men stood by the wayside, shouting encouragement, advice, or both.

"Tell him to pull over," Laramie said.

While the men continued their lively debate, she and Shorty went to work. Shorty grabbed a shovel and jumped into the hole to see if he could dig the calf free. Laramie rubbed the calf's nose to calm it as clots of mud began to fly past its head.

"It's no use," Shorty said a few minutes later. "This stuff is like quicksand. The more I dig, the deeper he sinks." He grunted as the nearly six-hundred-pound animal leaned its weight against him. "Easy there, little fella. We'll find a way to get you out of this mess."

"I've got an idea." Laramie grabbed the two lengths of rope lying on the ground and handed them to Shorty. "Loop them under the calf's belly. I'll tie the ends to the ATV. I don't see a winch, but it should have enough horsepower for us to be able to pull him out."

Shorty shifted his eyes in Yevgeny's direction. "You think our friend will be nice enough to let you play with his toys?"

"I don't plan on giving him a choice."

Shorty chuckled. "I knew Thad raised you right."

After Laramie tossed him the ropes, Shorty plunged his arms into the mud and worked the ropes under the calf's belly. Shorty fished the ropes out of the mud and tossed them to Laramie so she could tie them to the hitch on the back of the ATV.

"Shove over," she said, signaling for Yevgeny to get out of the way.

He grumbled but acquiesced. As he angrily puffed on a cigarette, she turned the key in the ignition and gingerly pressed on the gas pedal. Feeling resistance as the ropes tightened around the calf's body, she gave the ATV a little more gas. Not too much, though. She didn't want the ropes to press too tightly into the trapped animal's flesh. She would have preferred using tow straps for this maneuver, but beggars couldn't be choosers.

"Easy now," Shorty said. "Easy."

Laramie couldn't tell if his words were directed to her or the calf, but she backed off the gas nevertheless.

"There we go. He's coming."

Laramie watched as the calf's body slowly began to rise from the hole.

"That's it. That's the way. Hold up." Shorty held up a closed fist, signaling for Laramie to hit the brakes. "You got him."

Laramie put the ATV in Park and shut off the engine as the exhausted calf sank to his knees. After she untied the ropes, she motioned for the men to clear out of the way. The calf's mother slowly made her way over to him. She nudged his head with her muzzle, then gave him a few cautious licks. After he had time to catch his breath, the calf clambered to his feet. The men applauded as he scampered off in his mother's wake.

Laramie pumped her fist as she watched the happy reunion. "That's what I call a good day's work."

A man with short black hair and the doughy body of someone with no apparent interest in counting carbs led the cheers. "Yay, Piotr," he said. "Yay, Lesya."

Hearing him address each cow by name, Laramie pulled off her gloves, walked over to him, and stuck out her hand. "You must be Andrei Dolgopolov," she said as Anastasia provided translation. "I'm Laramie Bowman. Pleased to meet you."

"Yes, I am Andrei."

He shook her hand with a wary look on his face. As if he feared he were being singled out because he had done something wrong. The three other men looking on appeared nervous, too. Laramie kept forgetting how different things were here. Back home, everyone longed for their moment in the sun. Their fifteen minutes of fame. Here, people wanted to go about their business without being noticed. Because any attention they received might result in negative consequences. She rushed to set Andrei's mind at ease.

"I hear you know your way around the herd. I'll need your help telling who's who. Can I count on you?"

Andrei nodded enthusiastically after Anastasia translated what she had said. Then he released a rapid torrent of Russian. Laramie turned to Anastasia to see what he was saying, but he was speaking so fast even Anastasia seemed to be having a hard time keeping up.

"He says it would be his pleasure to help you. He enjoys looking after the animals and can already tell which will fetch highest price at market. He was butcher for twenty years. He knows all about best cuts of meat."

"Tell him I'm glad he's on our team."

After Andrei stepped back, the rest of the men crowded around to introduce themselves, too. They spoke simultaneously, making it hard for Laramie to tell which name belonged to which man. She repeated their names and pointed to each man to make sure she had attached the right name to the right face. Vladimir Myskin, a former history teacher. Fyodor Kafelnikov, a one-time plumber. Ivan Rublev, an erstwhile baker.

She remembered the information she had read about them in their personnel files, but she set that aside. What was written about them didn't matter. She needed to see how they performed.

"If you're done making friends, I've got news for you," Shorty said. "Your day ain't done." He tried to climb out of the hole, but the mud held him fast. "Get me the hell out of here."

Laramie had wondered why he hadn't been in on the exchange of handshakes. Now she knew why. She reached for one of the ropes so she could use the same technique she had utilized on the calf in order to pull him out. Fyodor and Ivan stepped forward before she could toss Shorty the rope.

Fyodor pointed to the rope while Ivan moved his hands like was turning a steering wheel.

"They would like to try," Anastasia said.

"I gathered that."

Laramie hesitated. The men needed to learn the proper techniques to perform the various chores around the ranch, but she didn't want to risk Shorty getting hurt.

"I know what you're thinking," Shorty said, "but I ain't a piece of fine china. I don't break easy. Give the boys a chance."

Laramie handed Fyodor the rope. Grinning, he knelt in front of the mud hole and looped the rope under Shorty's arms the way Shorty had secured the calf. Ivan, meanwhile, slid into the driver's seat of the ATV and gunned the engine.

"Whoa now," Shorty said. "I think he's been watching too much NASCAR."

"Formula One," Anastasia corrected him. "He says Lewis Hamilton is his favorite driver."

"In either case, I think I'd better hold on to my hat."

Shorty placed both hands on his Stetson and braced himself as Ivan shifted the ATV into gear. The mud that had held the calf fast was obviously unwilling to release its grip on Shorty as well. As Ivan eased the ATV forward, he pulled Shorty right out of his boots. Everyone laughed as he stood before them, mud covering nearly every inch of him except for his thick white socks.

Vladimir fished around in the mud hole until he located Shorty's boots. A cheer went up as he brandished them over his head. More laughter followed when Shorty began to dump out the mud that had pooled in his boots.

Shorty shook each of their hands. "Thank you, fellas. I always like starting my workday with a good mud bath. It's good for the complexion."

Andrei said something and slapped him on the back.

"He says you should try sauna," Anastasia said. "Is good for the pores."

"I'll keep that in mind."

Laramie didn't know if Shorty had earned the men's respect, but he definitely seemed to have earned their goodwill. That was a positive sign.

"I don't want to hear you say nothing about me being no smarter than a farm animal," Shorty said as he stepped into his muddy boots.

"I promise you won't hear me say it, but that doesn't mean I won't think it."

CHAPTER TEN

Laramie and Shorty were so filthy Yevgeny refused to allow them to get back in the ATV. He drove alongside them as Shorty, Laramie, and Anastasia finished the tour on foot. Andrei, Ivan, Fyodor, and Vladimir trailed behind, listening intently to what was said, but not interrupting with questions of their own.

"No skin off my nose," Shorty said. "The way he drives, I'd rather walk anyway."

Though Anastasia didn't provide a translation, Vladimir chuckled as if he understood the meaning of Shorty's words. He had taught history at a small university just outside Moscow. Anastasia asked him if he had picked up some English during his own studies.

"My father gave me lessons when I was a boy. He taught himself during the Cold War because he didn't trust the government to accurately depict what the Americans were saying. I have forgotten most of what he taught me, but I never lost my desire to learn—or to teach others. I became a professor so I could watch the light of knowledge shine in my students' eyes. Now I get to be a pupil again." His weathered face took on a boyish enthusiasm. "I am excited for the opportunity."

"To clean stables and herd cattle? Teaching seems a lot easier. And less messy, too."

"I am excited to be able to learn new things. I am excited to be useful. To feel needed."

"I don't understand. Teachers—even the bad ones—are desperately needed."

The teachers she'd had at the orphanage often seemed as if they were operating on autopilot instead of truly engaging with their students, but she had felt transported each time she learned something new. Even if the person delivering the information couldn't seem to care less.

"One would think, but it doesn't feel that way to me. I quit teaching because most of my students showed more interest in their various electronic devices than they did in the material. I grew tired of looking out at a roomful of laptops rather than my students' faces. But enough about me. What did you do before you joined our small but hearty band? Have you always been a translator?"

Anastasia didn't know how to answer his question. She wanted to be honest and tell him she spent most of her time fighting for gay rights. In her experience, the most educated people were generally the most tolerant. The more knowledge people possessed, the less likely they were to hate what they didn't understand.

She couldn't come out to Vladimir, for obvious reasons, but she thought she could count on him not to assail her with a slew of ill-informed arguments if she mentioned the subject of homosexuality. She wasn't quite as certain about the others, though. Andrei, Fyodor, and Ivan had spent their lives toiling in working class professions. They weren't as erudite or as well-spoken as Vladimir. Therefore, they might not be as accepting.

As Elena had warned Laramie earlier, the men were too set in their ways to adapt to something new. She couldn't be a bridge of communication between them and the Americans if they refused to listen to what she had to say.

"I did as little as possible," she said. "I would rather spend more time living my life than wasting it working."

"Spoken like a true romantic." Vladimir's eyes twinkled as he laughed. "I will lend you my copy of the collected works of Lord Byron to read during your stay. The others prefer vodka, but I consider literature to be the best way to while away the evening hours."

"I'm afraid I have to side with the others. I like to read a good book every now and then, especially the scary ones that force you to stop every few minutes to make sure your doors are locked, but I have never liked poetry. It's too highbrow for me."

"But you like the songs you hear on the radio, don't you? Poetry is like a song without the music. You will like Lord Byron."

"What makes you so certain?"

"After spending almost thirty years in a classroom, I have a knack for reading people. Especially students who, for whatever reason, choose to downplay how bright they are. I trust Lord Byron's words will not be lost on you." He cocked his head as if appraising her, then closed his eyes and said, "*She walks in beauty, like the night. Of cloudless climes and starry skies; And all that's best of dark and bright Meet in the aspect of her eyes.*"

Anastasia felt lightheaded as Vladimir recited the poem. The words moved her. Touched her soul. When she tried to imagine the woman the poem described, Laramie's face swam into view.

Vladimir opened his eyes, a small smile of self-satisfaction on his face. "Have I got it right?"

"Yes," Anastasia said, trying not to stare at Laramie, "you did."

"Excellent. I will give you the book after dinner."

"I look forward to reading it."

And to committing one poem in particular to memory. In time, perhaps she could become equally familiar with Laramie Bowman.

Shorty was covered in mud from head to toe and Laramie was nearly as bad, but both looked happier than Anastasia had ever seen them. They looked almost content. As if they were fulfilling their purpose. Anastasia wanted to feel something similar. To know she was doing what she was truly meant to do. Her life had meaning, but did it have purpose?

"The incident with the calf," she said as she, Laramie, and Shorty slowly walked across the gently rolling land. "Have you experienced such things before?"

Curious cows looked up as they approached. A few skittered away from the sound of the ATV's engine, but most quickly returned to grazing or napping in the warm sun. Some trotted over to the fence and poked their noses at Andrei's hand like dogs begging for treats. He chuckled like a proud father as he petted their furry heads. Anastasia couldn't reconcile his obvious love for animals with either his former or current professions. Perhaps he was trying to make restitution in some way in order to clear his conscience.

"Too many times to count," Laramie said. "Sometimes, I feel more like a member of a search and rescue squad than a rancher."

"I know what you mean." Shorty spit out a dark brown stream of tobacco-infused saliva. The stream landed squarely on the side of the ATV. Accidentally or on purpose? "Remember the time we almost had to call the fire department to lend us a hand? That steer was stuck so bad it took us nearly half a day to dig it out."

"Everybody was tuckered by the time we were done," Laramie said. "I slept like a log that night."

"Tonight should come a close second," Shorty said. "That calf was trapped pretty good."

Laramie nudged him with her elbow. "So were you, as I recall."

"Next time, I'll get one of our newfound friends to jump in the hole to see if he can do any better."

"They seem to pick things up pretty quickly."

"They're eager to learn, that's for sure," Shorty said. "They've just been waiting for someone to teach them."

Anastasia didn't bother translating Shorty's last sentence, which seemed to be a critique on Yevgeny's efforts—or lack thereof.

"What would have happened if you had not been able to free animal?" she asked instead.

Laramie's smile faded, a dark expression taking its place. "We would have had to put it down."

"You mean kill it?"

"If we had left it there, the predators in the area would have been attracted by its cries. They would have ripped it to pieces. We had only two choices: free it or put it out of its misery."

The pool of wetness gathered in Laramie's eyes let Anastasia know she had also performed that odious task on countless occasions as well.

"How can you kill something you care for?"

Laramie looked off into the distance as if the answer to Anastasia's question could be found there. Anastasia suspected, however, Laramie was searching her soul rather than the horizon.

"Sometimes," Laramie said, "you do what hurts you because you know it's the best thing for someone else."

Friends and lovers alike had often accused Anastasia of being selfish rather than selfless.

"Mischa's always saying I put my own needs ahead of those of other people."

"Is he right?"

"That depends on what I am doing at the time. At certain moments, I make sure someone else is satisfied before I think of myself."

Laramie's tanned cheeks reddened at Anastasia's risqué comment. She reminded Anastasia of the horses Shorty so frequently mentioned: strong and reliable but filled with a coltish energy. A spirit that couldn't be broken. Or perhaps she simply hadn't found the right rider.

Yevgeny glared at the large tobacco stain on the side of the ATV. "What would they like to see next?"

"Tell him to take us to the stables," Laramie said.

Anastasia felt her own cheeks warm at the thought of finding out if she had what it took to stay in the saddle while Laramie took her on the ride of her life.

"If that day ever comes," she said to herself, "I'll bet Shorty won't be the only one holding on to his hat."

Laramie smelled the stables long before she walked inside. The earthy odors of hay and horseflesh assaulted her senses. She took a deep breath, drawing the aroma deep into her lungs. Anastasia covered her nose as if she wished she had a gas mask.

"Is this too much for you?" Laramie asked.

As a city girl, Anastasia was probably more accustomed to the smell of car exhaust than horse manure. She looked like she could use some fresh air.

"Thank you for asking, but I am fine."

Anastasia's answer was unexpectedly formal and also an utter fabrication, but Laramie admired her stubbornness. Among other things. Anastasia had a nimble mind and thought quickly on her feet. She instinctively knew when to share what Laramie and Shorty were saying and when to keep it to herself. If they worked this well together on their first official day on the job, Laramie couldn't wait to see how they would perform after they had known each other for a while. Then again, Anastasia already seemed to know her better than most. She could read her moods. Anticipate her needs. How could a virtual stranger see her more clearly than some of her oldest friends?

Six quarter horses filled the stalls. Two thoroughbred types, two bulldog types, and two intermediate types. The bulldog type of quarter horse was instantly recognizable because of its huge muscles, large hindquarters and shoulders, and its substantial barrel. The other two types of quarter horses were not nearly as powerful but possessed greater speed and agility, both valuable assets when they were needed to cut or rein in cattle.

Laramie's favorite horse was an intermediate named Sorghum, a palomino mare who was strong and durable enough to ride on the ranch and fast enough to enter in barrel racing competitions. Chuck and Grant had promised to give Sorghum plenty of exercise while she was gone, but Laramie was looking forward to once more being the one putting her through her paces.

Shorty walked up to a stall occupied by a sorrel-colored mare. "Who's a pretty girl?"

Laramie looked at the horse's ears to judge her body language. When a horse's ears were flickering or pinned forward on its head, the horse was alert and paying attention to what was in front of it. If a horse pinned its ears back, that meant it was angry about something and was apt to lash out in some way, either through biting or kicking. When its ears were lowered, it was relaxed, bored, or not feeling up to par. Laramie wished women's moods were as easy to read.

Shorty scratched the mare between her flickering ears and offered her a handful of grain from the feed bucket hanging on the outside of her stall. The mare shook her large head, then lowered it to feed from Shorty's palm. Shorty beamed.

"Like I said, nothing beats a good horse."

Andrei stepped forward and said something in Russian.

"That is Raisa," Anastasia said. "The brown stallion next to her is Nikita. The dappled roan on the other side is named Dimitri. The large ones are Yuri and Viktor."

"What about this one?" Laramie approached a mare with a shiny black coat, a wavy black mane, and eyes the color of midnight. "What's her name?"

Anastasia flashed a curious smile as she listened to Andrei's response. "Her name is Krasota, which is Russian word for 'beauty.'"

"Fitting."

Laramie ran her hand along Krasota's long neck and gave her a pat. When she pulled away, Krasota ducked her head, rested her chin against Laramie's shoulder, and drew her closer.

Anastasia gasped, fearful the horse was about to attack, but Laramie laughed and enthusiastically scratched the animal's neck. As her strong hands dug into the horse's flesh, the mare pawed at the hay-covered floor of her stall and heaved what sounded like a contented sigh. Anastasia was transfixed by the scene.

"I think someone likes you, Laramie." Even though Shorty lowered his voice to a whisper, Anastasia heard his words loud and clear. "Then again, you've never had a problem convincing pretty things to throw themselves at you."

Anastasia felt a pang of jealousy as she remembered how Natalia kept touching Laramie in an overly familiar way at her farewell party. How many women had Laramie slept with in the past? Did she have a lover now? Did she prefer one-night stands or long-term relationships?

Anastasia didn't know the answer to the other questions, but the answer to the last one was fairly obvious. When Laramie took a woman to bed, it wasn't for the night. It was in the hope that it would be forever. Anastasia didn't like putting that kind of pressure on a sexual encounter. Sex was supposed to be hot. Sex was supposed to be fun. It wasn't supposed to make you want to send out wedding invitations and spend holidays with each other's parents. It was supposed to make you long for more, not something you never had.

"They have seen the ranch," Yevgeny said, interrupting Anastasia's thoughts. "What do they want to do next? Spend even more of Sergei's money?"

"No, they would like to see how you have been spending it." Anastasia recalled the conversation Laramie and Elena had shared in the main house. "She would like to see the accounting ledgers and all the documentation on the animals so she can make sure the records are in order."

Yevgeny's face blanched and his mouth fell open in shock. "Sergei invited the Americans here to show the men how to do their jobs. He didn't invite them here to tell me how to do mine. Why does this—this *woman* need to see the ledgers?"

Anastasia relayed Yevgeny's question so Laramie could speak for herself. Laramie was silent for a long while. As if she were trying to find the right words to get her point across without driving the wedge between her and Yevgeny even deeper than it already was.

"Shorty and I are here to help in any way we can. Tomorrow, Shorty, Ivan, Fyodor, and Vladimir will start working on some much-needed repairs and improvements. While they're doing that, Andrei and I need to inventory and tag the herd. In order to accomplish those tasks, I need to review the records. *All* the records." Laramie paused to allow Anastasia to translate what she had said, but she didn't give Yevgeny time to raise any objections. "I'm told your official accountant quit several months ago."

The muscles in Yevgeny's jaw crawled as he tried to figure out who had given Laramie the information she was using against him. Anastasia was having so much fun watching the confrontation, she almost forgot to do her job.

"I'm sure you've done an adequate job in Maria's absence," Laramie continued, "but you're only human. Mistakes are inevitable, especially when you're working on such a large scale. A second set of eyes can prevent a small mistake from turning into a much bigger one. I've handled my family's business accounts for years. I know how to save money, which you seem to have a keen interest in. If I can find ways to run the ranch more efficiently, we all win. And if I can't, well, you'll be no worse off than you are now and you can be the first to say, 'I told you so.'"

Even though Shorty had said he and Laramie didn't stroke egos, she was doing a fine job of it. Instead of criticizing Yevgeny, she offered flattery. Slowly, her words began to have an effect.

"The sales and immunization records are a mess," Yevgeny admitted. "Maria tried organizing them but could never make much headway. Perhaps you can have better luck. I will give you access to those records tomorrow. When you are done with them, then you can see the ledgers."

Laramie nodded as if she agreed with everything Yevgeny was saying. He had agreed to fulfill one of her requests, but he was dragging his feet on fulfilling the other. One way or another, she would get her hands on those ledgers. Thankfully, she wouldn't be sitting around twiddling her thumbs in the meantime. From the sound of it, she and Andrei—and everyone else—had their work cut out for them.

"He would like to know if there is anything else you require today," Anastasia said. "Men have work to do."

"I won't keep them from it," Laramie said. "We can have a team meeting after dinner."

"He says try not to ruin anyone's appetite."

"No can do," Laramie said. "I never make promises I might not be able to keep."

Chapter Eleven

After the tour of the property ended, Yevgeny went for a joyride on the ATV. Andrei, Fyodor, Ivan, and Vladimir stayed behind to feed and water the herd. Anastasia accompanied Shorty and Laramie to the main house so they could get cleaned up for dinner. Elena held out both hands like a police officer directing traffic when she saw them coming.

"Stop!"

Even though Elena uttered the command in Russian, Laramie and Shorty pulled up short.

"I just finished mopping the kitchen," Elena said at a slightly lower volume.

"Tell her we don't have any intention of tracking mud on her clean floors," Shorty said. "All we need is a hose and a spigot with good water pressure."

Elena led them to the back of the house and pointed to a rubber hose coiled in the yard.

"I will get some towels they can use to dry off. Tell them to give me their clothes when they're done. I normally do laundry every Friday, but I will make an exception in this case. The longer I wait, the more work it will take to get those stains out."

"Thank you, ma'am," Laramie said after Anastasia repeated what Elena had said. She tossed her hat aside and unbuttoned her denim shirt, revealing a form-fitting white tank top underneath.

After Laramie peeled off her dirty work shirt, Anastasia admired the sight of her toned arms and narrow waist. Even though she wanted to continue staring, she forced herself to look away so no one, Laramie included, could see the desire she felt burning in her eyes.

"Do you plan to bathe out here?" Her voice sounded so strange she almost didn't recognize it.

Even though they were in the middle of nowhere, there was a distinct lack of privacy. There were no outdoor shower facilities and the ranch hands could wander through the area at any moment. Unless they wanted to compare penis sizes, they probably wouldn't be too interested in seeing Shorty naked. Seeing Laramie in the nude was a different story.

Anastasia wouldn't mind sneaking a peek either, though she suspected one fleeting glance wouldn't be enough. It would most likely whet her appetite rather than curb it.

How am I supposed to share a bathroom with her? If I walk in on her stepping out of the shower, I might make a fool out of myself. If I haven't already.

Laramie was like a walking caution sign. Anastasia kept telling herself to be careful around her, but the more time she spent with her, the more she felt like throwing caution to the wind.

"I want to rinse some of this mud off before it dries any harder," Laramie said. "My jeans are so stiff I can barely walk."

The thick mud on Shorty's jeans sounded like ice cracking when he bent to turn on the water. "Now I know how the Tin Man must have felt before Dorothy found an oil can in *The Wizard of Oz*." He let out a piercing whistle that prompted one of the horses in the nearby stables to whinny in response. "Jiminy Cricket, this water's cold."

His teeth chattered as he directed the stream toward his shirt and pants. Rivulets of mud flowed off his clothes and pooled at his feet.

"Don't forget to rinse the inside of your boots," Laramie said. "You've been squishing ever since the boys pulled you out of that hole."

Shorty pulled off his boots and stuffed the end of the hose in each one. When he turned the boots upside down, the liquid that streamed out looked like day-old coffee.

"Your turn."

He handed the hose to Laramie, then stripped off his shirt, socks, and pants, leaving him clad in only an undershirt and a pair of baggy boxer shorts. He didn't seem to have an ounce of fat anywhere. His thin arms and legs looked like matchsticks.

"Thank you, ma'am," he said after Elena tossed him a large bath towel. He dried his face and chest, then wrapped the towel around his nearly nonexistent waist.

Elena wiggled her fingers. "The underthings, too."

Shorty arched his eyebrows after he heard the translation. "If she wanted to see me naked, all she had to do was ask."

Elena grunted noncommittally. "As far as I can tell, there isn't much to see."

"I'm what you call a grower, not a show-er." Shorty tossed his wet T-shirt and boxers at Elena's feet. "I'd better get a move on if I'm going to make myself decent in time for dinner. Ladies."

Shorty tipped his hat and headed to the bunkhouse, water sloshing off his wet boots with every step he took. He was so skinny the towel practically swallowed him. Elena chuckled at the sight of Shorty's wiry frame fading into the distance.

"He has a nice face underneath all that tobacco juice, but he could use some fattening up. Remind me to give him an extra helping of mashed potatoes tonight and two extra *piroshki* for breakfast."

Anastasia nodded because she didn't trust herself to speak. She was struck dumb by the vision before her.

Laramie closed her eyes and stuck her head under the hose in order to rinse mud off her face. Water dampened her sun-bleached hair and splashed on her white tank top, rendering the undergarment nearly transparent. Anastasia could clearly see the black sports bra Laramie was wearing, along with the outline of her hardened nipples. The thin cotton material of her tank top clung to the rippled muscles in her abdomen.

Laramie played the water over her legs, soaking her jeans. Anastasia felt herself grow wet, too, even though she was nowhere near the hose.

Eschewing modesty for comfort, Laramie kicked off her boots and shimmied out of her jeans. Before she pulled her tank top over her head and wrapped the towel around her damp body, Anastasia committed the image of her in her underwear to memory. Laramie had the body of a goddess, and Anastasia was tempted to drop to her knees in worship.

"She looks strong," Elena said.

Strong was one word Anastasia would use to describe her. The rest she chose to keep to herself.

Laramie took off her socks, then used the towel as a cover-up as she removed her bra and boxer briefs.

"Do you have a boyfriend?" Elena asked.

Anastasia was taken aback by the sudden change in subject. When she heard the translated question, Laramie seemed to be as well. She looked at Anastasia as if she thought she wanted the information instead of Elena. The question might not have been her idea, but Anastasia was definitely interested in the answer.

"No, ma'am. Aside from my family, I don't have anyone special in my life." Laramie allowed her gaze to linger on Anastasia's face before she turned to Elena. "It's just me, my parents, and my brother. He's the main reason I'm here. He got hurt and needs some help with his medical bills."

In a way, Anastasia was disappointed by Laramie's response rather than relieved. If Laramie had a lover waiting for her—someone she had to be faithful to—it would make her obvious charms easier to resist.

"I am sorry to hear about your brother's misfortune," Elena said. "I hope he gets better soon."

"So do I."

"What about you, Anastasia? You're seeing Sergei's nephew, correct?"

Anastasia chose her words carefully so she wouldn't have to be dishonest. She didn't want to ruin her burgeoning friendship with Elena by lying to her on the first day of their acquaintance. "Mischa and I live together."

"Tell me about him."

"Mischa is—" *Like a brother to me.* "He is the best man I've ever known." She decided to turn the tables so Elena wouldn't ask her to reveal more details about her relationship with Mischa. She knew the questions would come eventually, but she wanted to put them off as long as possible. "Do you have someone?"

Elena looked wistful. "I gave up on finding companionship long ago. Work keeps me too busy to worry about foolish things like falling in love."

"So you don't have your eye on Yevgeny or any of the ranch hands?"

Elena laughed long and loud. "Andrei, Ivan, Vladimir, and Fyodor have women of their own, and the only thing Yevgeny cares about is money. I am safe here."

"Safe. That's an interesting choice of words."

"At my age, security is more important than sex."

Elena was a relatively young woman. Anastasia was surprised to hear her say she had taken herself off the market.

"Everyone has needs from time to time. You don't mind being out here all alone?"

Elena shook her head with an air of finality. "Sex has never been very important to me. I don't miss it. The men here, they respect me. They don't try to take advantage. They go their way and I go mine. You are young and still in thrall to your hormones. Eventually, you will learn there is more value in earning someone's respect than sparking their desire."

"Fortunately, that day hasn't come yet."

"It will. Just give it time." Elena gathered Shorty's and Laramie's wet clothes. "I will return these to you after I take them out of the dryer." She regarded the dirty water dripping from the sodden material. "It's a good thing Fyodor changed the filter on the washing machine last week. Because I'm about to put it to the test."

"I don't mean to be a bother," Laramie said, even though Elena and Anastasia had been speaking in Russian.

Her intuition took Anastasia by surprise sometimes. How did she always seem to know the right thing to say even when she didn't know what was being said?

"Do not apologize." Elena opened the back door with her foot and dropped the soiled clothes on the floor of the appropriately named mud room. "You and Shorty are providing me with job security."

Laramie grinned after she listened to Anastasia's translation. "Anything I can do to help."

Elena placed the clothes in the washing machine, poured in a cupful of detergent, and lowered the lid. "Believe me, you have done enough for one day. Get dressed. I will ring the dinner bell in an hour."

"Yes, ma'am." Laramie headed inside with her boots in her hand. The sight of her wearing nothing but a cowboy hat and a towel wasn't quite as comical as the sight of Shorty in his underwear, but it was pretty close.

Anastasia checked her watch. "You're serving dinner so soon? I thought you said you didn't normally feed everyone until eight."

Elena jerked her thumb in Laramie's direction. "If she plans on changing the schedule, I might as well start today so the men can begin getting used to it."

"But what if Yevgeny doesn't agree to the changes?"

Elena laughed again. "In a battle between those two, who do you think would come out on top? I would put my money on her."

Anastasia felt a kinship begin to form. "If I had any, so would I."

Laramie headed to her room and closed the door behind her. She released the tight grip she held on the towel wrapped around her body, then sat on the bed and stared at her hands. They wouldn't stop shaking. Elena's questions had reminded her why her presence in Godoroye was so important. She wasn't here for herself. She was here for her family. She was here for Trey.

Everyone she loved was depending on her. She couldn't afford to fail. If she kept butting heads with Yevgeny at every turn, she didn't see how she could possibly succeed.

If she forced Duke to choose between them, there was no telling how that situation might turn out. If Duke sided with Yevgeny, she and Shorty could be on the first plane back to the States. If he chose to side with her, she might end up getting stuck with someone even harder to deal with than Yevgeny was turning out to be.

"The reasonable thing to do is work things out," she said, thinking out loud, "but how am I supposed to do that if he refuses to meet me halfway?"

She sighed in frustration. She had dealt with difficult personalities before, but she had always managed to settle her differences with them. Yevgeny, however, didn't seem willing to talk things out over a couple of cold beers at the local bar. Wherever that was.

"Maybe I should offer to split a bottle of vodka with him instead."

Her stomach churned in protest at the memory of the last time she had drunk more vodka than she could handle. She didn't want a repeat of that dreadful scene. If she wanted to win Yevgeny over, she couldn't do it by puking her guts out in front of him.

She decided to take Anastasia's advice. Anastasia had told her to flatter Yevgeny. To appeal to his ego. She had done a bit of that today. As distasteful as the tactic had been, it had served its purpose. He had agreed to grant her request to see the sales and inventory records. He had also promised to show her the accounting ledgers once she got the other files organized. His promise had sounded half-hearted, but she was determined to make him keep his word. If he didn't, she would have to appeal to Duke. Going over his head was a surefire way to ruffle Yevgeny's feathers even more, but he wasn't leaving her much choice. She had a job to do, no matter who was standing in her way.

She placed her hands in her lap as the tremors slowly subsided. She hoped Yevgeny was simply being territorial or misogynistic. In time, those were obstacles she felt confident she would be able to overcome. If there was something else at play, that meant she had even bigger problems to deal with than the ones she had already uncovered.

"Like Mama always says, if it took God a week to create the world, I can't expect to solve all of its problems in one day."

Thinking of her mother made Laramie long to hear her voice. She reached for her cell phone. She had no idea what time it was in Wyoming because she was too stressed out to calculate the time difference. She dialed the number anyway. She could always leave a message if her mother didn't pick up.

"Laramie?" Her mother's voice sounded so close it brought tears to Laramie's eyes. "I was hoping you would call. What time did you get in? How was your first day?"

Laramie didn't want to worry her unnecessarily. Not when she already had Trey to fret about. "It was an adventure."

"I'll bet. Have you met everyone? Do you think the hands will have any problems catching on?"

Laramie laughed as she remembered them pulling Shorty out of the mud pit. "I could be wrong, but they don't seem like they'll have any trouble picking things up."

"That's good to hear. I know how impatient you can get when you have to explain something to someone more than once. And that's when both of you are speaking English."

"I'm working on that. How's Trey?"

Her mother sighed. "He has his good days and his bad days. That's to be expected, I guess."

"Is he being a good patient?"

"What do you think?"

"I think he's probably chomping at the bit to get out of bed and back on a bull."

"Yep. He's already planning his comeback. He's aiming to compete in the Cheyenne Frontier Days next year."

The Cheyenne Frontier Days were part of an annual ten-day festival that took place each July. The showpiece of the event was the rodeo, which was held in a magnificent nineteen-thousand-seat outdoor stadium. For Trey to complete his comeback there would be like a fairy tale come true. If he tried to do it before his body was ready to take the pounding, though, the fairy tale could quickly become a nightmare.

"That's a little over a year from now," Laramie said. "Do you think the docs will clear him to compete by then?"

"Probably not, but you know your brother. He's never been one to sit around wasting time when he could be risking his neck."

"That sounds like Trey, all right. I'll send some money home when I get paid in two weeks. I've got the direct deposit set up, and I can use my phone to log on and do the transfer."

"We appreciate your generosity, but don't try to send too much. Leave yourself something to live on. Like Thad said before you left, we'll make a way somehow. We always do."

"Yeah, I know."

She longed for the day when her family wouldn't have to budget so tightly, but that wasn't likely to happen until Trey's medical bills were paid. Whenever that was. She knew he would give what he could. He had promised to pay her back someday, but she wasn't counting on seeing a complete return on her investment. No matter. She knew he would do the same for her if their positions were reversed.

"Tell Trey I'm sorry I'll miss seeing him compete in Cheyenne next year, but I'll be rooting for him."

"The competition won't be the only thing you'll miss." Her mother sounded sorrowful. "Three years' worth of Fourth of Julys, Thanksgivings, and Christmases. Birthdays, too."

"I know, Mama." Laramie tried not to dwell on the unpleasant thought of spending holidays and special occasions away from her family. "We'll just have to make up for lost time when I get back."

"I'm counting on it. I'd best be going. I've got to get back to work and I'm sure you have things you need to do as well. You take care of yourself over there. Call me anytime you want to talk, okay? Day or night. I won't mind missing out on a few hours' sleep if it means I get to hear from you."

"I'll do that. I love you, Mama."

"I love you, too, Laramie. Make sure Shorty behaves himself, hear?"

Laramie scoffed. "I'd have better luck teaching one of the cows to turn somersaults."

"Don't I know it. He's a good man, though. I used to wish he'd meet a woman who could tame his wild ways, but I'm starting to give up hope."

Laramie thought of all the playful banter Shorty and Elena had exchanged that afternoon. If Shorty played his cards right, the statuesque cook could prove to be his match in more ways than one.

"I wouldn't give up hope just yet if I were you."

"In that case, I'll keep wishing for you to meet someone, too."

Laramie's heart sank at the realization that, while she was in Russia, her chances of embarking on a relationship were somewhere between slim and none. The risk was just too great.

"You know that's not the way things work around here."

"That's not how things work in Wyoming sometimes either, but that never stopped you from looking. Just because you have to be careful with your heart doesn't mean you should close it off completely, Laramie."

If they had been having this conversation face-to-face, her mother would have laid a hand on her arm or her shoulder to ground her. Since they were thousands of miles apart, her mother used her voice to achieve the same result.

"You might have been hired to share your expertise about cattle ranching," her mother said, "but that doesn't mean I can't still teach you a thing or two about life in the meantime."

The heavy burden Laramie was carrying lightened momentarily. Her shoulders rose in response.

"No, ma'am, I guess it doesn't."

CHAPTER TWELVE

The dinner table was laden with so much food Anastasia was surprised it didn't collapse under the weight. She stared at the steaming platters of beef stroganoff, meat-stuffed cabbage leaves, mashed potatoes, and blinis as Elena peered into the oven to check on the *ptichye moloko* cake she was making for dessert.

Elena pressed the batter with her finger, then closed the oven door and wiped her hands on a kitchen towel.

"Five more minutes. After the layers cool, I'll top them with the frosting and drizzle on some chocolate glaze."

Anastasia leaned against the sink and watched Elena hustle back and forth between the kitchen and the dining room. "Do you cook like this every night?"

"I splurge on special occasions, but we typically eat only half this much."

"What's so special about tonight?"

Elena arched an eyebrow. "If Laramie follows through on her plan to ban alcohol, the men will need something to take its place. A full belly might do the trick. Fat and happy is much better than drunk and discontent, don't you think?"

Anastasia treated herself to a sample of the chocolate sauce cooling on the counter. "Is there anything I can do to help?"

Elena slapped the back of Anastasia's hand with a mixing spoon. "You can keep your fingers out of that bowl and use them to set the table."

Anastasia yelped in both pain and surprise, then tipped her invisible hat and drawled "Yes, ma'am" in her best approximation of a Western accent.

Elena chuckled and waved her away. "Are the two of them always that polite?"

Anastasia grabbed knives and forks from the cutlery drawer and placed them on the table. "From what I've seen, yes."

The loose ponytail Elena was wearing was starting to come undone. Ignoring it, she blew a lock of hair out of her eyes.

"That's going to take some getting used to. The men give me an occasional compliment every now and then when I make a meal they especially like, but none of them says 'thank you' regularly or removes his hat whenever I enter a room. I hope Shorty's good manners rub off on them instead of the other way around. Do you think he'll be okay in the bunkhouse by himself without you to translate for him?"

Anastasia spotted the interest Elena tried to downplay. She couldn't resist teasing her about it. "You're not worried about him, are you?"

"Me?" Pretending to take offense, Elena drew herself up to her full height. "Of course not. I was just remembering how hard it was for me to make the adjustment when I first started working here. It was quite a change from what I was accustomed to. But he has lived this way and done this kind of work for quite some time now. I'm sure he'll be fine. They both will. I have my doubts about you, though."

The comment made Anastasia so anxious she nearly dropped the knife in her hand. Had Elena seen the way she had looked at Laramie when Laramie was using the hose to wash her face and rinse her muddy clothes? Had Elena guessed her secret?

"You have doubts about me? Why? What have I done to cause you concern?"

"Nothing yet," Elena said with a wink, "but it is only your first day here. You have plenty of time to stir up trouble."

Anastasia kept her eyes downcast so Elena wouldn't be able to see the relief in them. "I'm not looking for trouble. I'm just here to do my job. Nothing more."

"That's good. But sometimes you don't have to go looking for trouble. Sometimes trouble finds you." Elena looked at her hard. "You seem like you have run into your fair share of it over the years."

Anastasia focused her concentration on the remaining place settings. Two more to go and she would be home free. "Does it show?"

"It's in your eyes." Elena came over to her and held her face in her hands like a mother inspecting a young child's first attempt at washing its own face. "There's something—" She gasped and released her grip.

"What's wrong? Do I have chocolate sauce on my face or something?" Anastasia licked her lips and wiped the corners of her mouth with her forefinger and thumb, but she didn't taste any chocolate or see any telltale brown stains.

"It's nothing. It's just—" Elena tapped a finger under her own eye before she pulled the two layers of the cake out of the oven and set them on the counter to cool. "That's an interesting birthmark you have."

"Oh, this." A dark spot called the nevus of Ota covered part of the white area of Anastasia's left eye. "It looks unusual, but it doesn't affect my vision in any way. It often startles people the first time they see it up close, though. Just like it did you a moment ago. Aside from a nurse who passed me on the street and mistakenly tried to treat me for a head injury I didn't have, your reaction is one of the most dramatic I've ever received."

Appearing embarrassed by her outburst, Elena cleaned spilled flour off the counter. "I don't know why I didn't notice it earlier. I think I was so excited to hear you say you come from Drezna that I didn't pay attention to anything else. Have you always had the mark?"

Anastasia shrugged. "I suppose so. I don't have any pictures of me when I was a baby. The oldest photo I have was taken when I was six or seven. The mark was there then. I'm hoping it's hereditary. If it is, I might be able to recognize my mother or my father if I ever run into them on the street."

Elena paused. "What would you say to your parents if you were to meet them?" she asked hesitantly.

Anastasia felt a familiar heaviness weigh her down. At times like this, she envied Mischa. He had a lightness about him she doubted she would ever possess.

"I used to have a whole speech planned. It took me almost twenty years to draft it. I was proud of the finished product, but I don't see the point of reciting it anymore. All I want to know is why they decided to create me if they knew they didn't want me."

Elena resumed cleaning the spotless countertop. "Perhaps they didn't have a choice."

"We all have choices. And my parents made theirs the day they decided to leave me on the street like I was nothing but a bag of garbage." Anastasia slammed a dinner fork so hard it bounced off the table and landed on the floor. She bent and retrieved the utensil, then placed it in the dishwasher. "I'm sorry," she said, grabbing another fork from the cutlery drawer. "It's not your fault. I didn't mean to take out my frustrations on you."

"That's okay. You can talk to me." Elena placed a consoling hand on her shoulder. "That's what friends are for."

"Thank you." Anastasia felt a lump form in her throat. She had just met Elena a few hours ago, but it seemed like they had known each other all their lives. She didn't know if she could tell her all her secrets, but it felt good knowing she had someone other than Mischa that she could confide in. "Do you need me to do anything else?"

Elena stirred the frosting and began to spread it on the bottom layer of the cake. "Go ring the bell. Dinner's ready."

Anastasia peered through the kitchen window and eyed the large bell tied to a rope on the front porch. In a place as quiet as this, the sound probably carried for miles.

"Unless you want them to be ringing all night, be sure to cover your ears."

Anastasia sneaked another sample of chocolate sauce while Elena's hands were occupied. "I think I can manage that."

What she couldn't seem to manage was the one thing she wanted to control the most: her emotions. If she intended to last more than a few weeks at this job, she needed to get a handle on her feelings. And soon.

Laramie noticed the confused looks on the men's faces as they gathered around the dinner table. Yevgeny asked Elena a question in Russian. Elena pointed at her as she gave a short reply.

"Should I be worried?" Laramie asked as Yevgeny glared in her direction.

Anastasia closed the book Vladimir had given her when he walked in. "He wanted to know why we are eating an hour earlier than usual time. Elena told him to ask you."

Laramie felt like she had spent most of the day arguing with Yevgeny over matters both trivial and profound. She steeled herself for yet another confrontation when Yevgeny stomped his way over to her. He said something, then folded his arms across his chest. She could practically see smoke coming out of his ears while he waited for a reply.

"He would like to know why you changed the meal times without consulting him first. He says you were brought here to train the men, not the cook."

"Here we go," Shorty said under his breath.

Laramie knew he was expecting her to lose her temper. Yevgeny had been pushing her buttons all day and she was close to blowing a gasket, but she was determined not to do so in front of Yevgeny. She had dealt with people like him before. People who loved to sow discontent. She had always preferred chaos to tranquility. If she let Yevgeny see how much he irritated her, his behavior was guaranteed to get worse instead of better.

Two can play this game.

"Shorty and I were brought here to train the *team*," she said. "Elena is part of that team."

"He says she is just a cook."

"She's much more than that. If you ask me, this ranch wouldn't be able to run without her."

The translated comment brought a smile to Elena's face. A smile that quickly disappeared after Yevgeny turned to gauge her reaction.

"Are you turning against me, too?" he asked.

Not backing down, Elena held Yevgeny's gaze as she replied to his question.

"Don't be stubborn," Anastasia said, translating Elena's words. "Listen to her. What she says makes sense."

After Elena gave her an encouraging look, Laramie motioned for everyone to take their seats.

"I had planned to have a meeting after dinner, but we might as well do it now."

Yevgeny sat at the head of the table. Everyone else quickly assumed what were most likely their usual seats. Andrei and Vladimir sat on the left side of the table. Fyodor and Ivan sat on the right. Both Andrei and Fyodor left an empty seat between himself and Yevgeny, emphasizing the chasm that existed between Yevgeny and the rest of the team. Hoping to bridge the gap, Laramie took the empty seat between Yevgeny and Andrei. Anastasia sat across from her. Shorty and Elena claimed the seats next to Vladimir and Ivan.

At home, the meal would have started with a prayer. Laramie didn't expect this crew to hold hands while someone said grace so she closed her eyes and gave a silent invocation while Andrei and Vladimir began to fill their plates with offerings from the many platters of food. Everything smelled so good Laramie didn't know where to start. Deciding to follow Andrei and Vladimir's lead, she helped herself to a little bit of everything. Anastasia and Shorty did likewise. Shorty must not have taken quite enough food for Elena's liking, however, because she dumped a heaping spoonful of mashed potatoes on top of his already large pile.

"I could get used to this," he said as he tucked into his meal.

Laramie's stomach growled in anticipation, but she kept her hands in her lap rather than reaching for her fork. While everyone else ate, she slowly and methodically listed all the changes she hoped to instill in the coming days.

"I think it's obvious to everyone that there is a tremendous amount of work to be done around here." The men nodded in agreement after they heard Anastasia's translation. "If we begin the work day earlier, we can get more accomplished."

"What does an earlier work day have to do with eating dinner before the sun goes down?" Yevgeny asked. "It hasn't been that long since we had lunch."

"The schedule will begin to sort itself out tomorrow," Laramie said. "An earlier start time requires an earlier bed time, which means earlier meal times. Effective immediately, I want everyone to assume their posts by five a.m. each day. Breakfast will be served at four thirty and lunch at noon. Dinner might not be as elaborate as it was today, but it will take place at the same time."

Laramie heard more than a few grumbles of protest, but Ivan shrugged and said, "Getting up early is nothing new for me. When I was baker, I used to rise before dawn each day so I could have *vatrushkas* and *pirozhki* prepared before morning rush." He looked at his fellow ranch hands. "It is adjustment, but it does not take long to get used to."

Laramie nodded in Ivan's direction to thank him for his show of support. She hoped he would still be on her side after she revealed the other changes she had in mind. Her heart sank when Anastasia relayed Fyodor's question.

"He would like to know where vodka is. There is usually a bottle on table during dinner, but bottle is missing."

Laramie turned to Fyodor. "As I said before, there is a great deal of work to be done on the ranch. If we are to accomplish our tasks as quickly and efficiently as possible, we need to make sure we provide our best effort. That means getting plenty of rest. Thus the earlier dinner time." She glanced at Yevgeny before turning back to everyone else. "It also means no drinking during the work week." The grumbles she had heard when she announced the new schedule grew louder. "Some ranch owners use Breathalyzers to make sure their employees follow the rules, but I don't feel the need to go that far. You know why?" She looked each man in the eye. "Because I trust you. I trust you to do what's right. I trust you to take pride in your work. I trust you to be professionals."

"You cannot change way things are," Yevgeny said. "This is our culture. We are Russian, not American."

To emphasize his point, he grabbed a bottle of vodka from the liquor cabinet and placed it in the center of the table.

"You look thirsty, Fyodor," he said, slapping the much smaller man on the back. "Drink up."

The other men turned to Fyodor to see what he would do. Fyodor eyed the bottle but didn't reach for it. He patted his stomach and flashed a gap-toothed grin. "My wife says I need to lose weight. Less vodka means more room for dessert."

He licked his lips when Elena handed him a thick slice of cake.

"Coward," Yevgeny said.

Fyodor paused mid chew, then grinned again. "If you had met my wife, you would be afraid of her, too."

Everyone laughed good-naturedly. Once when Fyodor said it and again when Anastasia repeated it in English. The only person who didn't seem to find the joke amusing was Yevgeny. Laramie attempted to placate him.

"I'm not trying to change who you are. I'm trying to change what you do. My goal is to make this ranch not only successful but self-sufficient. If Shorty and I help you do your jobs, it will cost us ours because you'll be so good at what you do that you won't need us anymore."

"We don't need you now," Yevgeny said as he reached for another helping of beef stroganoff.

"Thankfully, Duke doesn't agree with you," Shorty said. "If he did, we wouldn't be here." He leaned forward as Elena pointed to the nearly empty platter of stuffed cabbage leaves. "Why, thank you, ma'am. I think I will have some more. Don't tell your mama, Laramie, but this is the finest meal I've had in a long time."

"*Spasibo*," Elena said after Anastasia relayed Shorty's compliment.

Shorty shook his head. "No, ma'am. I should be the one thanking you. A few more meals like this and I might forget how to find my way home."

Laramie tried to prevent Yevgeny's dark mood from turning pitch black. She leaned toward him so she could keep what she had to say between the two of them. And Anastasia, of course.

"You've made your position clear and I respect you for being up-front with us. But, like it or not, Shorty and I have jobs to do. Why don't you stop standing in our way and let us do them? The faster we get this place up to speed, the faster we can move on."

Yevgeny's bushy eyebrows shot up. The idea of her early departure obviously pleased him. "What about your contract?"

"Like promises, contracts are made to be broken. If the men prove they can run the ranch without us, do you honestly think Mr. Ivanov is going to pay us to stand around and do nothing? He'll either send us home or send us somewhere else. Either way, we'll be out of your hair. That's something we both want, isn't it?"

Yevgeny picked up the bottle of vodka and poured himself a generous serving. "Finally something we agree on."

Laramie seemed content as she ate her cold food, but Anastasia felt torn. If Laramie and Shorty returned to America before their contracts ended, what would happen to her? They had jobs waiting for them at home. She didn't. Sergei was generous with his money, especially when he was trying to impress a potential bedmate or business associate, but she doubted he would pay her to be a translator if she had no one to translate for. Teaching Elena English wasn't in her job description. It was something she had offered to do for fun, not for a fee.

She wanted to get out of Godoroye and go back to Moscow, but she wanted to keep earning a paycheck, too, and Sergei was the only one who was offering her one. That meant her future was inextricably tied to Laramie and Shorty's. If Laramie and Shorty succeeded, so would she. But if they did their jobs too well and were asked to leave, she might not be too far behind.

She considered sabotaging the Americans' efforts by intentionally providing incorrect translations, but she quickly discarded the idea. She didn't want to make Laramie and Shorty look bad in front of Yevgeny. Even though it might cost her in the long run, she would do everything she could to avoid having that blowhard think he had been right about them all along.

After dinner ended, Shorty thanked Elena for the meal and headed to the bunkhouse to get some sleep. Laramie returned to her room so she could do the same. Yevgeny went upstairs to brood over the dwindling bottle of vodka. Andrei, Fyodor, Ivan, and Vladimir, meanwhile, sat on the front porch and smoked.

"Andrei usually plays his balalaika after dinner," Elena said, "but I guess he isn't in the mood tonight."

Anastasia looked at the ceiling as the floorboards over her head creaked. From the sound of it, Yevgeny was pacing back and forth. She wasn't foolish enough to think he was trying to alleviate his anger. She knew it was more likely he was trying to think of ways to exact revenge. She was tempted to call Sergei to complain about Yevgeny's behavior or drop a word in Mischa's ear so he could say something to his uncle the next time they spoke, but she refrained. If Sergei already knew what Yevgeny was like and didn't care, she would be seen as the troublemaker, not him. She didn't want her actions to reflect badly on Mischa so she decided to keep quiet. For now.

"Andrei's either excited about the task Laramie has assigned him or he doesn't want to risk angering you-know-who," she said. "Is Yevgeny always this unreasonable?"

"He's like a bear waking up from hibernation. I find it's best to stay out of his way."

Unfortunately, Laramie and Shorty were already in his cross hairs. Anastasia set the book of poetry Vladimir had given her in a safe place, then began carrying plates from the dining room to the kitchen.

"What are you doing?"

"Auditioning to be your assistant. If things work out as well as Laramie hopes, I'll need another job."

Elena nudged her with her elbow when their paths crossed. "Are you trying to earn yourself a new position by costing me mine?"

"I'm a terrible cook so you don't have anything to worry about in that regard."

"The way I see it, you don't have reason to fret."

Anastasia scraped the remnants of Ivan's meal into a compost container. "Do you know something I don't? My finances are in dire straits. I'm counting on this job to make things better. If it ends too soon, I'll have nothing to show for it." But she would have a chance to get to know Laramie Bowman, and that opportunity could turn out to be priceless.

"You're dating Sergei's nephew," Elena said. "As long as you and Mischa are together, Sergei will make sure you're taken care of."

Anastasia bristled. "I don't need anyone to take care of me. I can take care of myself. I always have."

"I don't doubt it. But everyone needs a helping hand from time to time. If one is offered, don't be ashamed to take it. The only person you'll hurt is yourself. There is no need to be your own worst enemy when the world is filled with so many people who are willing to assume the role."

Elena's voice was as soothing as her words. Anastasia felt a rare sense of peace settle over her as she placed the dirty plates in the dishwasher.

"You make life sound so easy."

"It can be as long as you don't take it—or yourself—too seriously." Elena turned her around and gave her a gentle shove. "Go to bed. You have a long day tomorrow."

"We all do." Anastasia tucked the book under her arm, then looked around to make sure she didn't see Yevgeny lurking in the shadows. "The meeting went well, don't you think?"

She had expected the men to take Yevgeny's side. They had surprised her by pledging their loyalty to Laramie instead. It wasn't hard to see why. Laramie was something Yevgeny wasn't: a leader. And the men were willing to follow her.

Anastasia had seen a palpable change in Andrei, Fyodor, Ivan, and Vladimir's collective demeanor when Laramie had taken the time to explain the rationale behind her decisions instead of simply telling them that this was how things were going to be. When she had treated them like they were someone she wanted to work with instead of someone she sought to control. When she had shown them that Yevgeny's way might not be the best way. The only way.

"Andrei, Ivan, Fyodor, and Vladimir weren't nearly as upset about the changes as I thought they would be." Elena lowered her voice to a conspiratorial whisper. "And I loved watching Laramie put Yevgeny in his place."

"So did I."

Anastasia and Elena shared a laugh. Much too soon, though, Elena turned serious again. "Let's see how long he stays there."

The answer, Anastasia knew, could cement Laramie's success or begin her downfall. And no matter what the outcome, she would be there to watch it happen.

CHAPTER THIRTEEN

Laramie felt like a hypocrite. During dinner, she had spent several minutes explaining why she wanted everyone to start turning in earlier. Despite some initial resistance, she had managed to convince the ranch hands that her idea had merit. When the meal ended, she and Shorty had gone straight to bed so they could provide a good example for the men to follow. The bunkhouse had been dark for well over an hour now. Shorty and the rest of the ranch hands were probably snoring to beat the band, but she couldn't relax enough to fall asleep.

She rolled from one side of the bed to the other as both her body and mind rebelled against her. Her muscles were in knots and her thoughts wouldn't stop racing. She kneaded the back of her neck in a vain attempt to ease the tension. She hadn't expected every step of this journey to be smooth, but she had no idea the trip would be this hard. And she and Shorty were just getting started.

She shot a glance at the clock. Nine thirty. Only six and a half hours before her alarm was scheduled to ring.

"So much for getting eight hours' sleep."

She tossed the covers aside, pushed herself out of bed, and walked over to the window. Outside, the moon was full, shining brightly on the rugged terrain. Some might consider the ranch an eyesore, but she thought it had the potential to be spectacular. One of those fixer-uppers most of the home design shows specialized in on TV.

She was excited by the opportunity. Perhaps that was why she was so anxious. This was the first time she had a chance to leave her mark on something. No matter how good a job she did at home, the family ranch would always be thought of as her father's place. In Godoroye, she had a chance to change that.

Here, she wasn't Thad Bowman's daughter or Trey Bowman's sister. Here, she could be herself. Well, almost. She had to keep quiet about her sexuality, but she was already used to that. Being discreet was a small price to pay for being able to prove she was not only ready to carry on her family's legacy but craft one of her own.

She decided to make herself a glass of warm milk, one of her mother's tried and true remedies to treat sleepless nights. She crept out of the room and tiptoed into the hall. She tried to be as quiet as she could so she wouldn't disturb Anastasia.

A sliver of lamp light was visible underneath Anastasia's door. Was she still awake? Curious, Laramie pressed her ear to the door but didn't hear any sounds coming from the other side.

She started to open the door to see if Anastasia had fallen asleep with the light on like her mother was prone to do when she was watching one of the cheesy made-for-cable movies she loved so much. She reached for the doorknob but pulled back when she remembered she didn't know Anastasia well enough to walk into her room unannounced—or uninvited.

"Elena?"

A shadow passed through the shard of light, and Laramie heard footsteps padding toward the door. "Crap."

She hastily moved away, but too late. Anastasia opened the door before she made it more than a couple of steps down the hall.

Anastasia was dressed in an outfit similar to the one she had worn while she slept on Laramie's hotel room couch in Moscow: a tank top and a pair of boy shorts. Laramie avoided checking out her legs this time, but it took a serious act of will.

"Oh, Laramie. I did not expect to see you. I promised to help Elena learn English. She is so eager to begin, I thought she might have come by for first lesson."

"I'm sorry to disappoint you."

"No, I am glad you are not her. I have not had chance to prepare. I need time to make cards I plan to use during lessons. If I write down English word for objects she sees every day and tape cards around house, she can practice even when I am working with you."

"That's a good idea."

"It is not my idea. I saw it in movie once. With Whoopi Goldberg. *The Purple Color*, I think it was." Anastasia folded her arms in front of her chest as if she were self-conscious. "Do you need my help with something?"

"No, I was just passing by. I couldn't sleep and I was about to head to the kitchen to..." Feeling like she was babbling, Laramie allowed her voice to trail off. "It's not important. I'm sorry I bothered you."

She turned to leave, but Anastasia's voice drew her back.

"Is no bother. Would you like to come inside for few minutes, or would we get into trouble for breaking curfew?"

Laramie laughed. Even though the joke was at her expense, the jibe seemed playful rather than malicious. She followed Anastasia into the room.

"I didn't know you had such a sense of humor."

Anastasia closed the door behind them. "There are many things you do not know about me."

Suddenly, Laramie wanted to know everything. "Such as?" she asked, taking a seat on the storage bench at the foot of the bed.

"Such as I have new appreciation for poetry."

Anastasia picked up a book resting on the nightstand. Laramie recognized it as the tome Vladimir had given Anastasia earlier. She couldn't read the title, though, because the words were printed in Cyrillic. "What's that?"

Anastasia ran a finger along the book's spine. "The collected poems of Lord Byron. Vladimir thought book would appeal to me."

"Does it?"

Anastasia blushed and looked away. "Very much."

"Read it to me."

"All of it?"

Anastasia sounded so shocked Laramie couldn't help but laugh again. "Not the whole book. Pick one of your favorite poems and read it to me. In Russian, not in English."

Anastasia looked at her quizzically. "Why? Is my English not good enough? I know I am out of practice. I do not get to use it every day. I will try to do better."

"Don't worry. You're doing fine. Your English is much better than my Russian, that's for sure."

Laramie had never been very good at expressing her feelings, especially when she was put on the spot. Like her father, she preferred to leave things unsaid. They didn't need words as long as their intentions were understood. She couldn't do that here. Not with both language and cultural barriers in the way.

"You seem different when you're speaking your own language," she said. "More relaxed. More at ease. I don't know. More *you*."

She recalled how laid-back Anastasia had appeared when she was with Mischa, and how tense she often seemed around her. She and Anastasia were strangers, yes, but Anastasia and Elena were strangers, too, and they already seemed to have attained a level of comfort she and Anastasia had yet to reach.

She leaned closer, drawn to Anastasia in a way she couldn't begin to explain. Attraction certainly had something to do with it, but desire only skimmed the surface of what she was feeling. She wanted more. More of what she knew she couldn't have.

"Let me see you, Ana. The real you. Just for a little while. Please?"

Anastasia was struck. She and Laramie had found themselves in several intimate situations in the short time they had known each other—first in Moscow and now here—but Laramie had never addressed her in such a familiar way. She had never called her Ana before. The longing she heard in Laramie's voice pierced her heart like an arrow.

She wanted to go to her. Caress her face. Stroke her hair. Take her in her arms and feel the strength exuding from her tight, firm body. But she couldn't. Not when there was so much at stake. Laramie had her family to think of, and she had Mischa.

I hope he appreciates the sacrifice I'm making for him.

She opened the book, found the poem that had quickly become her favorite, and began to read. What would Laramie do if she knew the poem made Anastasia think of her? Would she smile and say, "Thank you, ma'am," in that strange accent of hers, or would she forget words and let her actions speak for themselves?

She could feel Laramie's eyes on her as she recited the words. She couldn't meet Laramie's gaze. If she did, she knew she would lose her resolve and do something they might both regret. Not tonight. But tomorrow and all the days that followed.

"That was beautiful," Laramie said when she was done.

Anastasia closed the book. "Did you understand a single word I said?"

"No, but I didn't have to." Laramie's face was filled with emotion. Her eyes glistened as if the poem had touched her as deeply as it had affected Anastasia the first time she'd heard it. "Can we do this again sometime?"

Anastasia told herself to say no, but when she opened her mouth, something entirely different came out. "Of course." She walked Laramie to the door. "Come see me next time you have trouble sleeping. You will be so bored you will not be able to keep eyes open."

And I won't be able to keep my eyes off you.

CHAPTER FOURTEEN

Yevgeny was a no-show at breakfast. The missing bottle of vodka provided a probable reason why. If he had polished off the rest of it, chances were good he was nursing a monster of a hangover. Laramie had felt like crap for hours after drinking four shots of vodka. If Yevgeny had downed half a bottle of the stuff, he might be out of commission for a whole lot longer.

The mood, she observed, was noticeably lighter without him. Despite the early hour, everyone laughed and joked with one another as they ate the "typical American breakfast" Elena had prepared: scrambled eggs, bacon, sausage, and a heaping platter of hand-cut breakfast potatoes.

Elena said something, then looked at Laramie expectantly. Laramie turned to Anastasia to find out what Elena had said. Anastasia's hair was still wet from the shower. They had taken turns using the bathroom that morning. At Anastasia's insistence, Laramie had showered first. Anastasia had claimed it took her longer to get ready and she didn't want Laramie to sit around waiting for her to finish her preparations, but Laramie suspected she had simply wanted a few extra minutes of sleep. The nap must have done her good because, like the ranch hands, Anastasia looked eager to face the day.

"She researched American food on internet," Anastasia said, reaching for another fresh-baked biscuit. "She wants to know if she got it right."

"It's perfect. Thank you, Elena."

"All that's missing is some ketchup," Shorty said. He typically covered his potatoes and eggs in so much of his preferred condiment his plate looked like a crime scene by the time he finished eating.

"She says she will remember that for next time. Will you need some when she prepares steak, too?"

Shorty looked at Elena and Anastasia like each of them had just said something bad about his mama. "No, ma'am," he said firmly. "A good piece of beef don't require no adornment. It's plenty flavorful on its own."

Elena's reply drew laughs from Andrei, Ivan, Fyodor, and Vladimir. Even Anastasia was forced to hide her smile when she said, "In that case, she will be sure to have plenty of ketchup on hand."

"Is good beef that hard to find around here?" Laramie asked.

"Not if you can afford to pay for it," Anastasia said. "Best beef is imported, which costs more. Elena is reluctant to buy from local producers because she does not want Sergei to think she favors his competitors over him."

Laramie decided to have a case of steaks shipped from her family's ranch so her new co-workers could taste what they were missing.

"Ivan asks if you have brother," Anastasia said. "I told him yes. He would like to know if brother is older or younger than you."

"Trey is four years older than I am." Old enough to know better than to perform most of the stunts he pulled but too young to care about the consequences if they went wrong.

"If brother is older, why are you here instead of him?"

Laramie wasn't offended by Ivan's question because his query seemed to have more to do with her age than her gender. The ranch hands were older than she had anticipated. Aside from Fyodor, who was in his mid thirties, the rest of the staff, Yevgeny and Elena included, were well over forty. She and Anastasia were the youngest ones here. She wasn't used to being the baby of the bunch. Not when Wyoming was crawling with high school and college kids dying to be shown the ropes.

"Unless you want to learn how to ride bulls rather than take care of them, you're better off working with me than my brother."

"Your brother does rodeo?" Anastasia asked.

"He did before he got hurt. His career's on hold until he heals up."

"Do you ride bulls, too?"

"No, I used to barrel race every once in a while, but I haven't competed since Trey got hurt."

"Does that mean your career is…on hold, too?"

"For me, barrel racing is a pastime, not an occupation. I'm not cut out to travel the circuit for weeks and months at a time. I'm more of a homebody." She explained the term in case Anastasia didn't know what it meant. "I prefer to stay in one place rather than roam the countryside."

"I would like to watch you compete."

Laramie felt a surge of excitement at the idea of winning an event while Anastasia looked on. She wanted to see the expression on Anastasia's face while she showed off her skills. She wanted to feel how Trey felt each time some groupie screamed his name. She always seemed to perform better when someone she cared about was in the audience. Had Anastasia become one of those people?

"You'll have to come to Wyoming sometime. We would be happy to have you."

"Perhaps Miss Elena could accompany you," Shorty said, joining the conversation. "There's plenty of room on the ranch for visitors. Especially pretty ones like you two."

Elena smacked Shorty on his shoulder as she passed by him on her way to the kitchen.

"She says you should get to work instead of sitting at her table telling lies," Anastasia said.

Shorty wiped his mouth with his napkin and tossed the soiled cloth on his empty plate. "We do have a long day ahead of us. I can't deny that. We need to start shoring up the fence before half the herd makes a break for Moscow. Where do you fellas get your wood from? I'm assuming there ain't no Lowe's or Home Depot around here."

Anastasia translated Fyodor's response. "There is lumber mill about twenty kilometers away. They have all kinds of wood. Oak, pecan, walnut. Quality products, but not too expensive."

"Now you're talking my language. I took some measurements yesterday so I have a ballpark idea of how much wood we'll need for slats and posts. Does he know where we can find barbed wire and nails?"

Fyodor nodded fervently after Anastasia relayed the question.

"Then you're my new best friend, Freddy."

Fyodor placed a hand on his chest and slowly said his name. "Fyodor. My name is Fyodor," he said in halting English.

Shorty waved a hand. "Fyodor. Freddy. Close enough."

"What about the rest of us?" Ivan asked.

"I'll need Andrei's help going over the sales records," Laramie said. "Shorty should have plenty for you, Fyodor, and Vladimir to do."

"And me?" Anastasia asked. "Would you like me to accompany Shorty and the others to town or remain with you and Andrei?"

Laramie felt a moment of abject panic. Anastasia couldn't be in two places at once and neither she nor Shorty could afford to sit around and wait for her to complete one task before she began another.

"I don't need no help, Laramie," Shorty said. "Russian or English don't matter. I can haggle in any language."

"Vladimir speaks some English," Anastasia said. "He can be big help to you."

"You've been holding out on me, Vlad," Shorty said. "You speak English?"

Vladimir held his thumb and forefinger a few centimeters apart. "Only a little."

"As long as you know the words for hammer and nails, that's all I need. Come on, boys. Let's get the cattle fed and watered before we head to town. You're driving, Ivan, but make sure you take it easy on those potholes, hear?"

It seemed Shorty had amassed a new collection of acolytes. Vladimir, Fyodor, and Ivan reminded Laramie of Chuck and Grant as they followed him outside.

"We go to work now?" Andrei asked.

"Yes, we go to work now."

Laramie finished her cup of coffee. If the sales records turned out to be as disorganized as Yevgeny had said they were, she might end up drinking the whole pot.

❖

Anastasia had never seen so much paper in her life. The large desk in the office upstairs was covered with so many receipts, notes, and spreadsheets it looked like a giant rat's nest. She turned to Andrei as Laramie tried to put the mess in order.

"What did Yevgeny do, toss everything in the air to see where it would land?"

"He has unusual methods, but we usually manage to make things work."

"In spite of him, not because of him."

"I think it will be different from now on." Andrei cut his eyes in Laramie's direction. "She's tough. A fighter. I like having someone who will stand up for me instead of talking down to me."

"You don't mind that she's a woman?"

"She can be whatever she wants to be as long as she knows what she's doing."

Anastasia wondered if he would say the same thing if he knew Laramie was a lesbian. She had learned from experience that most people's opinions about her changed as soon as they learned she wasn't heterosexual. Then she went from being someone they liked to someone they wanted nothing to do with. Laramie couldn't afford to face the same kind of rejection. Her success at her job was contingent upon retaining her co-workers' respect. Something she could lose in an instant simply by being honest about who she was.

Nearly thirty minutes after she started sifting through the paperwork, Laramie pointed to one of nearly a dozen stacks of paper she had created from the original mess. "What are these?"

Andrei peered over Laramie's shoulder. "Tell her those are the immunization records. The veterinarian we use is Dr. Yeltsin. He comes out every few months to check on the animals. His next scheduled visit is in two weeks."

"Have all the animals had their shots?" Laramie asked after Anastasia translated what Andrei had said.

Andrei nodded. "Yes. A few cried like babies when Dr. Yeltsin stuck the needle into their backsides, but most did pretty well."

"How is their overall health?"

"A few members of the herd are a bit small for their ages, but most of the cattle are healthy."

That got Anastasia's attention. "Most? Is there something she should know? Something you're trying to keep from her?"

Andrei looked nervous. "A few of the calves developed foot rot a couple of months ago and we had to put them down because they didn't receive treatment in time," he said, wringing his hands. "I tried to tell Yevgeny something was wrong, but he didn't believe me until it was too late. When he finally called for help, Dr. Yeltsin said the cows had a mineral deficiency. He prescribed supplements for the rest of the herd, and that seemed to resolve the problem."

"Is that all?"

"Yes." He pointed to one of the stacks of paper. "The bill for Dr. Yeltsin's visit should be in the records. He is very good about documenting all of his expenses."

Laramie looked up from the chart she was examining. "Is something wrong?" She grimaced when Anastasia told her what Andrei had said. "How many is a few?"

Anastasia conferred with Andrei, then relayed the bad news. "Ten."

Laramie sighed as if she had been expecting a higher number. "That's bad, but it could have been worse. We lost a sizeable chunk of our herd to Johne's disease a few years ago. They were infected right after they were born, but the symptoms didn't appear until they were adults. It damn near broke Shorty's heart when the affected animals started dropping weight. Mine, too, when I found out that the man who had sold us the cattle suspected they were sick all along but didn't say anything because he was so desperate to make the sale. I helped raise those cattle from the time they were calves. It was awful watching them start to waste away."

That was why Anastasia had never owned a pet. Because she had known the memories of the happy times they had shared in the past wouldn't be enough to offset the pain she felt when they eventually passed away.

"What did you do?" she asked.

"After I talked my father out of breaking every bone in his body, I convinced the seller to refund our money. At that point, word had gotten out about what he had done, and he was willing to do whatever it took in order to salvage his reputation."

Andrei tugged on Anastasia's sleeve. "Is she satisfied I did nothing wrong?"

Anastasia saw genuine fear in his eyes, making her wonder yet again how bad the working conditions had been when Yevgeny was the only person who had any say over everyone's fate. She placed a hand on Andrei's arm to reassure him.

"Yes, she is satisfied."

"That is good to hear. I made good money in Moscow, but I like this job much better than my old one. I am closer to my family, the cost of living is lower here, and I don't have to worry about getting mugged if I go out at night."

"That's because there's nowhere to go."

Andrei laughed. "Newcomers always say that, but that's because they do not know where to look. Vladimir knows the history of this town and the surrounding area. Ask him to show you the sights sometime. There is much more to this part of the country than you might realize."

Anastasia didn't care about Godoroye's history. She was more concerned with its present. From what she had seen, there wasn't much to attract her interest. Nothing in town, anyway.

"Are these sales prices listed in rubles or euros?" Laramie asked.

Andrei peered at the receipt in Laramie's hand. "Rubles."

"What was the conversion rate at the time of the sale?"

Andrei turned to Anastasia. "I used to run my own butcher shop. I know how the market works. Tell her the prices are fair. I checked them myself before Maria left. Nine hundred US dollars for a calf and up to two thousand for an adult."

"Have we added any more cattle to the herd since Maria moved away?" Laramie asked after Anastasia imparted the information Andrei had shared.

"Yes."

Andrei frowned as he shuffled through the stack of receipts. Laramie had taken the time to place them in chronological order. The most recent receipt was dated prior to Maria's departure seven months before.

"I don't see the sales slips here. Yevgeny must have shredded them. He says there is no need for paper. He prefers digital files. The current paperwork must be stored on his laptop."

"Password-protected, I'm sure."

"Of course. He is very secretive about the business side of things. He often acts like it is his money at stake instead of Mr. Ivanov's."

"Great," Laramie said sarcastically. "Then I guess our job here's done." She placed her hands on the desktop, rolled the chair backward, and pushed herself to her feet. "We can't audit anything else until we see the most recent records. And there's no way we're getting our hands on those until Yevgeny sobers up. If then."

"We have rest of day off?" Anastasia asked hopefully.

Laramie grinned. "Nice try, but there's always work to be done on a ranch. Especially one this size." She pointed at Anastasia's white canvas tennis shoes. "I hope you brought a good pair of boots with you because those weren't made to inventory nearly five hundred head of cattle."

"I do not mind getting a little dirty."

Especially if it meant she would be the one taking an impromptu shower in the backyard with Laramie this afternoon instead of Shorty. Even though nothing could come of the encounter, she felt certain she could use it as fuel for her fantasies for months if not years to come.

CHAPTER FIFTEEN

When Laramie, Anastasia, and Andrei went outside, a large box was sitting on the front porch. Laramie sliced the box open with her pocketknife and dug through the packaging to find the ear tags she had requested. Either Yevgeny had put the fear of God in the distributor when he placed a rush order the day before or he had been sitting on the tags all along. Whatever the reason, Laramie had what she needed to begin working in earnest.

She directed Anastasia and Andrei to return to the office and begin the time-consuming task of cataloging the serial number for each tag so it could later be cross-referenced to the cow it was eventually assigned to. She wasn't about to ask Yevgeny if she could borrow his laptop so she retrieved hers and booted it up. After she opened the program she wanted, she gave Andrei and Anastasia a quick tutorial so he could call out the numbers on the tags and she could log them into the computer.

She watched them for a few minutes to make sure they had a good handle on the process, then she got out of their way. Figuring the task would go faster and leave less room for mistakes with no translation involved, she grabbed her saddle and headed to the barn so she could take Krasota for a ride. She wanted to inspect the property and the herd at a more leisurely pace than Yevgeny had set yesterday. More importantly, she wanted a chance to clear her head. Her favorite place to do that was astride a horse.

Krasota's ears perked up as soon as she entered the barn. As Laramie drew closer, Krasota snorted and tossed her nose in the air as if she were nodding hello.

"Well, good morning to you, too." Laramie scratched Krasota between her expressive eyes. "Would you like some exercise?"

Krasota tossed her head again and added in a loud whinny for good measure.

"I'll take that as a yes."

Laramie retrieved a bridle from a hook on the wall and placed it around Krasota's head. Krasota chewed on the bit impatiently.

"Give me a second, missy. I'm moving as fast as I can."

Laramie reached for a pair of worn leather reins and attached them to the bridle. Keeping a tight grip on the reins, she opened Krasota's stall door and led her out.

"Almost there."

She grabbed her saddle with her free hand and placed it on Krasota's broad back. Krasota shifted her weight but didn't move. Her twitching ears, however, betrayed her excitement.

"I think you're looking forward to this as much as I am."

After she cinched her saddle into place and made sure it was secure, Laramie grabbed the pommel with her left hand, placed her left foot in the stirrup, and swung her right leg over Krasota's rump as she pulled herself up. She settled into the saddle and allowed Krasota to get used to her weight.

"Good girl," she said, patting the side of Krasota's long neck.

Mounting a horse was second nature to her now. When she had first learned how to ride, though, she had struggled to master the task. She had ended up flat on her back more times than she could count. Once, her foot had gotten tangled in the stirrups as she fell and the horse had dragged her on a couple of loops of the riding pen before she was finally able to free herself. Only Shorty had witnessed the embarrassing scene. She was still waiting for the day when he would finally allow her to live it down.

"Ready?"

Krasota's ears flicked forward in response.

"Then let's go."

Laramie clicked her tongue and gently squeezed Krasota's sides with her legs, urging the horse into a gentle trot. Once they were clear of the barn, she tightened her grip on the reins and signaled Krasota to go faster.

Krasota moved into a canter, then gradually increased the pace until she was running at a full gallop. Laramie held one hand on top of her hat to keep it from flying off as Krasota tore up one hill and down another.

So much for a leisurely pace.

After Krasota burned off some of her pent-up energy, Laramie pulled back on the reins and patted the horse's neck again.

"Thanks, girl. I needed that, too."

She paused to take a closer look at an especially rickety looking section of fence. She slid out of the saddle and gave the post a good shake to test its strength. The post was so dry-rotted her hand came away covered in dust. She pulled a piece of orange chalk out of her shirt pocket and placed a large X on the post so Shorty would know to use that section as a starting point when he and the ranch hands returned from town and commenced their repairs.

While she waited for Laramie to continue their ride, Krasota lowered her head and began to graze. A thought occurred to Laramie as she watched Krasota nibble on a patch of grass. When Anastasia had read the poem to her last night, she had said Krasota's name. Not her name exactly but the word. Krasota. Beauty.

Laramie had been transfixed as she listened to Anastasia read a poem in a language she didn't understand. She felt that way now as she remembered the look on Anastasia's face. Recalled the sound of her voice. Clear and bright yet muted as Anastasia spoke at an intentionally lower volume so she wouldn't disturb anyone in the otherwise quiet house.

Laramie was curious about the English translation of the poem Anastasia had read, but she was reluctant to find out what it was. Perhaps it was better that she didn't know. She didn't want anything to detract from the moment she and Anastasia had shared last night. The truth tended to do that.

In this case, she preferred fantasy to reality. Because in her fantasies, she could pretend that Anastasia hadn't been simply reading a poem to her. She had been reading a poem about her.

"Like that would ever happen."

She chided herself for thinking such foolish thoughts. She mounted Krasota again and resumed their slow circuit of the property.

"You're here to do a job, not moon over someone you're not even supposed to look at, let alone touch."

If she repeated the words often enough, perhaps she would eventually start to believe them.

❖

Anastasia's résumé was long but spotty, dotted with a string of jobs she had held for varying lengths of time. Some for as little as a few days, others for several months. One of the gigs was a data entry position she had hated at the time but was grateful for now. The countless mind-numbing hours she had spent plugging in figures on a seemingly endless number of spreadsheets had perfectly prepared her for the task Laramie had assigned her today.

She and Andrei finished cataloging the thousand ear tags Yevgeny had ordered in a little over ninety minutes. She thought they had made pretty good time, even though it wouldn't have been fast enough to meet the strict quota of the company she used to work for. That was probably why she no longer worked there. The messy affair she'd had with the boss's daughter hadn't helped matters much either.

She smiled at the memory. She didn't consider sleeping with Dinara a mistake exactly. More like a pleasant diversion that had gone awry. If Dinara hadn't flown into a jealous rage every time she saw her talking to another woman, they might still be together. Or not. Being with Dinara had been a rush, but in all the wrong ways. She hadn't been nearly as excited by the reality of being with Dinara as she had by the possibility of getting caught. Perhaps that was why she was so intrigued by Laramie. Because she represented the lure of the forbidden. Or was it because she represented something else? Something Anastasia had never experienced: stability.

She nearly jumped out of her skin when Yevgeny lurched into the room. His eyes were bloodshot, his hair wasn't combed, and his clothes were so rumpled they looked like he had slept in them.

"What are you two doing in here?"

"Working." Anastasia closed the laptop so Yevgeny couldn't see what was on the screen. Even though the job she and Andrei had performed wasn't a secret, she didn't feel comfortable sharing the details with Yevgeny. If he could hold out on Laramie, she could help Laramie hold out on him, too. "What does it look like we're doing?"

"Snooping. Isn't that what most women do?" Hot ash dropped from the end of his lit cigarette as he tapped the stack of sales receipts. "Did your friend find everything she needed?"

He made the word *friend* sound almost unseemly.

Anastasia brushed the smoking ash away before the papers it had landed on could catch fire. "For now."

"Good." Yevgeny unlocked a large floor safe and pulled out a laptop that was stashed inside. "Now get out of my chair so *I* can get some work done."

Anastasia tucked Laramie's laptop under her arm and left the office with Andrei in tow. He didn't speak until they were downstairs.

"I think he is stealing from Mr. Ivanov. From the company." Even though they were well out of Yevgeny's earshot, he practically whispered the words.

"Why do you say that?" She had her own suspicions about Yevgeny, but she wanted to hear Andrei's.

"Most people who act like they have something to hide usually do. Why else would he be so secretive about the missing documents? Or so protective of his computer? None of us want to steal it and we do not care what he has stored on it. We just want to do our jobs and get paid. There is no need for him to lock the computer and ledgers away each night as if we are common criminals. He is the thief, not us."

"Calm down," she said, trying to prevent his voice from rising any higher. She had made sure to close the office door behind them when they left. If they were lucky, Yevgeny hadn't heard Andrei's accusations. "Have you said anything to anyone?"

"It isn't my place. Plus I do not want to get into trouble. What if I spoke up and no one believed me? What if I'm wrong? I have a wife and two children. We have some money saved and my wife works at the hospital, but my family wouldn't be able to survive for long on one salary. I would have to return to Moscow to find work. When I left, I vowed I would never go back. I want my children to grow up in the same town I did. My life is here."

He was just as passionate to stay as Anastasia was to leave. Perhaps she needed to give Godoroye a second look. She was going to be here for quite some time, so she might as well try to get used to it.

"I might be able to help," she said.

"How?"

"I used to—" She barely stopped herself from saying *date*. "I used to know a woman who's really good with computers. She can hack into anything if given a chance. If I send her the IP address for Yevgeny's laptop, I bet she can help us take a look at those files."

"How do you know you can trust her?"

"I don't, but what do we have to lose?"

"If she turns out to be a bigger thief than Yevgeny? Millions."

"Then I guess I'd better come up with another plan."

One that didn't involve a potential prison sentence. Perhaps it was time to give Mischa a call.

"How would you like a chance to be a hero?" she asked when she got him on the phone.

"Would I be able to wear tights and a cape?"

"No, but you might be able to prevent someone from stealing your uncle's money."

Mischa didn't hesitate. "I will be on the next train."

CHAPTER SIXTEEN

L aramie stiffened when she saw the ATV speeding toward her. What had she done to piss off Yevgeny now? It was way too early to deal with his latest hissy fit. She blew out a sigh of relief when she realized Andrei was behind the wheel instead of Yevgeny.

"That was fast," she said as Andrei and Anastasia spilled out of the vehicle.

"We checked entries twice to make sure they were accurate." Anastasia thrust her chin in the air with a hint of pride rather than defiance.

"You two make a good team."

Andrei sported an ear-to-ear grin as he grabbed a box of ear tags from the storage area in the back of the ATV.

Anastasia opened the laptop and accessed the program Laramie had taught her how to use. "Are you ready to begin? I make entries while you and Andrei tag cows. I place name of cow next to serial number on list. Then you use other program to track its signal, yes?"

"Yes."

Anastasia tied Krasota to a nearby tree and squeezed through the fence. A piece of barbed wire snagged her shirt, ripping a hole in her sleeve. She checked to make sure she wasn't bleeding. If the rusty metal had pierced her skin, she would need to go into town and get a tetanus shot. Considering how much she disliked doctors, she wasn't looking forward to the trip. Thankfully, her skin was unblemished.

"Hand them over, Andrei."

Andrei handed her the box of ear tags and stepped over the fence, pressing down on the barbed wire so it wouldn't jab him in the crotch on his way over.

"He asks if tags will hurt cows," Anastasia said.

"Tell him the sensation will be no worse than getting his ears pierced."

Anastasia laughed as Andrei rubbed his ears with both hands. "He says he will have to trust you on that one."

Laramie pointed to the gate several hundred feet away. "Drive down there and come inside the fence. You can follow us in the ATV while Andrei and I hoof it. That way, those dazzlingly white tennis shoes of yours can stay relatively clean."

Anastasia rolled her eyes. "If I go on internet tonight and buy boots, will you stop making fun of me then?"

Laramie kind of hoped she wouldn't. She enjoyed teasing her too much.

Anastasia sped down to the gate, maneuvered the ATV inside, and closed the gate behind her. Avoiding the piles of manure along the way, she drove back to where Laramie and Andrei were standing.

Laramie pulled her work gloves out of her back pocket. "Call 'em over, Andrei, and I'll show you what to do. Don't rile 'em up too much, though. We don't want a stampede on our hands."

Andrei cupped his hands around his mouth, took a deep breath, and shouted something in Russian. It didn't sound like "Come, boss," the phrase she used whenever she wanted to get a cow's attention, but it worked just as well if not better.

The cattle approached and began to circle, some sniffing curiously at the computer on Anastasia's lap. Anastasia recoiled when one licked her face.

"If I had known I would end up getting bath, I would have stayed in bed this morning instead of taking shower."

Laramie tried to focus on the cow she was trying to wrangle instead of imagining Anastasia slipping into a warm bath filled with scented bubbles.

"Here's how you do it, Andrei." She held up the two-piece ear tag. "You place the visual panel on the back part of the ear and put the button on the front. A little squeeze on the applicator and it's all over." She held up a tool that looked like a pair of pliers. "Which cow is this?"

"Ekaterina," Andrei said.

Laramie turned to make sure Anastasia had matched the cow to the correct serial number. "Got that?"

"Yes, got it."

"Hold her head still while I put the tag in, Andrei. You're supposed to immobilize them when you do this, but I don't want to put them through that if we don't have to."

"He says cows are well-behaved. They will not move if he tells them to remain still."

Laramie turned to Andrei. "I kinda like having a cow whisperer on staff. I'll let you watch me do the first few, then you can take over for a while."

The cow didn't budge when Laramie applied the ear tag, but Andrei jumped as if he had been goosed.

"See? It isn't so bad." Laramie slapped Ekaterina on her rump to shoo her away. "One down, four hundred eighty-nine to go."

"This will take all day," Anastasia said.

"If we round 'em up fast enough. If not, we'll be back at it tomorrow." Laramie tagged another cow and sent it on its way. "Is there something else you would rather be doing than dodging cow pies?"

Anastasia wrinkled her nose. "The smell of these pies makes me never want to eat real one again."

"If you feel that strongly about it, you'd better tell Elena to drop pies from the dessert menu. Make sure she keeps that chocolate cake she made last night, though. That was one of the best things I've ever put in my mouth."

The mischievous twinkle in Anastasia's eyes hinted she was tempted to ask Laramie a follow-up question on the subject. Instead, she dropped her gaze to the computer screen and prepared to make the next entry.

When she was growing up, a slip of the tongue had gotten Laramie nothing more serious than a box on the ears. Here, she reminded herself, the punishment could be much worse.

"Your turn." She handed the tag applicator to Andrei. "Show me what you can do."

She held the next cow's head while he tentatively put the pieces of the tag in place.

"There you go. You're doing fine. Now finish the job."

Andrei closed one eye and screwed up his face as he slowly applied pressure to the handles of the applicator. Anxious to be set free, the cow mooed and bobbed her head. Andrei reflexively squeezed his hand, securing the tag.

"That's the way. But try to do it a little faster next time, okay? These cows are a hell of a lot stronger than I am. I can't hold them forever."

"You are stronger than you look," Anastasia said.

"Thank him for noticing."

Anastasia looked up and met her gaze. "He was not the one who noticed."

Wrangling the cows had already made Laramie start to work up a sweat. Feeling Anastasia's eyes bore into hers caused her body temperature to spike even more. She tipped her hat. "In that case, thank *you*."

Anastasia didn't know why she had said what she had to Laramie. Because it needed to be said? Because it was true? Perhaps, even though they couldn't act on it, she wanted Laramie to know the attraction she felt was mutual so she wouldn't have to endure this torture alone.

Yes, torture was a strong word, but it was the only one that could appropriately describe how it felt living and working in such close quarters with someone she was starting to desire. Starting to? No, she was already there. How much longer would she be able to hide the effect Laramie was having on her? Every time Laramie looked at her, she felt a flood of moisture pool between her legs. And that was before Laramie's sweaty work shirt started clinging to her skin.

Anastasia imagined peeling the damp shirt off her. Dragging her into the shower, turning on the spray, and rubbing soap over her tight, toned muscles. She couldn't think of a more perfect way to spend the day. Or the night.

"I invited Mischa to visit us," she said, trying to banish the images she had conjured up from her mind.

Laramie dragged her arm across her forehead to dry the sweat on her brow. "Are you feeling lonely already?"

"I thought he could help you. Help *us*."

"Help how?"

"He works in accounting office. He would be able to tell if ledgers are in order."

"I know what to look for," Laramie said defensively. "I can tell if the ledgers are in order."

"Yes, I am sure you can," Anastasia said, trying to appease her, "but Yevgeny is not giving you chance to look. He can say no to you, but he cannot say no to Mischa. It would almost be like saying no to Sergei, don't you think?"

Laramie was quiet, which compelled Anastasia to fill the silence.

"Mischa should arrive later this afternoon. He can look at books tonight. Or maybe tomorrow if train is delayed. If we do not tell Yevgeny he is coming, he will not have time to undo anything he might have done. To—What is expression Americans use? Cover his tracks."

She forced herself to stop talking so Laramie could have a chance to respond.

"That's a good plan," Laramie said. "So good I wish I had thought of it first." She broke into a grin. The suddenness and brightness of it took Anastasia's breath away. "You're right. We do make a good team."

In a perfect world, Anastasia thought as she watched Laramie sprint after a runaway calf, they could be a whole lot more. In Russia, that world didn't exist. At least not for people like them.

CHAPTER SEVENTEEN

Determined to finish tagging the cows before the end of the day, Laramie decided to work through lunch. By the time she handed Andrei the final tag and Anastasia entered the data in the computer, the sun was starting to dip toward the horizon and all three of them were dragging. But at least she was finally able to cross off one of the many items on her to-do list. She was so happy to complete something she had set out to do instead of running into another brick wall, she felt like turning a cartwheel. She didn't want to spook the cows or her new co-workers, though, so she convinced herself to remain upright.

She looked around. In the distance, she could see Shorty and his crew start to pack up their tools so they could head in for the day. They had made substantial progress on the fence repairs. They were by no means done, but the weakest parts had been shored up and the rest would be fixed in a few days. After that, they could mend the barn roof and start sprucing up the bunkhouse. A fresh coat of paint and a new set of shingles and both should be as right as rain. There was only so much that could be done to the bunkhouse's drab décor, but she doubted Shorty and his roommates would feel the need to call an interior decorator to spruce the place up.

By this time next week, they should be in position to stop playing catch up and start trying to get ahead of the game. She looked forward to being able to establish a routine. One she hoped would take the ranch from so-so to successful. If she did, Duke had promised her a substantial bonus in addition to the base salary they had agreed on.

The extra money would be nice, but it wasn't her main incentive. Turning the ranch's fortunes around had become a point of pride. Shorty had told her on numerous occasions that she had what it took to run her own ranch. Now she just had to prove it to everyone else. Starting with herself.

She untied Krasota and climbed into the saddle. Perched in the driver's seat of the ATV, Anastasia watched her as she did so.

"Want a ride?"

Anastasia eyed Krasota warily. "I already have one."

"You sound like Yevgeny." Laramie patted Krasota's neck. "Are you sure you want to miss out on a chance to ride a creature as magnificent as this one?"

"She is beautiful animal."

"Then what are you waiting for?"

Anastasia continued to hold back, even though she seemed tempted to give in. Laramie could already feel Anastasia's arms wrapped around her waist as they slowly made their way back to the main house. She would make sure to take the scenic route so she could prolong the trip as much as possible. Then Anastasia's cell phone chirped, breaking the spell.

"I just received text from Mischa," Anastasia said, staring at the phone's display. "His train is half hour from station. If I take van and leave now, I should arrive same time he does. Would you like to come with me so you can help me explain what we need him to do?"

Laramie didn't relish the thought of taking another bumpy ride in the smelly van, but she loved the idea of spending time with Anastasia away from prying eyes. So they could bond in a way they couldn't with everyone else around. Like they had last night.

"Give me a few minutes to wash the dust off my face and hands and put on a clean shirt."

"I will follow you. I need to change shoes." Anastasia's once-white tennis shoes had turned a dusky gray. "Whatever you do, do not say, 'I told you so.'"

Laramie held up her hands as if the thought hadn't occurred to her because it hadn't. She had already made her point. There was no need to go rubbing it in. She liked to tease, but she knew when to pull back. Picking at a sore spot only caused the pain to get worse, not better.

"I'll race you to the main house," she said. "The loser has to sit in the back of the van."

That was the area where the smell had been most potent during their ride from the airport.

"Contest is only fair if you know how to find way into town. If you do not, you will have to sit in back of van anyway because I will refuse to give you directions."

Laramie wasn't deterred by Anastasia's humorous threat. "I've got a GPS app on my phone. As long as I have a signal, I can find anything. Even way out here."

Anastasia secured the laptop in the ATV's storage area. "I take bet. Try not to be sore loser, okay?"

Laramie started to say she didn't intend to lose, but Anastasia put the ATV in gear and stomped on the accelerator before she could get the words out. She dug her heels into Krasota's haunches.

"Come on, girl! Get after 'em!"

Krasota snorted and took off after the ATV. She managed to close the gap but couldn't erase it completely before Anastasia reached the stables. By the time Laramie and Krasota arrived, Anastasia and Andrei were exchanging high fives to mark their victory.

"You don't play fair."

"No," Anastasia said, "I play to win."

Laramie dismounted and led Krasota into her stall. "Good night, girl," she said, rubbing Krasota's nose. "I'll see you in the morning." She turned to Anastasia, who had followed her inside. "I'll keep that in mind before I consider making another bet with you."

"Why? You do not like odds?"

Anastasia handed her the laptop. Their fingers grazed as they exchanged possession of the device. The contact was brief, but Laramie felt it in her whole body. Like the horseback ride they hadn't had a chance to share, she wished she could have made it last longer.

"If I keep betting on a long shot, I'm bound to win eventually."

Provided she didn't crap out before her bet finally paid off.

❖

Anastasia grabbed the keys to the van and lingered in the kitchen while she waited for Laramie to finish washing up.

"Where are you going?" Elena asked. "It's almost time for dinner."

Anastasia noticed the meal wasn't nearly as elaborate as it had been the night before. Meat dumplings, buckwheat porridge, and *sushki* for dessert.

"The train station," she said, grabbing one of the crunchy, mildly sweet bread rings usually served with tea.

She hadn't thought about food once while she, Laramie, and Andrei were working. Now she couldn't stop. She reached for another *sushki*.

"Stop snacking or you'll ruin your appetite." Elena didn't have a mixing spoon this time so she shooed her away with a dish towel instead. "Who's at the train station?" she asked after Anastasia moved away from the stove. "Are we expecting someone else to join us?"

"In a manner of speaking. Mischa is on his way from Moscow."

Elena put her hands on her hips. "I feel like I'm cooking for an army as it is. Now I have another mouth to feed. How long will he be staying?"

"A few days. Maybe a week."

She didn't reveal any details about the reason for Mischa's visit so Elena couldn't slip and say something in front of Yevgeny. She didn't want him to see what he had coming to him until it was too late for him to do anything about it.

"And where will he sleep? With you?"

"No."

Anastasia realized she had said the word more sharply than she had intended because Elena gave her a strange look. Even though she and Mischa would have to keep up the pretense of being lovers during his visit, she didn't want to do it at the expense of moments like the one she had shared with Laramie last night.

She and Laramie couldn't be alone if Mischa was crowded in the room. They couldn't be as open. As intimate. She would feel self-conscious having him there, watching her dance an awkward tango between lust and loyalty.

"My bed is barely big enough for me," she said, trying to offer a plausible explanation. "Mischa would never fit."

Elena flashed a conspiratorial smile and returned her attention to the steaming pots on the stovetop. "He shouldn't need much room if he's on top of you. I know many things have changed over the years, but some things remain the same."

"As you said before, it's been a while since you were on the market. You would be amazed how many new techniques there are."

Elena's muscles flexed as she stirred the large pot of porridge. "I'll leave the new techniques to young people like you. If I ever give that foolishness another chance, I will stick to what I know best."

"I'm sure Shorty will appreciate it, no matter what you do."

Elena banged the lid on the pot of *pelmeni*. "Don't start that nonsense again. He seems to be a nice man, but I barely know him." A look of regret washed over Elena's face. "We don't even speak the same language."

"Tongues weren't made only for speaking, you know. They can be used in a wide variety of ways. Would you like me to show you some of them?"

Elena frowned. "Be careful before someone hears you talking like that. You don't want anyone getting ideas about you, do you?"

The lightness Anastasia had felt all afternoon grew heavy. She mentally chided herself for feeling too comfortable around Elena. Elena was straight and had lived in small, conservative towns all her life. Anastasia should have known she would be able to push a risqué conversation with her only so far before she found resistance.

"What kind of ideas?"

She knew what Elena was hinting at, but she wanted—needed—to hear her say it.

Elena turned away as if she couldn't bear to look at her as she said the words. "Ideas that you might be interested in women as well as men."

Anastasia pressed her lips together to remind herself to phrase her response carefully. "I can assure you I am only interested in one of the two."

Elena sighed in obvious relief. "That's good to hear, but you know how people talk. Yevgeny's already whispering about..." She jerked her head in the direction of Laramie's room.

Anastasia felt a knot form in the pit of her stomach. Anxiety began to eat away at her. "What is he saying about her?"

"A woman who's strong, good with her hands, and can do a man's job just as well as if not better than he can? What do you think he's saying?"

The van keys rattled as Anastasia's hands started to shake. "Do you believe him?" she asked, tightening her grip to muffle the sound.

"She is not my daughter, so I do not care one way or the other."

"And if she were your daughter?"

As Elena gave the question some thought, Anastasia hoped to hear her say she wouldn't care who Laramie slept with as long as the person made her happy.

"I would still love her, of course," Elena said without seeming to mean it, "but I would make sure she knew I did not approve of her choices. Laws exist for a reason."

Anastasia clenched her hands into fists as if she were preparing for a fight. "Laws should exist to punish criminals, not prevent two people from loving each other."

"Why are you getting so upset? You're straight. You have a boyfriend. It's not like you're one of them."

But I am.

The words resounded in Anastasia's head and her heart, but she couldn't force herself to say them out loud. Elena's opinion of her mattered, and she didn't want it to change. She didn't want to lose the acceptance that had been so readily given. Even if, as she knew now, Elena's acceptance was based on the idea of her being something she wasn't.

"Are you ready to go?"

Laramie's voice startled her. She was so happy to hear it, she almost ran for the door.

"Yes, please."

"Did I interrupt something?" Laramie asked as they walked to the van. "You and Elena seemed to be in the middle of a rather serious conversation."

Anastasia climbed into the driver's seat and started the engine. She waited until Laramie buckled herself in the passenger seat before she said, "Yevgeny told Elena he thinks you are a lesbian and she does not like it."

Laramie propped her arm in the open window like she didn't have a care in the world. "Which part? The fact that Yevgeny is talking about me behind my back, or the fact that I'm a lesbian?"

Anastasia eased the van through the front gate and turned onto the main road. "Does it matter?"

"No, because I can't control either one. People are going to say whatever they want to say about me, and there's nothing I can do about it except continue to live my life the best way I know how. If Elena or anyone else has questions they want to ask, they know where to find me. But if you're expecting me to gather everyone together, stand in front of them, and make some dramatic coming-out speech, don't. Because that's not going to happen. Not now. Not ever."

"Don't you want people to know who you are?"

"When people look at me, I want them to see a person who lives her life with honor and integrity. Who I sleep with is my business, not theirs."

A sharp pang of disappointment pierced Anastasia's heart. "I thought you were out and proud."

"I am, but we apparently have different interpretations of the concept."

Anastasia dragged her eyes away from Laramie's face so she could focus on the rutted road.

"I would love to trade places with you for just one day. You have ability to walk down street holding lover's hand without having to worry about who might see you. You can kiss her without fear of being arrested. If I want to show affection to woman I love, I must hide behind closed doors like I am doing something wrong. You have everything I want—everything I am fighting for—and it means nothing to you. How can you let such valuable opportunity go to waste?"

"Because being gay is only part of who I am," Laramie said. "I'm a woman. I'm a rancher. I'm a daughter. I'm a sister. And, yes, I'm a lesbian. Despite what you might think, I've never shied away from any of those labels. Why are we arguing about this anyway? You're the one who shot me down before I could even think of making a move on you. Why should I put myself at risk when you're not willing to do the same?"

"I am activist. I put myself at risk every day. I cannot count number of protests I have planned, marches I have participated in, or flyers I have disseminated. I have been arrested. I have lost jobs. I have even lost some friends. But, still, I keep going. I keep fighting for what is right, no matter how steep the cost."

"I applaud you for your efforts, but what have you really accomplished if you're still living a lie?"

Anastasia wanted to counter Laramie's argument, but she couldn't. Most people thought Mischa was her boyfriend, and she did her part to continue the ruse. Only those she trusted most knew the truth. Most of them were in the closet, too, hiding their true selves for fear they would be ostracized or reported to the authorities. The few who were out had paid the price for their bravery. A price she didn't have to pay as long as she had Mischa at her side.

"I guess you and I are not so different after all."

She took Laramie's hand and gave it a squeeze. Laramie briefly returned the pressure, then let go. Anastasia immediately missed the contact.

They drove in silence for a while before Laramie said, "I'm thinking of making a change."

"Another one?"

"Yes, another one." The mood had been so dark for most of the ride, Anastasia was glad to see Laramie smiling again. "This one, I think everyone will like."

"What is it?"

"I want to turn Sunday into family day. We'll still have chores to take care of, but everyone can invite their families to the ranch for lunch."

"Family day is good idea. I am sure the men would love to spend time with their wives and children—to show them around ranch and let them see what they do for work every day—but Elena's family is too far away to make the journey."

"Tell her anyway. Maybe they'll decide to surprise her one weekend. I'd like to meet her family. I'd love to see if she inherited her height from her mother or her father. Does she have brothers and sisters? Do they look alike, or, like me and Trey, are they as different from one another as night and day? I'm curious about everyone else's family, too."

"So am I. I can't wait to see what poor devil has agreed to spend the rest of her life with Yevgeny."

"If the steaks I ordered arrive in time, we can fire up the grill and have a cookout this Sunday. Do you like your steaks underdone, overdone, or done done?"

"There is difference?"

Laramie looked at her as if she had said the sky was green instead of blue.

"Stick with me, Ana. There are so many things I need to teach you."

And Anastasia couldn't wait to learn.

CHAPTER EIGHTEEN

At the train station, Anastasia parked the van and shut off the engine. She waved when she saw Mischa standing on the crowded platform. Laramie almost didn't recognize him because he was dressed much differently than the last time she had seen him.

His makeup was gone. So were the sequined T-shirt and brightly colored jeans. Instead, he was wearing a brown cardigan, matching corduroy pants, and a white dress shirt. He looked conservative but uncomfortable. His personality seemed different, too. Muted as opposed to outgoing. To say he wasn't himself was an understatement.

His dour expression changed as soon as Anastasia jumped out of the van and ran toward him. Smiling broadly, he dropped his bags and wrapped her in a huge bear hug as if he hadn't seen her in months rather than a few days.

Laramie could sense the genuine affection they had for each other. No wonder it was so easy for them to convince people they were lovers.

They kissed each other on both cheeks, then walked toward her arm in arm. As they approached her, Laramie idly wondered if their close friendship would be a help or a hindrance if one of them met someone else. The person they fell for would undoubtedly find themselves in a relationship with not only their lover but their lover's best friend as well.

"Whoever it is, I hope they like threesomes."

None of the women she had been involved with had ever been forced to compete for her attention. Not with her friends anyway. The long hours she put in on the ranch had often gotten in the way, preventing her from establishing relationships that were more than superficial. She had gotten close once, but it hadn't panned out.

She and Claire Snowden had grown up together. Their families knew each other and they shared the same ideals. It was perfect. Laramie had pictured them settling down together one day, either on her family's ranch or on a place of their own. Except Claire had different aspirations. She didn't want to watch the sun set over the mountains. She wanted to move to California and watch the waves roll in on the beach. She had no concrete plans about what she would do for a living once she got there, but she didn't care as long as she didn't have to be a rancher's wife. She had said the words as if the job was the worst thing in the world, but Laramie couldn't think of anything better. Her mother was the best woman she had ever known and she would consider herself truly blessed if she could find someone with half as much intelligence, backbone, and tenderness.

Claire had asked Laramie to move to San Diego with her, but Laramie had declined. The beach was a nice place to visit, but she didn't want to live there. She preferred the prairie. She needed the wide open spaces. Big cities made her feel trapped. Hemmed in. Exactly how Claire had felt before she left Broken Branch.

The two of them had stayed in touch for a while, then Claire had fallen for a woman she had met on the way to her favorite yoga studio one day. Since then, their conversations had been few and far between. Laramie missed her every once in a while, but Claire had a new life now. The life she had always wanted. Laramie was already living hers. One day, perhaps she would be able to meet someone she could share it with. Until then, she could only keep doing what she was doing: working to secure her and her family's future.

"It is good to see you again." Mischa spoke hesitantly, but his handshake was firm.

"You, too. Did Anastasia tell you what we need you to do?"

"Yes, she said you need me to look over books and let you know if I find any abnormals."

"Abnormalities," Anastasia said, gently correcting his mistake.

Mischa placed a hand over his lips apologetically. "So sorry for my English. Ana speaks it much better than I do."

"Sometimes, I think she speaks it better than me, too." Laramie played up the country bumpkin angle to make him feel better. When she saw him relax a bit, she returned to the subject at hand. "Does Duke normally give his business managers such free rein?"

"Yes, he owns so many companies he must delegate day-to-day responsibilities to other people. His accountants audit bank statements to make sure there are no unusual expenses."

"I told him ranch accountant quit seven months ago and Yevgeny has been in charge of books since then," Anastasia said.

"A business associate originally recommended Yevgeny for job," Mischa said. "According to friend I know in Uncle Sergei's office, Yevgeny has kept costs low and there have been no complaints."

"The men are too afraid to speak out against him," Anastasia said. "They do not want to draw attention to themselves and lose jobs."

Laramie noticed Anastasia and Mischa share a look that hinted they'd had a similar conversation themselves.

"Perhaps Uncle Sergei trusted Yevgeny more than he should."

"Perhaps," Laramie said.

In business, as in life, trust went only so far.

"What would you like me to do if I find something out of order?" Mischa asked. "Should I tell you or my uncle?"

"It's Duke's money. If some of it's missing, he deserves to be the first to know. Just between you and me, though, I wouldn't mind being a close second."

"I will do my best."

Laramie hoped his best would be good enough to uncover whatever it was Yevgeny was trying so desperately to keep under wraps. Then she could discover if the truth was better or worse than she had imagined.

When they reached the van, Laramie climbed in the back and ceded the seat next to Anastasia to Mischa.

"Why is she sitting back there?" Mischa asked in Russian. "Did you two have a fight before I arrived?"

Anastasia smiled to herself as she noticed Laramie had made a point of sitting in the very back of the van, leaving the other two rows of seats empty.

"No, she lost a bet."

"What kind of bet?"

As she drove back to the ranch, Anastasia told him about the race she had won that afternoon. She also filled him in on everything that had happened since she had arrived. Almost everything. She told him about the book Vladimir had let her borrow, but she didn't tell him she had read one of the poems to Laramie. It wasn't like her to keep secrets from him, but some memories were too precious to share. This one she would treasure like a flower pressed between the pages of a scrapbook, returning to it time and time again even as the once-vibrant colors began to fade.

"You've had more adventures in a few days than I've had all year," Mischa said. "And you thought this job was going to be boring."

"Didn't you?"

"Yes," he said with a sheepish grin. "Now I almost wish I had taken it."

"You wouldn't like it. All of the ranch hands are straight, and none of them is your type."

"Aw, I was looking forward to sneaking off to the bunkhouse with a strapping cowboy while I was here."

"Ivan looks like a cross between Dolph Lundgren and Jean-Claude Van Damme without the muscles and spray-on tan. Is that close enough?"

"Only if his bank account looks like theirs, too. It looks like you get to have all the fun." He took a quick glance behind him. "Does she mind us speaking Russian? I don't want her to feel like we're intentionally excluding her from the conversation."

Anastasia took a peek in the rearview mirror. Seemingly impervious to the lingering smell of manure, Laramie was staring out the window with a peaceful look on her face.

"She's fine."

Mischa shifted his weight and turned toward her. "Then tell me what it's really like working for her. Is she as tough as she looks? I'll bet she can be really mean when she loses her temper. She reminds me of a teacher I once had in school. When she was having a bad day, she would take it out on everyone. We could tell what kind of mood she was in just by the way she greeted us when we walked into the room. If she said 'good morning,' it was going to be a good day. If she stared at us without saying anything, we knew we would be in for it."

"She's tried really hard not to lose her temper. I haven't seen her go off on anyone yet, though I'm sure Yevgeny has tempted her a time or two. She gets her point across without yelling."

"How is she as a trainer?"

"I thought she would be a stern taskmaster, especially when she started making all sorts of changes no one was expecting, but she isn't like that at all. She shows people how a job should be done, then gives them a chance to do it. If they mess up, she lets them try again until they get it right. She's so encouraging, you find yourself wanting to do anything you can to please her."

"What have you done to please her?" Mischa asked with a cheeky grin. "And did you enjoy it as well?"

"She and I don't have that kind of relationship."

"Do you really expect me to believe nothing has happened between you? You spent the night with her in her hotel room in Moscow. Now you're living under the same roof. Are you sure you haven't slipped across the hall at least once in the middle of the night?"

"There are too many people around for us to get physical here, and she was too wasted in Moscow to do anything except sleep it off. You know I'm not that kind of girl. Whenever I have sex with someone, I want to make sure she enjoys it as much as I do. I don't want to be the only one bragging about my performance the next day."

"Still as humble as ever, I see."

"Did you expect my personality to change that much overnight?"

"No, I thought it would take longer, but you do seem different."

"In what way?"

He leaned his back against the door and looked her up and down. "I don't know. I'm still trying to figure it out."

"Let me know what you come up with, okay? I'm dying to know."

"Tell me more about Elena. Does she really expect me to share a room with you, or was she just getting back at you for all the teasing you've done about her and Shorty?"

Anastasia mentally replayed the conversation she and Elena had shared.

"I'm not sure. Until today, I thought I had a pretty good read on her. Then she made all those hurtful remarks about what she would say if she discovered her child was gay. Now I don't know what to think."

"You got really close to her, didn't you?"

"I didn't expect it to happen so fast, but we just clicked right away. I was looking forward to us growing even closer. I've had plenty of female friends, but never one who is that much older than I am. It was nice. It was kind of like—"

"Having a mother?"

A lump formed in Anastasia's throat when Mischa verbalized what she hadn't been able to put into words.

"I was going to say mentor, but your description is more accurate. Maybe that's why it hurt so much when she said the things she did. I felt like I was getting rejected by my mother all over again."

"What are you going to do about it?"

"What can I do? It's not like I can come out to her. That would only make things worse. For me and for you."

He placed his hand on her arm. "I'm sorry I got you into this. We're in so deep now, I don't know how we can find our way out."

"You know the way forward as well as I do. You just have to be brave enough to take it. We both do."

Mischa's eyes welled with tears. "I don't want to lose my family, Ana."

She felt for him. His pain was her pain. This time, however, she didn't know how to make the pain go away. Ignoring it no longer seemed like the best solution.

"I don't want you to either, Mischa, but what good would you be to them if you lose yourself along the way? You have another family, you know. One that loves and respects you for who you are, not who they want you to be. I am a part of that family. So are all our friends."

Mischa sniffed and dried his eyes. "Now I know what's different about you. You've grown up."

She appreciated the compliment but didn't feel certain she had earned it. Not yet.

"It's only temporary, I'm sure. Just wait. I'll revert into the immature brat you know and love before you know it."

"Not this time." He took another furtive peek over his shoulder. "And I know exactly who to blame."

CHAPTER NINETEEN

W hat is he doing here?"

Laramie heard the suspicion in Yevgeny's voice even before Anastasia told her what he had said.

"How would you like me to respond?" Anastasia asked.

"Tell him you invited Mischa to visit you for family day and explain what the day's about."

The ranch hands' faces lit up one by one as they listened to what Anastasia said. They started talking excitedly well before she was done. When they pulled out their cell phones, Laramie knew they were calling home to invite their families to attend the festivities.

"Will your family be joining us, Yevgeny?" Laramie asked.

"He says if he wanted to spend time with his family, he would live at home instead of here."

"I'm sure his wife would say the same thing about him," Shorty said under his breath. Laramie shot him a look to remind him that Vladimir spoke English, but Shorty wrapped an arm around Vladimir's shoulders and said, "It's okay. He's on our side. Aren't you, Vlad?"

Laramie couldn't tell if Vladimir was more uncomfortable with the hug or the question.

"You don't have to answer that, Vladimir. Shorty didn't mean to put you on the spot. There's no need to choose sides until war has been declared."

Vladimir's response would have been funny if it weren't true. "I think war broke out on day you arrived, don't you?"

"Unfortunately, I have to agree with you." She turned to Elena, who was busy ferrying steaming bowls of food from the kitchen to the dinner table. "Will you invite your family to join us as well?"

"She says Drezna is a long way from Godoroye," Anastasia said. "Train tickets are very expensive. Who will pay for them, you or Sergei?"

Now it was Laramie's turn to be put on the spot. At home, the ranch hands' families were within driving distance. That wasn't the case here. She wanted Elena to be able to participate, but it wasn't the kind of line item she could add to an expense report and she didn't want to take money out of her own pocket when she needed to hold on to as much of it as she could.

"I'll see what I can do."

"*Spasibo.*" Elena pointed at Mischa and said something in Russian.

"She wants to know what we are supposed to do with him," Anastasia said. "There is plenty of room in bunkhouse. Only available space in main house is in attic. He can sleep on rollaway bed if he does not mind moving a few boxes around. I told her it will take more time to clean attic than Mischa will spend here. He can sleep in office as long as Yevgeny does not mind sharing."

"Believe me," Mischa said, "I have slept in worse conditions."

He and Anastasia shared a laugh at the private joke.

"What did he say?" Laramie asked after Yevgeny growled something that didn't seem to sit well with everyone else.

"He said he agreed to arrangement only because Mischa is Sergei's nephew. He also told Mischa to make sure sleeping is only thing he does in office," Anastasia said. "This is place of business, not a brothel."

"Brothels are places of business, too," Shorty said. "Some make very good money. Or so I'm told."

"You wouldn't have any firsthand experience, would you, Shorty?" Laramie asked.

"I'm afraid I'm gonna have to plead the Fifth on that one. I wouldn't want to incriminate myself in front of our charming hostess."

Mischa headed upstairs to place his suitcase in the office. Yevgeny watched him go, obviously upset by the prospect of having to share the space with someone else. Laramie didn't care if Yevgeny got his feathers ruffled. She just wanted to make sure he couldn't get rid of any potentially damning evidence before they had a chance to examine it.

"He wants to know if this is how you plan to win everyone over," Anastasia said. "By planning parties and inviting their friends for sleepovers."

"Tell him if he has any better ideas, he's free to share them at any time."

"He says he will think about it while he has dinner."

Laramie pulled out a chair. "In that case, let's eat."

Anastasia noticed Laramie didn't eat her dinner with quite as much enthusiasm as she had the night before. Neither did Shorty. They cleaned their plates, but they didn't look too happy about it. She didn't have the heart to tell them that tonight's meal was more like a typical Russian meal than last night's feast had been.

After dinner, Yevgeny headed upstairs just as he had the night before. Laramie and Shorty deviated from their pattern, however. Instead of going straight to bed, they joined Andrei, Fyodor, Ivan, and Vladimir on the front porch. Andrei played an old folk song on the balalaika. Applause broke out when he was done, but the tune must not have been to Shorty's liking because Anastasia heard him say, "That was pretty good, Andy, but can you play something peppier? You wouldn't happen to know any Garth Brooks, would you?"

Curious, Anastasia pushed the door open and joined them.

Andrei shook his head after Vladimir translated Shorty's question.

"No?" Shorty pointed to the balalaika. "Well, hand that thing to Laramie and let her take a stab at it. It can't be much different than a guitar or banjo, can it?"

"A guitar has six strings and most banjos have five," Laramie said. "That only has three."

"Applying the math, that means you should be able to play twice as well as you normally do," Shorty said with a wink.

Laramie shook her head when Andrei tried to hand her the balalaika, but the ranch hands egged her on. She reluctantly accepted the instrument from Andrei and took a few tentative plucks at the strings. Once she was satisfied with the notes, she began to sing. Like her speaking voice, her singing voice was a clear, rich alto.

Anastasia didn't recognize the song. The lyrics seemed to be a celebration of friendship, whiskey, and beer. That was ample reason for her to like it. She found herself clapping along with everyone else as they kept time with the music.

Everyone applauded wildly when Laramie was done. Just like at a concert, the crowd begged for an encore. Laramie obliged them. The second song was much slower than the first. As soon as the first few notes rang out, Shorty slapped his hand on his knee and said, "Oh, you went and done it now."

He pushed himself to his feet, bowed in front of Elena, and extended his hand to her. Anastasia had been so entranced by Laramie's performance, she hadn't noticed Elena and Mischa had joined everyone on the porch.

"Is he asking me to dance?" Elena said. "Tell him I don't know this song."

"It doesn't matter if you don't as long as he does. Just follow him wherever he leads you."

Elena tucked her hair behind her ears and took Shorty's hand. While Laramie sang about life being better left to chance, Shorty led Elena down the steps and waltzed her around the front yard.

When Anastasia turned away from them, she noticed Laramie was staring at her. It was as if Laramie was performing a private concert and was singing directly to her. The lyrics seemed to be a blueprint of Anastasia's life. She was thankful for all the pain she had endured over the years because it had given her the opportunity to share this dance with Laramie.

"She's good," Mischa whispered.

Anastasia nodded in agreement but didn't say anything.

"You like her, don't you?"

Anastasia glared at him to make him stop talking. She wanted to hear Laramie's voice, not his.

He put his arm around her and kissed the top of her head. "I'll stop, but only because I know I'm right."

Laramie continued to hold her gaze long after the song ended. Long after Shorty kissed Elena's hand and said, "Thank you, ma'am." Long after the ranch hands treated Laramie, Shorty, and Elena to a standing ovation.

Laramie didn't look away until she turned to Andrei and said, "Thanks for the use, Andrei. I hope I didn't do it any harm."

Andrei said something, and Laramie looked at Anastasia with an expectant look on her face. Mischa gave her a gentle shake to let her know it was her turn to speak. "Oh, he says you played instrument much better than he ever has."

Laramie squeezed Andrei's shoulder. "You're sweet, but I'm going to need some practice if I want to catch up with you."

Andrei laughed. "Tell her I will train her to be a good balalaika player if she trains me to be a good ranch hand."

Laramie shook his hand. "It's a deal. With that said, I'm going to turn in." She tapped two fingers against her forehead in an impromptu salute. "Good night, everyone."

Anastasia joined everyone else in bidding Laramie farewell. After Laramie entered the house, she looked back and caught Anastasia's eye. Anastasia longed to follow her so she could tell her how much she had enjoyed her performance, but Elena touched her arm and beckoned her to accompany her inside.

"Do you need help clearing the table?" Anastasia asked.

"No, I wanted to apologize for what I said to you earlier. I didn't mean to upset you."

Like she had with Mischa, Anastasia nodded but didn't respond. She needed to hear what Elena had to say before she could decide whether she could forgive her.

"Do you have friends who are homosexual?" Elena asked.

"Several."

"Women or men?"

"Both."

Elena looked at her as if seeing her for the first time. "And you aren't afraid they might...do something to you?"

Anastasia decided to be honest with her. "I feel safer with them than I do with most of the straight people I know."

"Just because we have a difference of opinion doesn't mean it has to become an issue with us, does it?"

"I will still give you English lessons, if that's what you're wondering."

Elena moved closer. Her voice was as earnest as her expression. "I don't care about the lessons. I care about you. About us. I want to be your friend. Today, I felt we were more like enemies."

"I felt it, too."

"Can we start over?"

Elena opened her arms and Anastasia stepped into them. If she could give Elena a second chance, perhaps Elena would eventually be able to return the favor.

"I didn't know you were such a good dancer," she said after Elena finally let go.

Elena blushed. "I had a good partner."

"The singer wasn't half-bad either."

"She's a good person."

Elena sounded as if she were trying to convince herself that the words were true. Anastasia, however, didn't need convincing. She knew without doubt that Laramie was the best woman she had ever met. And quite possibly the most attractive. She knew Laramie was attracted to her, too. Before this long journey was over, perhaps they would be able to do something about it.

CHAPTER TWENTY

L aramie was so tired she fell asleep almost as soon as she assumed a horizontal position. She woke the next day with a full bladder and a heart brimming with regret. A trip to the bathroom resolved one problem, but she had no idea how to fix the other.

The time she had spent sitting on the porch and strumming a couple of her favorite Garth Brooks tunes on Andrei's balalaika was the most fun she'd had since she and Shorty had arrived in Russia. It was also the most bittersweet.

As she sang the lyrics to the up-tempo song, she had realized how much she had in common with the members of her new team. As she sang the words to the ballad, however, she had realized how many differences they still had to overcome.

The men had applauded wildly after Shorty and Elena finished their dance. Would their reaction have been as positive if she and Anastasia had been the couple moving in slow circles as they held each other close? Not a chance. She and Anastasia probably wouldn't have even made it down the steps before all hell would have broken loose.

As she looked into Anastasia's eyes while she sang, she had sensed that Anastasia knew exactly how she was feeling because she was feeling the same way. Like they were a part of the group but separate from it at the same time.

Laramie had wanted to go to her last night. To sit in her room and watch her face transform while she read another poem from the book Vladimir had given her. To talk with her afterward about whatever subject came to mind. To feel connected rather than left out.

She hadn't had a chance to do any of those things because Elena had pulled Anastasia aside. Laramie hadn't been able to understand any of the whispered conversation she had overheard before she closed her bedroom door behind her, but Elena's tone had sounded apologetic.

She hoped Anastasia and Elena had been able to put yesterday's argument behind them. Good friends were hard to come by. Before their disagreement, Anastasia and Elena had seemed well on their way to becoming just that. In a way, Laramie felt responsible for their rift. After all, it had been Elena's disapproval of her lesbianism that had driven the pair apart. Her relationship with Elena hadn't changed as a result of the revelation. It had always been purely professional, and Laramie didn't see any reason why it wouldn't continue to remain that way. Anastasia and Elena's relationship was different. And perhaps forever changed.

"Time will tell," she said with a sigh as she finished putting on her work clothes.

Before she could tap on Anastasia's door to let her know the shower was free, Elena came running up to her, wild-eyed and speaking Russian so rapidly Laramie couldn't tell where one word ended and another began.

"Wait. Slow down. Has something happened to the cattle?"

Laramie began imagining and discounting all sorts of unpleasant scenarios. She didn't smell smoke so there wasn't a fire. She didn't hear the cattle making any sounds of distress so there weren't any predators attacking the herd. Elena looked fine, but one of the ranch hands could be having some kind of medical emergency.

"Is someone sick?" she asked, trying not to panic. "It's not Shorty, is it?"

He kept claiming he was indestructible, but he wasn't as young as he used to be. Then again, neither was anyone else, herself included.

Frustrated by her inability to get her point across, Elena grew more and more agitated.

"Hold on."

Laramie pounded on Anastasia's door. The sound was startling, especially so early in the morning, but she didn't have time for niceties. When she didn't receive a response, she banged on the door again. This time even harder than before.

"Ana, wake up! I need you."

A few seconds later, Anastasia finally came to the door. When she pulled it open, her hair was tousled and she was still wearing her pj's. "What is happening?" she asked, rubbing her sleep-reddened eyes. "It is not yet time for alarm. I had fifteen more minutes left."

Anastasia's voice was gravelly and her accent thicker than normal. Both were almost unbearably sexy. Ignoring the pleasant effects this version of Anastasia was having on her, Laramie focused on discovering the cause of Elena's distress.

"Please tell me what she's saying."

Elena gripped Anastasia's hands in hers and began to speak. While she listened, Anastasia's expression changed from confused to apprehensive to angry. When Mischa joined them, she said something to him and pointed over her head. His face drained of color, then he turned and ran back up the stairs, his baggy T-shirt flapping on his lanky frame. Laramie heard his feet pounding on the ceiling as he ran down the second floor hallway.

"What—"

Anastasia held up a hand, cutting her off. She shouted something in Russian and cocked her head while she waited for Mischa to respond. He appeared at the top of the stairs and shook his head. Whatever he said made Anastasia's shoulders droop.

"Will you please tell me what's going on?" Laramie asked.

"It is Yevgeny," Anastasia said reluctantly. "He must have figured out real reason Mischa is here."

"Why? What did he do?"

"His room is empty. He has packed belongings and taken van. Keys are kept in same place every day so they do not get lost. When Elena went into kitchen to make breakfast, she noticed keys were missing. She looked outside and saw van was gone. When she went upstairs, she discovered Yevgeny was gone, too. He is—How do you say? In the breeze."

"In the wind," Laramie said. "What about his laptop and the ledgers? Did he take those, too?"

"Safe is locked," Mischa said. "Unless he took them while everyone was outside yesterday night, laptop and ledgers are still there."

"Call a locksmith," Laramie said. "We need someone to crack that safe. Do any companies offer twenty-four-hour service around here?"

Anastasia quickly conferred with Elena.

"She says there is one place that does, but the owner charges more than the other businesses in town."

"Get them on the phone. Right now. Cost is no object."

Anastasia relayed the information, and Elena ran down the hall to complete her assigned task.

"I will call my uncle," Mischa said. "Members of his security team are former agents with Federal Security Service. It is still early. Perhaps they can use contacts to find Yevgeny before he leaves country."

"What will they do if they manage to track him down?" Laramie asked.

Mischa answered her question with one of his own. "What would you do if someone stole from you?"

"Whatever the law allows."

"In Russia," Mischa said with a sad smile, "law does not apply to everyone."

"That's something else our countries have in common."

Anastasia felt defeated. Based on the dour expressions she saw on the faces of the people surrounding the breakfast table, everyone else felt the same way.

A few hours ago, she had been confident that the plan she, Laramie, and Mischa had concocted would allow them to catch Yevgeny by surprise. Instead, they had been the ones who were caught unawares. It was if they were playing checkers and he was playing chess. While they were focused on the next move, he had been thinking about the end game. This morning, he had reached checkmate.

Had they done or said something to tip him off, or had he decided he had enough and it was time to get out? In most criminals' minds, there was no such thing as enough. Whatever the reason, he was gone and they were left trying to take the puzzle pieces he had left behind and form them into a cohesive whole with nothing to use as a guide.

Elena set a platter of cheese pancakes and a platter of sausages on the table. The *sirniki* and sausages looked delicious, but no one seemed to feel like eating.

"Uncle Sergei said his security team will do everything they can to find Yevgeny," Mischa said. "They have already alerted agents along the southern border to be on the lookout if he tries to drive into Kazakhstan or Ukraine. Two people are heading for his hometown in Estonia in case he winds up there. Several others are staking out the train stations and airports in Moscow."

"That's fine for them, but what are we supposed to do?" Fyodor asked disconsolately.

Even though Mischa had started the conversation, everyone's eyes naturally gravitated to Laramie.

"When the locksmith pops the safe open," she said, "Mischa's going to take a look at what's inside. Unless he finds something that puts us out of business, we're going to do what we're being paid to do: work. The cattle still need to be looked after, the fence still needs to be mended, the hole in the barn roof isn't getting any smaller, and the bunkhouse isn't going to paint itself. So let's fuel up and keep doing what we're doing until someone tells us to stop."

"What will we do for transportation?" Vladimir asked. "Yevgeny left the ATV, but it is not allowed to be driven on main roads."

"Like I keep telling ya," Shorty said. "Nothing beats a good horse."

"The horses will get us around the ranch," Laramie said, "but they're not practical for hauling loads back and forth. Especially heavy ones. We can rent a truck until Duke gives us the okay to buy something new."

"You heard her, boys." Shorty speared two sausages and three pancakes. "Let's dig in so we can get at it. I want to get the fence surrounding the back forty patched up by the end of the day."

Now that they had a goal to achieve, the men's spirits lifted. Following Shorty's example, they filled their plates and attacked their food with gusto. Some topped their *sirniki* with jam, some with sour cream. Obviously in a better mood than he'd been in a few minutes before, Fyodor opted for both.

Fyodor had ceded his normal seat at the table so Mischa could sit next to Anastasia. While Fyodor chatted animatedly with Ivan and Vladimir about who would be the first to drive the new truck, Mischa leaned toward her. "You were right about her," he said softly. "She makes me want to do anything I can to please her, too."

"Back off," she replied with a smile as Elena rose to answer the knock on the front door. "I saw her first."

"That's okay. She isn't my type anyway." He paused as he reached for his coffee. "But he certainly is."

Anastasia followed his line of sight. Elena and a tall bearded man who looked like a dark-haired version of the movie star who played Thor were heading up the stairs. If he had a hammer clutched in his hands instead of a grease-stained tool bag, the image would have been complete.

"If that's the locksmith," Mischa said, "he can crack my safe any time." He wiped his mouth on his napkin and pushed his chair away from the table. "I think I'll go see if Elena needs help supervising."

"So I don't have to worry about you being bored today?"

"Not a chance. I think I like it here," he said as he climbed the stairs two at a time.

Anastasia knew the feeling.

After breakfast, Anastasia followed Laramie to the feed storage bin. Laramie wanted to make sure Yevgeny hadn't sabotaged the food and water supplies before he slipped away in the middle of the night.

"I know I'm probably being paranoid," Laramie said, "but better safe than sorry." She shined a flashlight around the base of the overhead bin. "No fresh footprints or ATV tracks. That's a good sign."

Anastasia tried to see what Laramie was seeing, but she couldn't differentiate one set of tracks from another. They all just looked like shoe prints to her.

Laramie pulled a lever and allowed some of the feed to pool in the palm of her hand. She looked at it from several angles, then brought it to her nose and took a tentative sniff.

"Is okay?" Anastasia asked.

Laramie put some of the feed in her mouth, allowed it to rest there for a few minutes, then spit it out. "Yes, it's okay. Andrei's taking a peek at the dugouts and stock tanks. Let's check the water storage tank."

Anastasia had no idea what some of those things were. While Laramie and Shorty conducted their walking tour of the ranch a few days ago, she had heard one of them say the storage tank was large enough to hold a seven-day supply of water.

Laramie drank some of the water in the main storage unit. Satisfied it hadn't been tampered with, she headed toward the pasture. As the rising sun changed the sky from black to dark gray, they spotted Andrei kneeling in front of one of the many man-made watering holes dotting the property. He and nearly a dozen cattle were drinking greedily from its depths. Anastasia pointed toward them.

"That is dugout?"

"Yes," Laramie said. "Beef cattle like to drink three to five times a day, and grazing can often take them far from home. Some have to walk long distances to get water. Dugouts are constructed so the cattle don't have to cut down on grazing time or expend too much energy looking for something to drink."

In the field, Andrei clasped his hands together and lifted them over his head in a gesture of triumph.

Laramie took a deep breath and slowly released it. "That makes me feel better."

"I am glad. Did you really think Yevgeny would do something to hurt cows?"

"I wouldn't have put it past him. Disgruntled employees have been known to pull a whole host of stunts before they make their way out the door, especially when they have to head that way against their will."

"I do not think Yevgeny cared about cows. Only money that could be made from them."

"Unfortunately, I think you're right."

Laramie leaned against one of the new fence posts. Anastasia stood next to her. She enjoyed the comfortable silence for a few minutes before she said, "I waited for you last night, but you did not come. You no longer like poetry?"

"Spending time with you was on my mind, but Elena seemed to have the same idea. Did you two patch things up?"

"She apologized for things she said yesterday and hopes we can go back to being friends. She asked if we could start over. I agreed to try."

"That's good. I can see how much her friendship means to you. Shorty's kinda sweet on her. Do you know if she feels the same way about him?"

"She says he is excellent dancer."

Laramie grinned. "I'll be sure to tell him she said so."

"I did not know you could sing so well."

Before Laramie turned away, Anastasia saw her cheeks redden at the compliment.

"I'm not ready to try out for one of those talent shows you see on TV, but I hold my own."

"Will you sing again tonight?"

"Oh, no. You've already heard the extent of my repertoire. I don't want to go to the well too often."

"I cannot speak for everyone else, but I would like another taste."

When Laramie turned to face her, her eyes glowed like the white-hot embers beneath a roaring fire.

"And I would like a taste of you."

Anastasia tried, but she couldn't look away.

Come see me tonight, she wanted to say. *Then we can give each other what we both want.*

Her phone chimed before she could get the words out.

"Is that Mischa?" Laramie asked as Anastasia read the text printed on the phone's display.

"Yes. Locksmith has drilled through safe."

"Are the laptop and ledgers still there? Has Mischa found something?"

"Yes, and he says news is not good."

"I didn't think it would be." Laramie pressed her lips into a tight, thin line before she pushed herself away from the fence. "Well, let's go see what he's discovered. Standing here won't make it any better."

But leaving, Anastasia knew, was guaranteed to make everything worse.

CHAPTER TWENTY-ONE

Laramie's feet felt leaden as she climbed the stairs to the second floor of the main house. A refreshing breeze hit her in the face when she entered what had once been Yevgeny's office. Mischa had opened the windows, most likely to alleviate the smell of the unfiltered cigarettes Yevgeny favored. The heavy glass ashtray overflowing with crumpled cigarette butts had been emptied, but the odor lingered, competing with the aroma of scorched metal. The door of the floor safe was open, a gaping hole where the lock used to be. The lock's mangled remains rested on one of the safe's empty shelves.

Mischa was sitting behind the oversized desk. Two rectangular leather-bound ledgers lay open in front of him. Off to his left, Yevgeny's laptop was powered on, the password screen displayed on the monitor. Another laptop sat to his right. He compared the entries in the two ledgers, then made an entry in the spreadsheet displayed on the second laptop.

"What did you find?" Laramie asked, taking a seat in front of the desk.

Mischa saved the spreadsheet he was working on and turned the ledgers around so she could get a better look at them. She could see the differing dollar values, but the corresponding entries were written in Cyrillic so she couldn't tell what the numbers meant.

"Sorry, but you're going to have to give me a hint about what I'm looking at."

"Of course. Is okay if I speak Russian? I do not wish to get anything wrong."

"That's fine."

Anastasia sat next to her and began to translate what Mischa was saying.

"Problem began six months ago. Yevgeny began managing accounts after Maria left. First month of entries are similar to previous records. After that, Yevgeny began keeping two sets of records. Entries in first ledger appear to be legitimate. Entries in second ledger do not. Amount of expenses in second ledger is higher, and there is additional payee not listed in first ledger. Amounts that company received are small so individual entries would not have caused concern. Over time, small amounts add up to much larger one."

Mischa tapped his finger on a set of entries in the second ledger.

"If you look at this date," Anastasia said, leaning closer, "you will see line item for feed is listed for less than what is listed in first ledger. Difference is listed as being paid to company that does not exist. Mischa searched internet but could not find address or name of owners."

"That's because it's most likely a shell corporation Yevgeny set up so he could siphon funds," Laramie said.

"What is shell corporation?" Anastasia asked.

Laramie thought back to some of the business classes she had taken while she was in college. "A shell corporation is a company that exists in name only. It has no physical address, no employees, no assets, and no business operations. Not all of them are illegal, but most are used to prevent law enforcement from knowing who truly owns and benefits from them. Money launderers open them all the time so they can hide some of their ill-gotten gains."

"*Da*," Mischa said, nodding.

He continued in Russian and Anastasia picked up the thread.

"He thinks Yevgeny doctored invoices and receipts to make numbers in second ledger match new calculations. Original forms have been shredded and copies are stored on laptop. He has called Sergei's office and spoken with internet technology department. They have program that allows them to determine password someone has assigned to computer. They are running program now."

"How long will it take for them to come up with the password?" Laramie asked.

"Person he spoke to told him it could take from as little as few minutes to as long as few days. Perhaps weeks. Depends on complexity of password."

"So close and yet so far. Can he at least tell how much money Yevgeny has managed to divert?"

After Anastasia relayed the question, Mischa turned the second laptop around so Laramie could see the screen.

"He says he has to look through another month of entries, but here is what he has found so far."

Anastasia looked at the screen. Even in rubles, the figure she saw listed at the bottom of the spreadsheet was astounding.

"He has informed Sergei of discoveries and will report to him with final results. Sergei has contacted bank to block Yevgeny's access to all accounts related to ranch. Workers will still be paid. Money will be sent from main office until new foreman is hired. Sergei has approved purchase of new van as well as truck for ranch. He will wire money to automobile dealer when vehicles are selected. Van has been reported stolen and claim will be sent to insurance company. He thanks you for calling attention to this matter and would like to know what you wish from him in return."

"He doesn't have to thank me. Mischa's the one who did all the work."

"I assumed you would say that so I made request on your behalf."

Laramie tried not to show her irritation. Translating for her was one thing. Putting words in her mouth was something else.

"What did you ask for?"

"Sergei plans to visit on family day so I told Mischa to ask him to stop by Drezna and bring Elena's family with him."

Laramie felt silly for assuming Anastasia would make some sort of ridiculous request on her behalf. In fact, she couldn't think of a better way to take advantage of Duke's generosity.

"How did you know I wouldn't ask for something for myself?"

"Because, unlike me, you are not selfish person," Anastasia said with a smile. "I always see you place own desires second to others'. Main reason you are here is to help brother, not yourself. I knew you wanted to make sure Elena did not feel left out on family day. This way, you can do it and let someone else take credit."

"How do you know me so well?"

"That kind of thing tends to happen when you spend sixteen hours a day with someone. Would you like to stop?"

"I've already gotten used to you. Why would I want to start over with someone else?"

"New translator might be more to your liking."

"Thanks anyway, but I like the view from here just fine."

For the second time that day, Anastasia felt herself getting lost in Laramie's eyes. Mischa had to clear his throat three times before she remembered he was in the room.

"Is there something else you would like me to say?" she asked.

"Not about Yevgeny."

"Then what is it?"

He looked as if he had done something he shouldn't. "I invited Pavel to attend family day. Do you think she will mind?"

When she shook her head to let Laramie know that Mischa didn't have anything to add regarding the missing money, Laramie excused herself to check on Shorty's progress.

"I will join you as soon as I can."

"Take your time. That boulder we've been pushing up the hill every day isn't going to come rolling back down anytime soon."

Anastasia noted Laramie's allusion to the mythical tale of Sisyphus. For someone who claimed not to know much about anything except cows, Laramie seemed to be more well read than she let on.

"Who's Pavel?" Anastasia asked after Laramie left her and Mischa alone.

"The incredibly handsome man who drilled into the safe for us."

"You mean Thor?"

"Is that what you're calling him? I don't know if he has the body of a Norse god underneath his coveralls, but I'd love to find out. We wouldn't have any of this information without his help." He indicated the laptop and ledgers. "I'm sure Uncle Sergei would like to show him his appreciation, too."

"And if Sergei doesn't, you certainly would, right?"

"I wouldn't be averse to the idea, no."

"How did the invitation come about? Did you beg him to be your date as soon as he showed you his drill?"

Mischa leaned back in his chair and laced his hands across his stomach in a pose that was a touch too casual, which meant he was trying to downplay his obvious excitement.

"Actually, he asked me out first. He invited me to go for a drink with him tonight. It seemed only fair for me to return the favor."

"A drink? Where?"

"There's supposed to be a pub in town. The floor show, if there is one, probably pales in comparison to Lyubov's, but I'm going for the company, not the ambiance. Would you like to come with us? I don't think Pavel would mind."

"I would if I were him. When I invite someone on a date, I don't want her dragging her best friend along. It sends a clear signal she doesn't expect the evening to go well."

"If you bring Laramie with you, you wouldn't be my chaperone. It would be more of a double date."

"I would feel comfortable walking into Lyubov with her because no one would notice us. In a small town like this, everyone would."

She finally realized that was probably the reason why Mischa had asked her to join him. Two women and two men sharing a booth would draw considerably less attention than two men alone. Not only would Mischa have to deal with first date jitters, he would feel exposed while doing so. She empathized with the difficult situation he was in, but she couldn't do anything about it.

"It sounds like fun, but she will never agree to the idea."

"Why not? I saw her doing vodka shots at your farewell party so I know she likes to drink."

"Exactly my point. She banned alcohol on the ranch so the men could get better at their jobs. She can't go out drinking tonight and not expect them to resent her for it. I can't go either because I don't want her to resent me. You're just visiting so you can do whatever you want. I have to work with her. You don't."

Mischa looked pensive. "Now I feel guilty about saying yes. Should I call him and cancel?"

It had been ages since Anastasia had seen him this enthused about meeting someone new. She didn't want the spark to fade.

"Of course not. Go, enjoy yourself, and tell me all about it in the morning."

"You mean you get to live vicariously through me for once instead of the other way around? Talk about a change of pace."

"You said it yourself. I'm all grown up now, remember? That means I get to stay home at night while you go out partying until the wee hours of the morning."

She looked out one of the open windows after a subtle movement caught her eye. In the distance, she could see Laramie leading Krasota out of the stables.

"Text me if you find out anything else. I've got to go before I miss my ride."

She ran downstairs and out into the yard. When Laramie placed her foot in the stirrups, Anastasia called to her to get her attention.

"You are not leaving without me, are you?"

"I wouldn't dream of it. Grab the ATV and let's check on the boys."

Anastasia touched her arm. Laramie seemed surprised by the contact and stunned by the request that followed.

"I was hoping I could ride with you."

"Would you like the front or the back?"

"Is question same as asking if I like top or bottom? If so, answer is it depends on who I am with at the time."

"If you were with me?"

"If I were with you, I think I would enjoy myself in any position."

Even though there wasn't a cloud in the sky, the air between them seemed to crackle with electricity.

"Then let's start with one and work our way through the rest."

Laramie stepped toward her, bringing Krasota closer. Anastasia thought Laramie meant to kiss her. Instead, she bent, adjusted the stirrups, and gave her instructions on how to mount the horse.

Anastasia stepped into the stirrups the way Laramie told her to, but she couldn't manage to pull herself up. She felt herself start to fall, but Laramie's strong arms caught her before she hit the ground.

"It's okay. I've got you."

Laramie held her close. Even closer than Shorty and Elena had held each other while they were dancing last night. Anastasia could feel Laramie's heart beating against her back. Like her grip, Laramie's heartbeat was strong and sure.

"Ready to try again?"

Anastasia didn't want to move. She wanted to stand there forever. With Laramie's arms around her and a gentle breeze blowing against her skin.

"Yes, I am ready."

She stepped into the stirrups again. With a not-so-gentle push from Laramie, she managed to mount Krasota. As she sat in the saddle, she felt awed by her achievement—and the power she could feel surging through the animal she now sat astride.

"What do I do next?" she asked as she fought to maintain her balance.

"Simple. Try not to fall off." Laramie effortlessly mounted Krasota, then placed her arms against Anastasia's sides. "Hold on to the pommel. I'll try to keep you from swaying too much. Between the two of us, you should manage to stay upright."

Anastasia latched on to the rounded knob on the front of the saddle with both hands.

"Here we go," Laramie said. "Giddyap, Krasota. Easy now."

Laramie clicked her tongue and Krasota slowly began to move. The horse's gait felt awkward at first, but Anastasia quickly adjusted to it. Her fear and apprehension soon faded away. She felt safe. Protected. She was with Laramie. What could possibly go wrong?

"Make her go faster."

Laramie's soft chuckle vibrated against her back. "Have you ever heard the expression you've got to crawl before you can walk? Today, you have to walk before you can gallop."

"Well, look at what we have here," Shorty said when they finally reached the area where he and the other ranch hands were working. "Was I right or was I right?"

As Shorty and the rest of the men looked on, Anastasia slid out of the saddle and into Laramie's welcoming arms.

"You are correct. Nothing beats good horse."

Nothing except the cowgirl who had taught her how to ride one.

CHAPTER TWENTY-TWO

Laramie was so worked up she didn't know what to do with herself. She felt like Krasota before she had given her some exercise yesterday: filled with pent-up energy she desperately needed to release. Unable to resort to her preferred method—taking Anastasia to a secluded place and kissing her breathless—she pulled her work gloves out of her back pocket and pulled them on.

"Need a hand?"

Shorty lowered a new fence post in the hole that had been left by the previous one and stamped the dirt into place. "Andy, Vlad, and I've got a handle on this section. Why don't you take Ivan and Freddy to the next section? Remove the old barbed wire, pull up the posts, and start sticking new ones in. We'll hook the wire on this section and take care of yours when you're done."

"All right then."

By Laramie's reckoning, the fence posts were situated ten feet apart, a sufficient amount of space for a six-wire barbed fence. Steel fence posts, commonly known as T-posts, were more durable since most were made of rail steel, but she and Shorty had always been partial to wood. It didn't rust over time and it just plain looked better. Not to mention it was far better to use a wooden fence post to scratch an itch you couldn't reach. As long as you didn't mind picking up the occasional splinter along the way.

"How can I help?" Anastasia asked, shading her eyes from the sun.

"The way I see it, you've got three choices. You can keep Krasota company, you can fetch the ATV and start hauling off some of the old barbed wire, or you can act as a lookout."

"What would I be looking out for?"

"Now that we've taken some of the wire down, a few of the cows might make a break for it. It'll be your job to make sure they stay put."

"Yes, I can do that job."

As skittish as Anastasia was around animals, it remained to be seen how good a job she would do keeping the cattle at bay. Laramie decided to reserve judgment.

The work was backbreaking, but the ranch hands performed their assigned tasks without complaint. They fell into a rhythm, working quickly and efficiently.

"At this rate," Laramie said as she paused to wipe her brow with her shirtsleeve, "we'll have the whole thing patched up by the end of the day."

Shorty looped a strand of barbed wire around a fence post and clamped it into place. "Unless you keel over from pushing yourself so hard. I've never seen you move this fast unless something was chasing you. What's got you so het up?"

Laramie glanced at Anastasia, who was holding her hands in front of her like a traffic cop to prevent a curious calf from moving any closer.

"Oh, I see what your problem is." Shorty peeked over his shoulder to make sure Vladimir was out of earshot. "You two did look awful cozy when you came riding up."

"I keep telling myself not to think about her that way, but I just can't seem to stop."

Anastasia had felt so good in her arms. So right. Like she belonged there. Every time Anastasia had leaned against her, her head had swum and she had come close to swooning like some silly damsel in distress. It wasn't like her to lose her head over a woman, but she had never met a woman like Anastasia Petrova. Outgoing, yet reserved. Open, yet secretive. A veritable study in contradictions.

"It's like me and sweets," Shorty said. "The more my dentist fusses at me to give them up, the more I seem to crave them. You've got yourself a good, old-fashioned addiction."

"Yeah, but how am I supposed to fight it?"

Shorty began to roll out another strand of wire. "Don't ask me. At this point in my life, I've got more fillings than teeth."

Laramie had a hole inside her, too, and she was starting to think it was one only Anastasia could fill.

Anastasia didn't like the way the cow was looking at her. Like she was the last obstacle standing between it and freedom. The cow bellowed at her. The noise was so loud it made her eardrums vibrate. More angry than frightened, she impulsively stuck out her tongue. The cow cocked its head as if confused, then turned and trotted off. Anastasia didn't breathe until the cow lowered its head and began to graze.

"Ha. I showed you who's boss, didn't I?"

She didn't say the words too loudly, though, in case the cow decided to take her on again. Hearing the ATV approach, she turned to see Elena slowly making her way toward them. Elena parked the vehicle, turned off the engine, and pointed to the large cooler sitting in the storage area.

"You look like you could use cool drink."

Elena said the words haltingly, but she said them in English. She had responded so well to the flash cards that Anastasia had started to teach her a few phrases. Nothing major. Just enough to be able to hold a basic conversation. As everyone lined up in front of the cooler, Anastasia hoped neither Laramie nor Shorty would say something she and Elena hadn't gone over yet.

"Now that you mention it, I was feeling a mite parched." Shorty held up his cup of water. "Spaceballs."

"*Spasibo,*" Elena said.

"Close enough."

Anastasia was so busy watching Elena and Shorty stare into each other's eyes she forgot to keep her own eyes on the cows. She heard a rumbling sound, then turned to see what was causing it. The cow that had confronted her a few minutes earlier ran past her and charged through the opening in the fence.

"We've got a runner!" Shorty said.

He dropped his cup and started after the cow, but Laramie held up a hand to stop him.

"I'm on it."

Shorty grabbed a length of rope off the ground and tossed it to Laramie. Catching the rope in stride, she ran toward Krasota and untied her. She mounted the horse in one smooth motion. She looped the rope over her shoulder, kicked her heels against Krasota's sides, and spurred her into action.

"That is Piotr," Andrei said.

"The calf that got stuck in the mud the other day?" Shorty asked. "That little devil's turning out to be a handful."

Anastasia spread her arms to prevent Lesya, Piotr's mother, from chasing after him. Behind her, Krasota ran so fast her long legs were a blur.

As Krasota began to gain ground on Piotr, Laramie transferred the reins from her hands to her mouth, gripping them between her teeth. She reached for the rope, formed part of it into a loop, and circled it over her head. Anastasia could hear the rope whistling as it spun through the air.

Laramie leaned slightly to one side, then tossed the rope in Piotr's direction. Spinning lazily, the loop flew through the air and landed around Piotr's head. Laramie quickly knotted the other end of the rope around the pommel on her saddle.

"Whoa, Krasota!"

Krasota skidded to a stop. The rope tightened. Krasota didn't budge, but Piotr was pulled off his feet. Laramie slid out of the saddle and ran over to him to make sure he wasn't injured.

Shorty slapped Laramie on the back with his hat as she led Piotr back to the pasture. "That was some darned good roping. Next time I see your brother, I'll be sure to tell him he isn't the only Bowman who knows how to wrangle a cow."

Laramie's response was characteristically modest. "I might not earn as many style points as Trey does," she said as she steered Piotr toward the rest of the herd, "but I get the job done."

Anastasia had never seen anything—or anyone—so amazing in her life. Ivan must have agreed with her.

"Did you see that?" he asked excitedly. "Tell her I would like her to teach me how to be a cowboy."

"Me, too," Fyodor said.

He grabbed the rope Laramie had discarded and tried to throw it around one of the new fence posts, but his arm got tangled up before he let go.

"Dang, Freddy," Shorty said as he helped free Fyodor from the loop that had closed around him. "I think that's the first time I've ever seen a cowpoke lasso himself."

Anastasia laughed along with the rest of the group. "At least I am not only person who embarrassed self today."

"You don't have anything to be ashamed of," Laramie said. "Some cattle can be sneaky. You have to keep your eyes on them at all times or they'll pull one over on you."

Laramie rested a hand on Krasota's neck. The tall horse protected them from view, giving them a semblance of privacy. Anastasia took advantage of the opportunity.

"Sorry I was not watching cows. I was busy watching you."

"Weren't you afraid someone might notice?" Laramie asked, even though she seemed pleased by the revelation.

"Only thing I feared was that you did not notice me, too."

"Then you can rest easy because it's getting harder and harder for me to notice anything else."

This time, Anastasia didn't let the words go unsaid.

"Tonight, I teach you different way to use rope."

CHAPTER TWENTY-THREE

Laramie tried not to wolf down her food—chicken kiev served with a side of beet salad—but she was anxious for dinner to be over so she could get to what was supposed to happen next.

Tonight, Anastasia had said while they stood in the pasture a few hours ago, *I teach you different way to use rope.*

Laramie felt a thrill every time she thought about Anastasia lassoing her the way she had snared the calf that had bolted through the gap in the fence. As Shorty said, the animal was a handful, but she liked his spirit. She might have to keep him around. Even though he was still just a calf, she could tell he would grow up to be sturdy and strong. If he showed an interest, he would make an excellent breeder.

She laughed to herself. Even when she tried to occupy her mind with other things, it kept coming back to sex. She didn't dare look at Anastasia. If she did, she knew the moonstruck expression on her face would surely give them away. If she didn't spontaneously combust beforehand.

She felt even giddier than she had before she won her first barrel racing competition. She had come close to taking a win before she finally earned her maiden first place ribbon so she'd known she had it in her to eventually come out on top. Thanks to the oppressive laws governing the society in which she now found herself, she had feared this night would never come. Now it was only a few minutes away.

"Elena says she has never seen you smile this much," Anastasia said. "She would like to know what has caused you such happiness."

Ignoring the knowing smile tugging at the corners of Anastasia's mouth, Laramie turned to Elena and said, "I received an updated tracking notification for the steaks I ordered. The shipment should arrive tomorrow. I'll marinate them overnight so they'll be perfect for Sunday."

"She says she is looking forward to watching someone else cook for a change. Would you like to borrow her apron?"

"Tell her to ask Shorty. He's going to be the one manning the grill."

Elena's laugh offered a hint that her reply was a comment about Shorty's relative lack of height. Anastasia's translation confirmed it. "She says apron will not fit, but he is welcome to try on for size."

Instead of flying off the handle like he normally did when someone kidded him about his stature, Shorty took the joke in stride. "She'll be singing a different tune after she tastes my meat on Sunday."

"Forgive me, but you are gentleman, yes?" Anastasia said. "Comment sounds more...sexual than you might have meant. Would you like me to tell her you said size does not matter?"

"Hell, no. I don't mean to offend her, but I sure as shooting don't want her to think I'm coming up short in other ways, too."

"What would you like me to say?"

"Tell her thank you kindly for the offer, but I should be able to manage just fine."

"*Spasibo,*" Elena said. "No burn steak. Like mine rare."

"Don't you worry. This ain't my first barbecue." He speared a piece of chicken with his fork. "She's really starting to pick up the lingo. I'd better up my game, too. Miss Ana, I would be much obliged if you could teach me a word or two here and there."

"I would be happy to. As long as you invite me to wedding."

"Let's not go getting ahead of ourselves. I ain't even asked the question yet."

"Would you like to?"

"Well, now, I think that's a subject that needs to be discussed between me and her. When the time comes, of course." Shorty cleared his throat and changed the subject. "Are Duke's IT people any closer to cracking the password on Yevgeny's laptop?"

"Program is still running. Technician says he is making progress. Mischa asked technician to text him if he discovers password so he can return early from date—I mean dinner."

Anastasia looked stricken. She visibly relaxed when she saw Vladimir, the only ranch hand who spoke English, was too caught up in his conversation with Fyodor to have noticed her faux pas.

"Tell Mischa to take his time," Laramie said with studied calm. "I'll keep an eye on things while he's gone."

When she wiped her mouth on her napkin and pushed her chair away from the table, Anastasia followed her lead.

"I will go with you. If technician is successful, you will need me to translate what is in files."

"Can't it wait until morning?" Shorty asked. "The boys and I were hoping you'd pick out a few more tunes tonight. A watched pot never boils, you know."

Perhaps not, but Laramie could feel the water in hers starting to heat up.

"Maybe tomorrow. I'll let Andrei do the honors tonight."

Anastasia went over to him and whispered something in his ear. He beamed when she nodded at his whispered reply.

"What did you say to him?" Laramie asked after Anastasia joined her at the foot of the stairs.

"I teach him how to say, 'May I have this dance?' in Russian. Perhaps you are not only one who will be getting lucky tonight."

"Perhaps not."

Anastasia trailed Laramie up the stairs. Laramie's ass looked so good in the tight jeans she favored that Anastasia was tempted to reach up and give it a squeeze.

When they reached the office, Anastasia closed the door and locked it behind her. She doubted anyone would pay them an unexpected visit tonight, but she didn't want to take any chances.

She took a quick look at the laptop to see if Sergei's IT guy had finally broken into it. Even though she longed to see the files stored on the laptop, she was grateful to see the display was still stuck on the password screen.

"Now what?" Laramie asked.

"Now we do what really came here for."

"We can't."

"Why not?"

Laramie pointed at Anastasia's empty hands. "You forgot the rope."

"Would have raised too many questions if I brought rope inside." Anastasia gripped Laramie's shirt with both hands and backed her against the wall. "Besides, I want you to be able to use hands."

Laramie flashed a lazy smile. "Yes, ma'am."

She slid her hands into Anastasia's back pockets and pulled her closer. Loosening her grip, Anastasia flattened her hands and placed them on Laramie's chest. Then she slowly slid them down until they rested on the rise of Laramie's breasts. As Laramie's breath quickened, Anastasia stared at the rise and fall of her chest.

Laramie put her finger under Anastasia's chin and slowly tilted her head up. "My eyes are up here."

"Those are beautiful, too."

Anastasia could feel Laramie's hardened nipples poking against her palms. Time seemed to slow to a crawl as Laramie parted her lips and bent to kiss her.

When their lips met, Anastasia forgot how to breathe. All she could do was feel. Laramie's hands on her ass. Laramie's tongue in her mouth. Laramie's body pressed against hers.

Laramie gasped when she broke the kiss. "Why did you stop?"

"Because you are wearing far too many clothes."

She unbuttoned Laramie's shirt and pushed it over her shoulders. Though the room was warm, goose bumps formed on Laramie's skin as Anastasia slowly trailed her fingertips down her arms.

Laramie held her arms over her head to allow Anastasia to remove her undershirt. Anastasia reached for her belt next.

"Wait," Laramie said when Anastasia started to unzip her jeans. "Let me make this easier for you. Now," she said after she kicked off her boots, "where were we?"

Anastasia pushed Laramie's jeans down and waited for her to step out of them. Laramie stood before her clad in only her sports bra, socks, and boxer briefs.

"Better?" Laramie asked.

"You tell me."

Anastasia parted the fly of Laramie's boxer briefs and slipped her hand inside. Laramie's eyes darkened as Anastasia cupped her mound in the palm of her hand. Laramie's clit was hard and she was so wet Anastasia could tell she was already close to coming.

Anastasia wanted to go slow, but she couldn't afford to take the chance. Mischa could return from town unexpectedly, and either Elena or the ranch hands could come upon them at any moment.

Laramie groaned deep in her throat when Anastasia began to massage her clit. Undulating her hips, she began to move against Anastasia's hand. Slowly at first, then with increasing speed.

"I go inside you?" Anastasia asked.

Laramie's reply came through gritted teeth. "God, yes."

Anastasia slid her fingers between Laramie's folds and slowly entered her. The sound Laramie made was just short of a primal scream.

"Kiss me," Laramie said. "Or pretty soon everyone's gonna come runnin'."

"Only person I want to come is you."

"Keep that up and you'll get your wish."

Anastasia pinched one of Laramie's erect nipples. Before Laramie could cry out again, she covered Laramie's mouth with her own.

Laramie groaned again and pulled her closer. Laramie was trembling from head to toe. Anastasia could feel her nearing the edge. Desperate to take her there, she increased her pace.

"Oh, Jesus, I'm about to—"

Laramie squeezed her eyes shut and arched her back. Her head bounced off the wall, but she didn't seem to feel the pain.

Anastasia could feel Laramie's smooth muscles gripping her fingers, pulling her deeper. She kissed her until the spasms subsided. Until Laramie's rapid breathing gradually returned to normal.

"That was amazing," Laramie said. "Now it's my turn."

Laramie led her to the leather couch and knelt before her. She unzipped Anastasia's jeans and hooked her thumbs inside Anastasia's underwear. Anastasia lifted her hips, allowing Laramie to drag her jeans and boy shorts down to her ankles.

Laramie pulled Anastasia to the edge of the couch and closed her mouth around her clit. Now it was Anastasia's turn to cry out. She buried her hands in Laramie's hair, holding her in place. She needed her to remain exactly where she was: at the center of her need.

Laramie varied her pace. Picking up speed. Slowing down. Bringing her to the precipice. Then pulling her back. Anastasia felt like she was on the ultimate roller coaster. She lay back and enjoyed the ride.

When it was over, her body was spent, but her heart was full.

"I have been dreaming about this since I met you," she said, finger-combing Laramie's tousled hair. "Is even better than I imagined."

Laramie rested her head in Anastasia's lap. "Ditto."

Anastasia heaved a contented sigh as she stroked Laramie's back and shoulders.

"Did you bring the book?" Laramie asked.

"I don't need it."

Anastasia recited her favorite poem from memory. Laramie lifted her head when she was done.

"One day, you're gonna have to tell me what the words mean."

"I can tell you now. They mean that I—"

She stopped speaking when she heard Yevgeny's laptop emit a series of electronic chimes. She looked up and saw dozens of icons displayed on the monitor.

"Hold that thought," Laramie said. "We're in."

CHAPTER TWENTY-FOUR

Laramie took the steaks out of the refrigerator and carried them outside so they could start coming up to temperature before Shorty placed them on the grill. When the case of boneless rib eyes arrived yesterday, Andrei had requested an opportunity to inspect the contents.

"Good marbling," he had said, running a finger over one of the plastic-wrapped cuts. "Looks tender. Like it will practically melt in mouth."

Anastasia had blushed a bit as she translated the last sentence. Laramie had avoided looking her in the eye so she wouldn't devolve into a fit of giggles.

She had been deliriously happy since she and Anastasia had made love. She tried not to let it show, but the feelings welling up inside her were almost impossible to hide.

"Tell him that's what we're aiming for," she had said, trying to keep her mind on business. "If we get there, we'll be able to corner the market in this part of the world."

"He asks if you truly believe we can compete with Khachanov brothers or if you are simply trying to make him feel good," Anastasia had said.

"Tell him I'm not in the habit of saying things I don't mean."

Anastasia had fixed her with a gaze that was unmistakable in its intentions. "I will keep that in mind, especially considering things you said to me last night."

Two little-used picnic tables had been brought out of storage, given fresh coats of paint, and put into use for today's get-together.

While Mischa and Pavel spread linen cloths on the tables, Anastasia followed behind them, positioning napkins and silverware at each place setting.

Laramie watched her work. She could still feel her. She could still taste her. And, oh, how she wanted more.

"Are you sure you don't need to borrow one of Elena's aprons, Shorty?" she asked as she set the tray of marinated steaks on the expansive work area next to the grill.

"Don't start," he growled as he held a hand over the grates to check the temperature of the coals. With a nod of satisfaction, he closed the lid so the briquettes could retain their heat. "You missed a real good shindig last night. The boys did a folk dance. You know the one where they fold their arms, squat like they're about to let one rip, and kick their legs out like they're trying to get up but can't?"

"It's called the Cossack dance. I've seen it on TV a time or two. I was tempted to try it once, but I didn't want to blow out my knees."

"I didn't think Vlad and Ivan were going to be able to pull it off either, but they managed it somehow."

"I'm sorry I missed it."

"You don't look too broken up about it." Shorty took a long look at her. "You don't have to bother telling me why. It's plum written all over your face."

Laramie had always been honest with him so she didn't opt to change their dynamic now. "You don't expect me to apologize, do you?"

"Of course not. I just want you to tell me you're happy and promise me you'll be careful. I'll do everything I can to protect you—same as I always have—but we both know this ain't Wyoming. The rules are different here."

"Don't I know it."

"Thanks for agreeing with me, but I'm still waiting for you to tell me what I need to hear."

"Yes, I'm happy, and yes, I'll be careful."

"Good. I know we ain't blood kin, but you've always been like family to me. Not to mention your parents would never speak to me again if I let anything happen to you."

"I'll try not to give you cause for concern."

"You best not. Otherwise, you'll have me to answer to, and neither of us wants that."

"No, we don't." At times, Shorty had been harder on her than either of her parents had. She was grateful for his tutelage. She wouldn't be where she was now without it. "Aside from the floor show, how was your night? Did you and Elena cut another rug?"

"Yeah, we did."

"You don't sound too happy about it." In fact, he sounded almost wistful. "Did something happen?"

Shorty looked across the yard. Elena and her two sisters sat at one of the picnic tables, chatting happily while they nursed cans of soda. One was two years older than Elena, the other five years younger. Despite the disparity in their ages, the three looked so similar they could have passed for triplets.

"You can tell a lot about a woman by the way she dances," Shorty said as if lost in thought. "How she moves. How she holds herself."

"What did you learn from Elena by dancing with her?"

"That's just it. I didn't learn a consarned thing." He poked one of the steaks with a two-pronged fork so the marinade could seep into the meat. "She seemed like she was enjoying herself, but she didn't want to enjoy herself too much."

"I don't understand."

"It's like she's holding something back. Like she's afraid of something. For the life of me, I can't figure out why she's so skittish."

"Maybe she's been hurt before and she doesn't want to take a chance on getting hurt again. Maybe she thinks you're just looking for a little fun."

"I'm not the love 'em and leave 'em type."

"I know that, but she doesn't." She tapped the back of her hand against his chest. "Have you thought about telling her so?"

"In case you haven't noticed, we don't speak the same language. And I'm not about to ask Anastasia to translate that for me. When it comes to matters of the heart, some things you have to say for yourself."

Elena looked over at them and said something to her sisters. All three burst into raucous laughter and simultaneously turned away.

"I tell you one thing, though," Shorty said. "I'm gonna keep knocking on that door until she lets me in. 'Cause that tall drink of water—"

"Makes a man a mite thirsty. You've said that before."

"I thought it was a sentiment that bore repeating."

Duke strolled over to them. He was wearing the same designer boots he had sported during their meeting in Moscow. Today, though, he had paired them with a colorful Western-style shirt and a pair of crisply ironed jeans instead of a tracksuit. He looked more like a rodeo cowboy than a rodeo clown. Laramie liked the change.

"May I talk to you for a moment?" he asked with no hint of his usual bombast. "In private."

"Sure."

Curious, she followed him a few steps away.

"I am told you do not like being center of attention, so I will not mention you in speech when I address workers. When I hired you to be trainer, I did not expect you to become my savior as well."

"I wouldn't go that far."

"No, is true. You saved my pork."

"I did what? Oh, you mean I saved your bacon."

"Yes, that is what I said. Bacon is pork. You saved my pork. Thanks to records you found on computer, my people managed to track down Yevgeny about an hour ago. He had trashed van and spent some of money, but we convinced him to return rest and repay what he owes."

Laramie didn't ask what methods had been used to persuade Yevgeny to make restitution. "So he was in Siberia after all."

The laptop had contained several stored internet searches focused on the area.

"Yes, we caught him while he was lying on beach working on tan."

"I thought Siberia was a place people were sent for punishment, not a destination they sought for pleasure."

"Is true weather is quite bad in winter. In summer, is very popular resort area. But enough about Yevgeny. He is old news. I am ready to move on to new and better things. I was hoping I would be able to do such things with you."

"What do you mean?"

"With Yevgeny gone, I need new ranch manager. I would like you to consider taking job. Your contract is for three years. For right price, maybe we can make position permanent."

Laramie was stunned into silence by the unexpected offer. Three years was a long time to spend away from her family. Now Duke was asking her to spend even more time separated from those she loved most. The money was good—great, in fact—but was it enough to compensate for the sacrifices she would have to make?

"I don't know what to say."

"Yes is good word."

"Yes *is* a good word. I just don't know if it's the right word for me to use in this particular situation. Let me make a suggestion. I'll assume the role until my contract is up. When it ends, I'll take your offer into consideration. If I choose not to accept it, I'll help you find someone to replace me. Someone you can trust. Does that work?"

"Is good compromise," he said, shaking her hand. "We will revisit matter later, yes?"

"Yes. In addition to a ranch manager, you're going to need a good accountant, too. Someone onsite, not three hundred miles away."

"I know. I plan to offer job to Mischa. He has good head on his shoulders and is ready to take step up in career." He looked over at Mischa, Pavel, and Anastasia, who were kicking a soccer ball around with one of Fyodor's kids. "Besides, it will be good for him to get out of Moscow and away from all those party boys he chases after. He deserves a chance to meet someone stable. Someone like Pavel."

Laramie took a moment to make sure she hadn't misheard what Duke had just said. "Are you saying—"

"That Mischa is gay? Yes, I have known since he was little boy."

"Why haven't you said anything to him?"

"Like him, I have been pretending. Saying what I thought he needed to hear. I do not want to force him to say anything he is not ready for. I want him to come to me when he feels time is right."

"Does the rest of his family know?"

Duke shrugged. "Some suspect. Some, I am sure, have no idea. Not all of them are as sophisticated as I am. I travel world, and I read things other than propaganda distributed by Kremlin."

"Is it safe for Mischa and Pavel to be a couple here?"

"Godoroye is small town. Lucky for me, I own seventy-five percent of it. Townspeople do not wish to cross me. If Mischa chooses to make a life here, they will treat him with respect as long as he gives it in return. If Pavel's business suffers, which I doubt, I can put him on payroll, too. I own several apartment buildings. I can use him to pop locks when renters refuse to pay."

"You have a solution for everything, don't you?"

"If that were true, I would still be married to first wife instead of paying alimony to her and two of the three that followed her. Look," he said after they shared a laugh, "Mischa is good man, no matter who he loves. Ana has been good friend to him. Maybe she will meet someone, too." He looked at her with a knowing smile plastered on his face. "Maybe she already has."

Laramie bit her lip to keep from confirming his suspicions. "Maybe."

❖

Anastasia's kick slid past Fyodor's daughter's foot. When Dominika went to fetch the ball, Anastasia looked up to find Elena and her sisters were staring at her. Again. It wouldn't have been quite as bad if they weren't so brazen about it. She was starting to feel like an animal on display at a zoo.

"They're doing it again," she said without moving her lips.

"I noticed." Mischa moved closer so they could talk without having to raise their voices. "What did you say when you met them? They hugged you like you were long-lost relatives instead of perfect strangers."

"They didn't give me a chance to say much of anything. They said Elena had told them all about me. Like her, they were happy to see someone from their hometown doing so well. I work as a translator on a fledgling cattle ranch. It's not like I'm nominated for the Nobel Peace Prize."

"Maybe they're overly friendly. What did they do when she introduced them to everyone else?"

Anastasia thought back to the various encounters she had witnessed after Elena's sisters climbed out of Sergei's limo.

"They were cool to Laramie. They were polite, but you could tell they weren't completely receptive."

"So they share opinions as well as a family resemblance."

"It seems so, yes. They giggled like schoolgirls whenever Shorty said more than two words to them. With everyone else, they were just…normal."

"That's how they were with me, too. I guess the disguise is working."

Anastasia cut her eyes at Pavel, who had taken advantage of the break in the action to grab them another round of drinks from the cooler. Soda and bottled water. Nothing fun. On a day like today, she could have used something stronger.

"How much longer can you keep it up?"

"I was about to ask you the same thing." He glanced at Laramie, who was deep in conversation with Sergei. "What will you do when she leaves?"

Anastasia's heart sank. Being with Laramie last night had felt so right. So natural. But even while it was happening, she had known that it couldn't last. That *they* couldn't last. Was that why it had felt so good to be with her? Because she didn't have to worry about a future she knew could never come to pass?

"I will do the same thing you'll do when you return to Moscow and leave Pavel behind: go back to my life."

"Would our lives be the same without them in it? I don't think so."

"Neither do I. Our lives would continue to have meaning, but there would be a void that didn't exist before."

"Not just one. At least two. Maybe more. The people here? They like me for me, not because I am Sergei's nephew. Would their opinion of me change if they knew I was gay? Call me naïve, but I like to think it wouldn't."

"Are you ready to come out?"

Mischa looked over at Pavel. "I don't know, but he makes me want to try."

"So soon? You just met him a few days ago."

"Sometimes it doesn't take long to know when someone is right for you. You just feel it in your bones. Along with other places that are a lot more fun."

Anastasia glanced at Laramie. Whenever she looked at her, she experienced feelings she had never felt before. Each time she started to feel overwhelmed, Laramie would say or do something to reassure her. To ground her. To remind her that she wasn't going through this alone. They were in this together. How long would it last? Anastasia had no idea. All she could do was live each day as if it might be their last. Because one day, it truly would be.

Sergei held up a hand and motioned to Mischa.

"Your uncle's beckoning you. You'd better see what he wants."

"Do I have to?"

"Don't look so worried. For the foreseeable future, you can do no wrong in his eyes. Use that to your advantage."

"And do what?"

"I could use a raise. Why don't you start with that?"

"I think I'll wait until he recovers all of the money Yevgeny stole before I ask him to spend some of it on you."

"Good idea."

Laramie joined her after Mischa took her place at Sergei's side.

"What were you and Sergei talking about?" Anastasia asked.

"He wanted to thank me without making a big production number out of it."

"Is that all?"

Laramie took a sip of her soda as she watched Ivan's young sons chase each other around the yard. "No, but this isn't the time or place to talk about it. I'll tell you later."

Anastasia didn't want to wait. "Our time alone is too precious to waste talking about other people. Tell me now."

Laramie hooked her thumbs in her belt loops. "Duke knows about Mischa. And about us."

This was the moment Anastasia had feared. The moment when the house of cards she and Mischa had built would come crashing down on top of them.

"What do you mean he knows? Did you tell him?"

"Of course not. Like you, I've never outed anyone other than myself and I don't intend to start now. He already knew about Mischa. He said he's always known. He's waiting for Mischa to broach the subject first. He's willing to play the game as long as you two are. When Mischa's ready to talk, he's ready to listen. You can say something to Mischa, or you can let him come to a decision on his own. It's up to you. I've said all I'm gonna say on the matter."

"How does he know about you and me? We have been discreet."

"That's a matter of opinion. According to Shorty, we couldn't be more obvious."

Anastasia ran her hands through her hair. "What are we supposed to do? If word gets out—"

Laramie cut her off.

"I thought this was what you wanted: to be open and honest."

"It is, but—"

She paused when she saw Elena and her sisters looking her way yet again. She turned her back to them so they couldn't see the confusion on her face. Elena would probably blame Laramie for that, but this wasn't Laramie's problem. It was hers. She had spent the past few years putting herself on the front lines of a war that seemed impossible to win. But the real battle was here. In the trenches. Instead of standing her ground, all she wanted to do was run away.

"This is all too much. I just want to be with you without wondering what everyone else is thinking. Without having to find places we can sneak off to in order to be alone. I just want to be with you."

"I want that, too."

"Then how do we make it happen without losing everything we have worked for?"

Laramie briefly squeezed her hand. "By sticking together instead of turning on each other. Let's enjoy today and worry about tomorrow when it comes. We'll figure things out in time."

Except time, Anastasia knew, was a luxury they didn't have.

"This was one of the best ideas you've ever had," Shorty said as the gathered family members began to say their good-byes.

"Everybody gets lucky sometimes. I guess today's my day."

Shorty waved at Elena and her sisters as they made their way to Duke's waiting limo.

"Looks like you've got two new fans," Laramie said.

"Yeah, it's pretty good being me. They don't seem to be fans of yours, though. Was it something you said?"

"More like something I am."

"Oh, that. Do you want me to say something to Elena? I can help her see what a good person you are."

"You shouldn't have to help her do anything. If I'm as good as you say I am, she should already know that by now."

"She does. It's just…Some people are funny about things they don't understand, you know?"

"You never were."

"That's because I've known you practically from the day you were born. You've never had to explain yourself to me. No matter who you fall for, you're always gonna be the same Laramie to me. Unless your intended turns out to be a vegetarian. Then we might end up exchanging a few cross words."

"Thanks, Shorty."

"For what?"

"Always being you."

"Someone has to, right? It might as well be me. You just keep on being you. Elena will eventually come around."

"If she doesn't?"

"Well then, it'll be her loss, won't it?"

"I know you're trying to get something going with her. I don't want to come between you two."

"Ain't nothing to come between. If she's got a problem with you, she's got a problem with me, too. Now let's quit jawing and get back to work before the new boss tans both our hides."

"Temporary boss."

"I know how much you like it here. You're not thinking of staying on after your contract runs out?"

"Who would run our place if I did? My parents won't live forever, and Trey has his heart set on being a rodeo star rather than a rancher. That leaves me. I can't be in two places at once, especially when the two places are this far apart."

"Good thing you have plenty of time to make up your mind."

"Extra time isn't going to make the decision any easier."

He reached up and draped his arm across her shoulder. "That's why it's good to be me and sucks to be you."

"Do you want to trade places?"

"Not on your life, kid. Not on your life."

Her life had never been more in flux. All the choices she had made in the past had led her to this point. And the most important choice was yet to be made: deciding whether she should support her family's dreams or embark on one of her own.

CHAPTER TWENTY-FIVE

Sergei tried to keep it quiet, but the drama surrounding Yevgeny's embezzlement and attempted escape ended up as front-page news. Most of the press attention was focused on Sergei's headquarters in Moscow, though Laramie, Shorty, and the ranch hands had to chase a few persistent photographers off the property after they gave Elena a fright.

Elena had been washing a load of laundry when she spotted three strangers sneaking across the backyard. Her scream had brought everyone running—Laramie and Anastasia from the office, Shorty and the ranch hands from the pasture. Laramie had grabbed a rifle from the gun cabinet and fired a warning shot in the air to get the photographers' attention. Shorty, Ivan, and Fyodor had done the rest.

Laramie had looked like an avenging angel as she stood on the back porch with the smoking rifle in her hands. Anastasia had a healthy fear of guns, but she couldn't deny she had found Laramie incredibly sexy at that moment. She didn't look half-bad in this moment, either.

Laramie was naked and on top of her. Her right hand was between Anastasia's legs, her fingers thrusting inside her. Her left hand was on Anastasia's breast, kneading it while she gently pinched her nipple. And her mouth was everywhere. Kissing her. Licking her. Whispering naughty things to her while Laramie took her to heights she never thought she could reach.

Then Anastasia did the same for her.

This was the ritual they practiced every night. After everyone else went to bed, they would spend hours locked behind closed doors, making love until their bodies were spent. Anastasia didn't know which was more physically taxing—the often strenuous work they did during the day or the gyrations they put themselves through at night—but she definitely knew which was more fun.

"There's something I have to tell you," Laramie said as they caught their breath between rounds. "Something I've been keeping from you."

"Something like what?"

Except for the one they shared, it wasn't like Laramie to keep secrets.

"Duke offered me a job."

"You already have job."

"He offered me one that's permanent instead of temporary."

"When did he do that?"

"During the first family day."

"That was almost two weeks ago. Why have you not said anything before now?"

"I didn't want to steal Mischa's thunder. Everyone was so excited to welcome him on board. I didn't want to detract from that."

Mischa had accepted Sergei's offer. He had put in his notice at the accounting office he worked for in Moscow and emptied out the apartment he and Anastasia had shared. In a few days, after he spent one last weekend partying in all of his favorite nightclubs, he would officially move to Godoroye.

Elena had tried to convince him to move into Yevgeny's old room, but he had chosen the attic so he could have more privacy whenever Pavel came to visit. Though he had taken the huge step of coming out to his family, who had proven to be more supportive than he had expected, he had not told Elena, Andrei, Fyodor, Ivan, or Vladimir that he and Pavel were more than friends. He planned to do that after he arrived, though he was nervous about what their reaction would be. Anastasia was, too. Because when Mischa revealed his secret, hers would be out in the open as well.

Would everyone on the ranch accept her for who she was, or would they be upset with her for lying to them all this time? Whether positive or negative, their reaction would be easier for her to take knowing Laramie would be by her side. Not just for a few months or a few years. For all the years to come.

For the first time in her life, Anastasia began to look on the future with optimism instead of pessimism.

"Did you take job?"

"No."

With one word, Anastasia's hopes were dashed.

"Why not?"

"I like it here, but I don't know if I like it enough to stay."

"Go ahead and leave me. Everyone else does."

Anastasia tried to pull away, but Laramie wouldn't let her go. "I'm not everyone else."

"Who are you?" Tears pricked Anastasia's eyes, making her vision blur. "Who are we?"

Laramie knuckled away Anastasia's tears and traced her fingers along the line of her jaw. "We're Laramie and Ana. Two women who care for each other and are doing their best to make it work even if they don't know how to go about it."

"How do you always know right thing to say?"

"One of the perks of being a cattle rancher is knowing how to deal with bullshit."

Anastasia laughed through her tears. She curled herself around Laramie's body.

"Stay with me. I am not asking you to stay forever," she said when she felt Laramie stiffen. "Stay with me tonight. I want to wake up in your arms. Is okay?"

Laramie kissed her, then held her tight. "Is very okay."

Laramie woke up disoriented. Nothing was in its usual place. It took her several minutes to remember she wasn't in her own room but Anastasia's. Last night, instead of heading across the hall after she and Anastasia made love, she had opted to stay. Now she didn't want to leave. Anastasia obviously felt the same way. She stirred, then snuggled closer.

"Five more minutes, yes?"

"If I stay, that five minutes will turn into five more. Then five more. Then who knows how many after that." She kissed Anastasia's cheek, then slid out of bed. "I've got to go."

Anastasia turned to face her. "What if I give you reason to stay?" she asked, tossing the covers aside.

Laramie's mouth watered as she stared at Anastasia's naked body. She had spent last night with that body pressed against her side. Now she wanted to feel it moving underneath her.

"Don't tempt me."

She gathered her discarded clothes and wadded them into a ball rather than putting them on. It would be foolish for her to get dressed when she would need to strip for a shower anyway.

She opened the door just wide enough to poke her head through the opening. She didn't see Elena wandering around so she dashed across the hall. She cinched her robe around her waist and gathered her work clothes. When she opened the door, Elena was standing in front of her with a stern look on her face.

"Is something wrong?" she asked. Elena had picked up a good deal of English, thanks to her daily lessons, but a few communication gaps remained. "Do I need to grab Anastasia?"

Elena leaned forward and sniffed melodramatically. "You smell like sex."

"I—What?"

"You," Elena said, slowly enunciating every word. "Smell. Like. Sex. I will not have such behavior under my roof. No daughter of mine—"

She tried to poke her finger into Laramie's chest, but Laramie brushed her hand away.

"I'm not your daughter," she said, trying to keep a lid on her temper.

Elena pointed behind her. "But she is."

Laramie looked past her, hoping to see Anastasia's door was still closed and Anastasia was sound asleep. No such luck. Anastasia stood in the open doorway, one hand on the knob and the other on the jamb. Her beautiful face was twisted in a rictus of pain.

Laramie wanted to go to her. To hold her and tell her everything was going to be okay. But she couldn't because she didn't know. She squeezed Anastasia's arm to show her support.

"Do you want me to—"

"No," Anastasia said softly. "Just go."

Laramie left them alone. In a way, Elena's revelation didn't come as a surprise. Their bond had been palpable since the moment they met. Would it remain intact now that Anastasia knew the reason behind it, or were there too many years of anger and resentment in the way?

Whatever the outcome, Laramie knew Anastasia and Elena's relationship would never be the same again. She could only pray that her and Anastasia's relationship wouldn't be irreparably damaged as a result.

❖

Elena gripped the lapels of her robe with both hands as if she were trying to protect herself from something. Anastasia almost laughed at the absurdity of the idea, considering she was the one who stood to be hurt the most.

"I did not mean for you to find out this way."

Elena extended a pleading hand toward her, but Anastasia jerked away. She bumped against the door, making it bang against the wall. The sound echoed through the quiet house.

Elena flinched, then slowly lowered her hand. Anastasia watched it descend. Was that the hand of the woman who had held her when she was a baby? The one that had tossed her away instead of caring for her?

"I have wanted to tell you so many times," Elena said. "From the moment I recognized you and knew you were mine." She pointed to her eye. "My baby, the one I gave away, had the same mark in her eye. She had forehead just like yours. And a smile that made my heart melt every time I saw it. Just like yours. We can get a DNA test if you want, but I don't need to see the test results to prove what I already know to be true. You are my daughter."

"Is that why you and your sisters couldn't stop staring at me on family day? Because you've convinced yourself and them that this fairy tale you're concocting is true?"

"It's not a fairy tale, Ana. It's true. I am your mother."

"Stop saying that!"

Anastasia said the words so loud Shorty and the rest of the ranch hands probably heard her all the way in the bunkhouse.

"Even if you do turn out to be the woman who gave birth to me, you are not now and have never been my mother."

"I deserve that."

"And I deserve an explanation. If you loved me as much as you're trying to convince me to believe, why did you give me away?"

Elena lowered her eyes. "It's complicated."

"I like puzzles. Help me solve this one."

"Come to the kitchen. We can sit and talk over a cup of coffee instead of standing here yelling at each other."

Anastasia would have preferred to remain where she was, but she decided to heed Elena's suggestion for Laramie's sake. Laramie could take refuge in the bathroom for only so long. She followed Elena down the hall so Laramie wouldn't turn into a prune while she cowered under the shower spray.

"If you're my...mother," she said while Elena poured two cups of black coffee, "who's my father?"

Elena didn't answer, forcing Anastasia to press her for a response.

"Please tell me it isn't Yevgeny."

"No, it is not him," Elena said firmly.

When she hesitated again, Anastasia waited her out.

"I do not know your father's name," Elena said at length. "He and I were never formally introduced."

Elena seemed ashamed by the confession. Anastasia could think of only one reason why. A reason both logical and unimaginable.

"You were raped, weren't you? That's why you couldn't bear to keep me. That's why you won't let Shorty get too close to you."

Nodding, Elena finally broke down. Her broad shoulders shook as tears rolled down her cheeks.

"How did it happen?" Anastasia asked.

"You already know the circumstances. Do you really need to know the details?"

"I don't want to. I need to. I have spent twenty-eight years wondering about my past. You are the only person who can fill in the blanks for me. *All* the blanks."

Elena got up and plucked a bottle of vodka out of the liquor cabinet.

"For this," she said, pouring a liberal amount into her cup, "I'm going to need something stronger than coffee."

"I'll take some of that, too."

Considering the enormity of the moment, she felt confident Laramie would forgive her for breaking the rules.

"I was twenty-five when it happened. Three years younger than you are now. One night, I went to dinner with friends. I left early because I had to be at work the next day. As I made my way home, a man ran up behind me and hit me on the head with something hard and cylindrical. It felt like a police baton. The blow knocked me unconscious. When I came to, he had pulled me into an alley and he was having his way with me. He put his hand over my mouth so I couldn't scream for help. I have no idea what he looked like because he wore a balaclava over his face. He didn't speak during the assault so there's no way I would be able to recognize his voice. I still remember the way he smelled. He had a very distinctive body odor. If I ever came across him again, I would recognize him right away."

Anastasia winced as she took a sip of the spiked coffee. Not from the sting of the vodka but from the pain inflicted by Elena's tale. *Her* tale.

"I told my sisters what had happened, but I didn't go to the police because I wouldn't have been able to give them a description and I didn't want any of the officers to act like it was my fault. Plus I couldn't be sure the man who accosted me wasn't one of them. If he was, they would be more likely to protect him than seek justice for me."

Anastasia had heard similar stories from friends who had gotten gay-bashed. Dealing with the trauma of the assault was often less stressful than dealing with the police's disdain afterward.

"I discovered I was pregnant two months after I was...attacked. I wasn't seeing anyone at the time—I stopped dating after the incident—so I knew the father could be only one person. My sisters told me to get rid of it—of *you*. A baby, they said, would only remind me of the worst night of my life. I struggled with the decision. I took too much time to make up my mind, and I had no choice but to bring the pregnancy to term."

"Why did you give me away?"

"I was living on my own, making barely enough money to support myself. I couldn't support you, too. I wanted you to have what I couldn't give you: a loving home with parents who could care for you the way I couldn't. I wanted to cry when you told me you had grown up in an orphanage. That no one ever claimed you. I wanted to tell you everything then. I wanted to tell you I was sorry I wasn't able to make your dreams come true. And for making you the way you are."

"The way I—You mean you think you're the reason I'm a lesbian?"

Elena spread her hands in a gesture of helplessness. "Perhaps my distrust of men seeped into you somehow."

The statement wasn't the most farfetched Anastasia had ever heard, but it came close.

"My best friend is a man. I trust him with my life. I just don't want to have sex with him."

"Mischa is not your boyfriend?" Elena seemed almost relieved by the revelation. "That changes my view on some things. Part of the reason I was so upset when I saw you flirting with Laramie was I thought you were cheating on him with her."

"Mischa and I aren't together. We just said we were to make things easier for both of us."

"And you don't blame me?"

"You didn't make me this way." Anastasia rolled her eyes heavenward. "Someone else did."

"That makes me so happy." Elena gripped her coffee mug with both hands as she started crying again. "I used to think the night you were conceived was the worst day of my life. It wasn't. The worst was the day I let you go."

"What was the best?"

"The day we met for the second time. When I looked into your eyes and realized you were mine."

Anastasia remembered that moment. When Elena had gasped after seeing the birthmark in her eye. The sound, she realized now, hadn't been one of horror or revulsion but recognition.

"I know you will need time to take everything in, but do you think you will ever be able to forgive me?"

"I don't know," Anastasia said honestly. "I've spent so much time wondering who you were and why you did the things you did. Now that I know, I don't know what to do with it. Or the realization that you don't approve of me being gay. Even if we put the past twenty-eight years behind us, I can't forget what you said last month."

"I was wrong to say those things. I didn't know—"

"That you weren't just talking about Laramie? That you were talking about me and Mischa, too?"

"I said the things I did because I didn't want you to be hurt. I didn't want her to take advantage of you and walk away with your heart in her hands. I was wrong to say what I did because I am in no position to pass judgment on someone else's life."

Anastasia must have lost her tolerance for alcohol over the past few weeks. After less than one shot, she felt the vodka begin to lower her defenses.

"I won't comment on your choice of partner if you don't comment on mine," she said.

"It's a deal."

Elena reached across the table. Anastasia felt a surge of emotion when Elena's large hand swallowed her smaller one in its grip.

"Is it safe to come out?" Laramie asked gently.

Anastasia turned to look at her. Laramie looked adorable standing there with her hat in her hands and an expression of concern on her face.

"Yes," Anastasia said, switching to English. "Everything is fine now."

She and Elena—She and her mother couldn't erase the past, but if they worked hard enough, they could create a future they had both dreamed of. One she had thought she would never achieve but was now within reach. If she was lucky, she would be able to spend it with Laramie Bowman by her side.

CHAPTER TWENTY-SIX

L aramie felt like a weight had been lifted from her shoulders. Her relationship with Anastasia was out in the open, and despite what she had been told to expect, the world had not come to an end. Quite the opposite. In fact, her world had never felt more idyllic. Sure, a couple of the ranch hands and their wives had acted a bit standoffish during the first family day after Mischa made his big announcement, and she and Anastasia had confirmed the rumors about them as well, but Elena had taken the guilty parties aside and given them a talking-to. Elena hadn't revealed what she said and Anastasia hadn't been close enough to overhear her, but Laramie had been able to tell by Elena's stern expression and the group's downcast looks that she hadn't tempered her words while vocalizing her disappointment in their behavior.

"She's taking this mama bear thing to heart," Laramie had said as she watched the fiery exchange.

The men had been receptive to the news that Elena was Anastasia's mother. Though she hadn't told them the unfortunate story detailing Anastasia's conception, she had admitted to giving Anastasia up for adoption—and confessed to being overjoyed by their most unexpected reunion.

"She is trying to make up for lost time."

"I'd say she's off to a pretty good start."

After they absorbed Elena's withering lecture, Fyodor and Ivan had each made their way over to Laramie, Anastasia, Mischa, and Pavel to offer their apologies. The gestures had seemed sincere, not feigned. Like the men were speaking from their hearts and not just paying lip service so they could get out of Elena's doghouse.

"This proves that everything I have been doing as an activist is worth it," Anastasia had said. "If I cannot change whole world at once, maybe I can change little bit of it at a time."

When Laramie had reached for Anastasia's hand, it had felt like much more than a gesture of solidarity. It had felt like she was making a statement. A loud one.

"Is time for you to make big coming-out speech you said you would not do?" Anastasia had asked with a teasing smile.

Laramie had squeezed the hand she held in hers.

"Who needs speeches? In my book, actions speak louder than words."

Things had been okay around the ranch since that slight bump in the road. More than okay. Better than before. Laramie didn't have to be on guard all the time or worry about keeping secrets—either hers or Anastasia's. She could just be herself. She had never felt more free. Or more wary.

As she had seen time and time again, life often gave you everything you wanted only to turn around and take it all away. She went to bed each night and woke each morning wondering when the other shoe was going to drop.

It took almost five months for her to finally receive the answer.

Her cell phone rang late one night in mid December. Despite the cozy covers piled on top of her and Anastasia's warm body lying beside her, a chill went down her spine when she heard the sound. She reached for the phone knowing the conversation she was about to have likely wouldn't be pleasant.

"Dad?" she said after seeing her father's name printed on the phone's liquid crystal display. "Is something wrong?"

"I tried and tried not to make this call, but I didn't know what else to do. I didn't know who else to turn to."

Her father was one of the strongest people Laramie had ever known, but she had never heard him sound so helpless.

"What's happened?"

"Your brother's taken a turn. I need you to come home."

As Laramie watched large flakes of snow fall outside her bedroom window, she felt the frigid winter temperatures began to seep into her.

"What?" she asked, trying not to tremble with fear. "I don't understand. The last time I talked to Mama, she said Trey was getting better."

"His body is healing, but his mind is…" Her father's voice trailed off as he let out a heavy sigh. "He says he's still in pain, even though Dr. Whitaker says he shouldn't be feeling much more than the normal aches from physical rehabilitation. He's not the kind who will admit when he's hurting, so logic says there has to be something to it. At least, that's what I thought in the beginning. I had a talk with Lloyd, though, and he told me Trey should have weaned himself off painkillers two months ago. Instead, he's taking more and more of them. At this point, it can't be for pain. I think he's just trying to escape."

"Escape from what?"

"Reality. If his rodeo career is over, he has no idea what he'll do with his life. Rodeo was always Plan A. He doesn't have a Plan B."

"What do you want me to do?"

"Talk to him. He'll listen to you. He always has. Your mother and I have been trying to convince him to go to a drug rehab center, but he won't hear of it."

"He's always been a stubborn cuss. He gets that from you."

"So do you. Unlike me and Trey, you allow yourself to see reason from time to time. I know you've made a commitment to Mr. Ivanov. I wouldn't dream of asking you to break it if I could see any other way around it, but—" Laramie could hear her father's control start to break. "I don't want to wake up one morning and find my only son dead of an overdose."

It broke Laramie's heart to hear her father suffering so. She wanted to wrap her arms around him and hold him as he cried, but she could only use words to offer comfort.

"It'll take some time for me to make my way, but I'll be there as soon as I can."

❖

Anastasia had been listening in silence throughout the call between Laramie and her father. She placed a hand on Laramie's slumped shoulders when the call ended.

"What is wrong?"

Laramie turned to her with tears in her eyes. "I have to go home."

Anastasia thought she had another two and a half years before she and Laramie would be forced to have this conversation. She thought she had time to prepare. She had thought wrong.

"For how long?"

"I don't know. For as long as it takes, I guess."

Anastasia wrapped her arms around her knees to hold in the pain of Laramie's impending departure.

"You do not know when you will be back?"

Laramie shook her head. "It's my brother. He needs me."

"I need you, too. We all do."

Anastasia didn't mean to sound petulant or selfish, but they were the only emotions her fractured soul could muster.

Laramie moved closer to her and caressed her cheek.

"I know, but—"

"He is your family and we are not."

Anastasia pulled away, even though what she really wanted to do was hold on and never let go. If Laramie returned home and remembered how much she loved it there, there was a very good chance this was the last time they would ever see each other. There was a very good chance that this good-bye could be for good.

"You're my family, too," Laramie said. "You all are."

"But we are not blood. Blood is thicker than water, yes?"

Laramie frowned. "You're acting like I'm leaving and never coming back."

"Aren't you?"

"Of course not. I'm just taking a leave of absence. I will be back. I promise you that."

"You once told me you never make promises you might not be able to keep. Do not start now."

❖

"Give me a few minutes to pack my bags," Shorty said after Laramie told him the news. "I'm going with you."

"Don't." She stopped him before he could head to the bunkhouse. "I need you to stay and hold down the fort."

"Nah, this'll be a good test to see if Elena and the boys can handle things without either of us around to run interference. I don't want you going through this alone."

"And I don't want anything to undo the progress we've made these past few months. We've worked too hard to let it get mucked up now. Stay here. I won't be alone. I'll be with my family."

"All right then," he said reluctantly. "But if you need me, you just say the word and I'll be on the fastest bird I can find."

"I will."

Shorty's voice softened. "Give Trey my best, won't you? Thad and your mama, too."

"I'll do that."

"How did Anastasia take the news that you're leaving?"

"About as well as you did."

"I'll bet. She's awful sweet on you. I'm sure she's gonna miss you something fierce. Elena and I will do what we can to make sure she doesn't get too down in the dumps while you're gone. You just concentrate on helping Trey get better."

"Thanks, Shorty. I appreciate that."

She grabbed her luggage from her room and set it at her feet before she knocked on Anastasia's door.

Anastasia opened the door just wide enough for her face to show through the crack. Her eyes were red, her face puffy from crying.

"Will you drive me to the train station?" Laramie asked. "I have to get to Moscow. Duke's booked me a flight that leaves from Domodedovo this afternoon. If I leave tonight, it will cut down on a day of traveling."

"Fyodor and Ivan love new truck. I am sure one of them would be happy to drive you."

"Yes, I know they would, but I was hoping I could spend a few more minutes with you, not them."

"You are leaving. A few more minutes together will not change that. Have safe trip."

Laramie continued to stand in the hall long after Anastasia closed the door in her face because she couldn't bring herself to walk away. She had told Anastasia over and over again that she would be back. Why wouldn't Anastasia believe her?

"Come," Elena said gently. "Fyodor is waiting. Do not want to be late for train."

Laramie stumbled down the hall as if in a daze.

"Why is she being this way?"

"She is feeling abandoned. First by me. Now by you."

"What should I say? What should I do?"

Elena cupped her face in her hands.

"Keep promise. Come back."

CHAPTER TWENTY-SEVEN

Chuck and Grant met Laramie at the airport in Cheyenne. They greeted her with handshakes and one-armed hugs.

"It's good to see you," Chuck said, "though I'm sorry it's under these circumstances."

"Me, too."

"How's the old man doing?" Grant asked.

"Better than you might think."

She pulled out her phone and showed them a couple of pictures of Shorty dancing with Elena while Andrei played the balalaika.

"Well, look at that," Grant said with a laugh. "He always did like the tall ones."

"Compared to him," Chuck said, "they're *all* tall ones."

"Do you want us to take you to the ranch first or head straight to your brother's place?" Grant asked after they grabbed her bags from the luggage carousel and headed to the truck.

"I haven't laid eyes on my parents in months. I want to see how they're doing before I check on Trey."

"You got it."

Laramie smiled to herself as Chuck and Grant fought over who would get to drive during the ride back to the ranch. Their bickering over the keys reminded her of Fyodor and Ivan having a similar argument. The language was different, but the argument was the same.

"What's so funny?" Chuck asked as she tossed her suitcase and saddle in the back of the double cab truck.

"It's good to know some things never change."

She couldn't say the same for her parents, however. Both seemed to have aged exponentially since the last time she had seen them. Trey's injury and rocky recovery had obviously taken a serious toll on both of them.

"Russia must be treating you good." Her father pointed at her stomach. "Too much vodka?"

"Too much food, more like. Elena, the ranch cook, doesn't believe in portion control. If you think my belly's big, you should see Shorty's. By this time next year, he won't need padding to dress up like Santa Claus."

"A couple of extra pounds never hurt anyone." Her mother patted her father's rounded stomach. "Right, Thad?"

"You know what winter's like around here. I need the extra insulation."

"Uh-huh."

Laramie was happy they were able to share a laugh, even if just for a little while. The way her father had sounded when he called to ask her to return home, lighthearted moments like this one had been few and far between.

"It is so good to have you home," her mother said, giving her a crushing hug. "Your room is the same as you left it."

Everything else was, too. Laramie sighed as she took in all the familiar sights, smells, and sounds. She was back in Wyoming. She was back in Broken Branch. She was home.

❖

Laramie's request to drive her to the train station had touched Anastasia deeply, but it hadn't convinced her to change her mind. Saying good-bye to Laramie one-on-one was hard enough. There was no way she would have been able to stand on a crowded train platform and hold in her roiling emotions as she watched Laramie's train slowly pull away.

She had looked out her bedroom window as Fyodor drove Laramie to the station in her stead. Drove her out of her life. Laramie had told her that she would come back one day, but Anastasia hadn't been able to allow her tortured heart to believe the words.

If Laramie didn't take her saddle with her, she had told herself, that would offer the sign she needed that Laramie truly meant to return to Godoroye one day. That she meant to return to her.

Her eyes, already sore from crying, had filled with fresh tears when she saw the saddle resting next to Laramie's suitcase in the bed of the truck.

That was three days ago. Anastasia had finally managed to stop crying, but she didn't feel any better. Laramie had texted her constantly while she made her way from Godoroye to Moscow, then from Moscow to Chicago, but Anastasia hadn't heard from her since Laramie's connecting flight from Chicago was supposed to land in Cheyenne. Had something happened to her, or was she too busy reconnecting with everyone she loved to reach out to those she had left behind?

Mischa tried to make her feel better by keeping up a constant stream of conversation, but seeing him so blissfully happy about his burgeoning relationship with Pavel made her resent his efforts. She didn't want to end up resenting him, too, so she decided to keep her distance.

When she wasn't working, she began to spend more and more time alone, seeking solace in the book of poetry Vladimir had given her. She returned to her favorite poem time and time again, reliving the moments she and Laramie had shared. Moments they might never share again.

She returned the book to Vladimir when continuing to read it proved to be unbearable.

"Was it worth it?" he asked.

"What?"

He fixed her with a smile that was both warm and sincere. "Loving her."

"Yes, it was," she said, trying not to cry. She might not know who her "real" father was, but in Vladimir and Shorty, she had two father figures she could count on whenever she needed them. "One day, I hope to feel that way again."

"You will."

Would it be with someone else, or would it be with Laramie?

CHAPTER TWENTY-EIGHT

The first time Laramie visited her brother, Trey didn't want to talk. No, that wasn't exactly true. He wanted to talk about everything except what truly mattered.

As she tossed the empty cartons of pepperoni pizza he had been living off of for the past month or so, she heard all about his adventures on the rodeo circuit, the women he had met along the way, and the pretty nurses who had tended to him while he was laid up in the hospital.

She had heard most of the stories so many times she could probably recite them just as well as Trey could. She let him tell them, though, so they could avoid the awkward silence that was sure to follow when it was her turn to speak.

"I know why you're here," he said when he finally ran out of things to say. "Mama and Dad think I need help, and you're the one they're counting on to make me see the light. Does that about sum it up?"

Laramie polished a decorative belt buckle that had begun to show a bit of tarnish. "If you have all the answers, what do you need me for?"

"I don't. I've got everything I need right here."

He held up a can of beer in one hand and a bottle of pills in the other. A set of crutches lay on the floor next to his lounge chair. Though his broken bones had healed, they weren't quite strong enough to bear his weight without additional support. He preferred to remain locked in his apartment rather than allow his friends and neighbors to see him at less than one hundred percent, which explained the string of food delivery people beating a path to his door.

"It figures they'd call you," Trey said after he took another sip of his beer. "You've always been the one they could count on, not me."

"Why are you selling yourself short? You can still turn this around."

"Have you taken a good look at me since you've been home?" His once-bulging biceps had lost some of their definition and the sweatpants he was wearing sagged against the emaciated muscles in his legs. "How do you expect me to turn this around?"

"You can stop using the crutches on the side table and start using the ones on the floor."

He popped a pill and downed it with a sip of beer. "These taste better than the ones on the floor."

"When was the last time you left this apartment? When was the last time you moved out of that chair?"

Trey rolled his eyes. "If you're trying to go the tough love route, forget it. Dad already tried that tactic. Mama, too. What makes you think you can accomplish something they can't?"

"I don't."

Trey's head whipped around so fast Laramie was surprised he didn't pull a muscle.

"You mean you're giving up on me, too?"

"You've already given up on yourself. Why shouldn't I follow suit?"

"Because—"

Trey faltered. Like Laramie and their father, he had a hard time expressing his feelings, but she needed him to find a way to do so now. They both did.

"Because you're the only one who's always believed in me. Even when I thought I couldn't do something, you're the one who always convinced me I could. When it sometimes felt like I was chasing a pipe dream, you're the one who made me believe the win I was looking for was just one rodeo away. Even if you didn't believe it half the time, you made me think you did, and that was all that mattered. If you give up on me, too, then I know I'm truly done for."

"Would I be here sitting in front of you right now if I didn't believe in you? If I didn't think you could pull yourself out of the hole you're in and become, perhaps not the man you once were but the one you're meant to be?"

"You think I don't want that?" Trey looked away so she couldn't see the tears welling in his eyes. When he spoke again, his voice was choked with emotion. "I think about it all the time and it kills me that I'm not strong enough to make it happen. That I'm not big enough to resist the lure of something so small."

He picked up the bottle of pills and hurled them against the wall. The supposedly childproof cap popped off from the force of the impact. The pills inside scattered all over the hardwood floor.

"Flush them," Trey said bitterly. "If you don't, I'll be crawling over there on my hands and knees after you leave, sucking them up like I'm some kind of goddamned vacuum cleaner."

Laramie swept the pills into a dustpan and dropped them in the toilet. She pulled the lever twice to make sure no trace of them remained.

"What's next?" he asked.

"Now you get clean."

He rubbed his scraggly beard. "I take it you don't mean a shave and a shower."

"There are several rehab centers in Cheyenne. If I can get you into one of them, will you go? They have both short- and long-term treatment options. You can stay for one month or up to four. It's up to you."

"How am I supposed to pay for it? My insurance is maxed out as it is."

"You let me worry about that."

"How much is that Russian guy paying you, anyway?"

"You let me worry about that, too. Let me call a few places and see if they have any openings."

She got up to retrieve her phone from its perch on the kitchen counter. He grabbed her hand before she could make it more than two steps.

"I can't do this without you, Laramie."

"You won't have to. I'll be with you every step of the way. When you're done, maybe I'll make a rancher out of you yet."

Trey grinned. "Did Dad pay you to say that?"

"He didn't have to. Some things are priceless. Having a chance to help you continue what Dad started is one of them."

❖

Laramie had been gone for close to two months when Shorty received a phone call from her. When the call ended, he whooped loudly and tossed his hat high in the air.

"Either you have received good news or you have lost mind," Elena said after Shorty kissed her cheek. Based on the sounds Anastasia heard emanating from Elena's room at night, Shorty's lips had been visiting more intimate places as well. "Which is correct?"

"Trey finally got out of drug rehab," Shorty said, spinning her around. "After Thad shows him how to be a real cowboy again, he's gonna start working on the ranch."

"I am glad to hear he is doing better," Anastasia said. "Why did Laramie not call me?"

"She said you didn't respond to any of her texts. I reckon she thought you didn't want to hear from her."

"Did you tell her that is not the case?"

"It ain't my place to go sticking my nose in other people's business." He slipped his arm around Elena's waist. "Besides, I'm too busy working on my own relationship to worry about someone else's. If you want Laramie to know how you feel about her, put your big girl panties on and tell her yourself."

Anastasia felt like kicking herself for not exhibiting some of the maturity Mischa had prematurely given her credit for. She hoped it wasn't too late for her to redeem herself for her mistake.

She headed up to the office, where Mischa was logging new invoices into the computer. She grabbed a few permanent markers off the desk.

"Thanks for these," she said as she turned to leave.

"What are you up to?"

"You're not the only person who has work to do around here."

CHAPTER TWENTY-NINE

The second time Laramie landed in Domodedovo Moscow Airport wasn't nearly as disconcerting as her first. As she made her way from the terminal to the luggage carousel, the signs leading the way seemed familiar instead of foreign. When she had called Duke to let him know what time her flight was scheduled to arrive, he had said someone would be waiting to take her to her hotel. He had booked one for her to stay in overnight before she flew to Bryansk the next day. She had tried to tell him she didn't mind taking the train to Bryansk tonight, but he had insisted he wanted her to be refreshed when she finally returned to work, and a long trip on a crowded train after two days of even longer flights wasn't the best way to go about it. Too tired to complain, she had let him have his way.

She plucked her suitcase and saddle off the luggage carousel and headed to the ground transportation area so she could meet up with her driver. As she waded through a sea of representatives from various tour groups holding up signs with their companies' names printed on them in a variety of languages, she spotted a hand-written sign with her name inscribed on it in English only.

The driver was dressed in a black chauffeur's uniform, complete with matching cap. The cap was pulled low, obscuring most of the driver's features.

"I'm Laramie Bowman."

When the driver looked up, Laramie found herself staring into Anastasia's distinctive blue eyes.

"You're my driver?"

Instead of responding, Anastasia held up the sign in her hands. As she looked closer, Laramie noticed Anastasia was holding not just one sign but several.

Anastasia placed the first sign behind the others.

Welcome back, the second sign read.

"Thank you."

Anastasia placed a finger over her lips, effectively shushing her.

"Oh, so that's how you want to play it? Okay, what else you got?"

I am sorry for the way I reacted when you left, the third sign said.

When Laramie nodded to let Anastasia know she had finished reading what she had written, Anastasia moved the sign so she could read the next one.

But I thought I would lose you and did not know how to react.

Laramie had felt the same way. As she made her way back to Russia, she hadn't been certain what she was making her way back to. Being greeted by Anastasia's smiling face gave her hope that the journey hadn't been in vain.

A few months ago, the fifth sign read, *Mischa told me I have grown up. While you were gone, I realized how much growing up I still have to do.*

Laramie had realized something, too: that family wasn't a matter of biology. Family was a matter of the heart. Anastasia and all the people she had met in Godoroye each had a place in hers.

I love you, the final sign read. *Please forgive me.*

"Is it my turn now?" she asked when Anastasia finally lowered her bundle of signs.

Anastasia nodded, and Laramie stepped toward her.

"I only have two things to say."

She pushed the brim of Anastasia's cap up so she could get a better look at her face. The last time they had seen each other, Anastasia's eyes were filled with tears. Today, they were filled with something else: hope.

"First of all, I love you, too."

Unconcerned about who might be looking on or what they might think, Laramie kissed her long and hard.

"What is second thing?" Anastasia asked after they finally came up for air.

"My brother's taking the reins back in Broken Branch, which means I'm free to accept the ranch manager job Duke offered me. We might have to fight Elena and Shorty for it, but I thought we could move into Yevgeny's old room. Spruce it up some and—"

Anastasia's eyes widened. "Does that mean you are staying?"

"If you'll have me."

Anastasia dropped the signs and jumped into her arms. This time, Laramie didn't intend to let go.

"You're gonna get us arrested," she said as Anastasia peppered her face with kisses.

"For me, would not be first time. I will show you ropes, yes?"

"I'm still waiting for that lesson you promised me back in Godoroye."

"Did you bring it?" Anastasia asked with a smile.

Laramie slowly lowered her to the ground. "I might've."

Anastasia reached for her hand. "In that case, let's go home."

About the Author

Yolanda Wallace is not a professional writer, but she plays one in her spare time. Her love of travel and adventure has helped her pen numerous globe-spanning novels, including the Lambda Award-winning *Month of Sundays* and *Tailor-Made*. Her short stories have appeared in multiple anthologies including *Romantic Interludes 2: Secrets* and *Women of the Dark Streets*. She and her wife live in beautiful coastal Georgia, where they are parents to two children of the four-legged variety.

Books Available from Bold Strokes Books

Comrade Cowgirl by Yolanda Wallace. When cattle rancher Laramie Bowman accepts a lucrative job offer far from home, will her heart end up getting lost in translation? (978-1-63555-375-8)

Double Vision by Ellie Hart. When her cell phone rings, Giselle Cutler answers it—and finds herself speaking to a dead woman. (978-1-63555-385-7)

Inheritors of Chaos by Barbara Ann Wright. As factions splinter and reunite, will anyone survive the final showdown between gods and mortals on an alien world? (978-1-63555-294-2)

Love on Lavender Lane by Karis Walsh. Accompanied by the buzz of honeybees and the scent of lavender, Paige and Kassidy must find a way to compromise on their approach to business if they want to save Lavender Lane Farm—and find a way to make room for love along the way. (978-1-63555-286-7)

Spinning Tales by Brey Willows. When the fairy tale begins to unravel and villains are on the loose, will Maggie and Kody be able to spin a new tale? (978-1-63555-314-7)

The Do-Over by Georgia Beers. Bella Hunt has made a good life for herself and put the past behind her. But when the bane of her high school existence shows up for Bella's class on conflict resolution, the last thing they expect is to fall in love. (978-1-63555-393-2)

What Happens When by Samantha Boyette. For Molly Kennan, senior year is already an epic disaster, and falling for mysterious waitress Zia is about to make life a whole lot worse. (978-1-63555-408-3)

Wooing the Farmer by Jenny Frame. When fiercely independent modern socialite Penelope Huntingdon-Stewart and traditional country farmer Sam McQuade meet, trusting their hearts is harder than it looks. (978-1-63555-381-9)

A Chapter on Love by Laney Webber. When Jannika and Lee reunite, their instant connection feels like a gift, but neither is ready for a second chance at love. Will they finally get on the same page when it comes to love? (978-1-63555-366-6)

Drawing Down the Mist by Sheri Lewis Wohl. Everyone thinks Grand Duchess Maria Romanova died in 1918. They were almost right. (978-1-63555-341-3)

Listen by Kris Bryant. Lily Croft is inexplicably drawn to Hope D'Marco but will she have the courage to confront the consequences of her past and present colliding? (978-1-63555-318-5)

Perfect Partners by Maggie Cummings. Elite police dog trainer Sara Wright has no intention of falling in love with a coworker, until Isabel Marquez arrives at Homeland Security's Northeast Regional Training facility and Sara's good intentions start to falter. (978-1-63555-363-5)

Shut Up and Kiss Me by Julie Cannon. What better way to spend two weeks of hell in paradise than in the company of a hot, sexy woman? (978-1-63555-343-7)

Spencer's Cove by Missouri Vaun. When Foster Owen and Abigail Spencer meet they uncover a story of lives adrift, loves lost, and true love found. (978-1-63555-171-6)

Without Pretense by TJ Thomas. After living for decades hiding from the truth, can Ava learn to trust Bianca with her secrets and her heart? (978-1-63555-173-0)

Unexpected Lightning by Cass Sellars. Lightning strikes once more when Sydney and Parker fight a dangerous stranger who threatens the peace they both desperately want. (978-1-163555-276-8)

Emily's Art and Soul by Joy Argento. When Emily meets Andi Marino she thinks she's found a new best friend but Emily doesn't know that Andi is fast falling in love with her. Caught up in exploring her sexuality, will Emily see the only woman she needs is right in front of her? (978-1-63555-355-0)

Escape to Pleasure: Lesbian Travel Erotica edited by Sandy Lowe and Victoria Villasenor. Join these award-winning authors as they explore the sensual side of erotic lesbian travel. (978-1-63555-339-0)

Music City Dreamers by Robyn Nyx. Music can bring lovers together. In Music City, it can tear them apart. (978-1-63555-207-2)

Ordinary is Perfect by D. Jackson Leigh. Atlanta marketing superstar Autumn Swan's life derails when she inherits a country home, a child, and a very interesting neighbor. (978-1-63555-280-5)

Royal Court by Jenny Frame. When royal dresser Holly Weaver's passionate personality begins to melt Royal Marine Captain Quincy's icy heart, will Holly be ready for what she exposes beneath? (978-1-63555-290-4)

Strings Attached by Holly Stratimore. Success. Riches. Music. Passion. It's a life most can only dream of, but stardom comes at a cost. (978-1-63555-347-5)

The Ashford Place by Jean Copeland. When Isabelle Ashford inherits an old house in small-town Connecticut, family secrets, a shocking discovery, and an unexpected romance complicate her plan for a fast profit and a temporary stay. (978-1-63555-316-1)

Treason by Gun Brooke. Zoem Malderyn's existence is a deadly threat to everyone on Gemocon and Commander Neenja KahSandra must find a way to save the woman she loves from having to commit the ultimate sacrifice. (978-1-63555-244-7)

A Wish Upon a Star by Jeannie Levig. Erica Cooper has learned to depend on only herself, but when her new neighbor, Leslie Raymond, befriends Erica's special needs daughter, the walls protecting her heart threaten to crumble. (978-1-63555-274-4)

Answering the Call by Ali Vali. Detective Sept Savoie returns to the streets of New Orleans, as do the dead bodies from ritualistic killings, and she does everything in her power to bring them to justice while trying to keep her partner, Keegan Blanchard, safe. (978-1-63555-050-4)

Breaking Down Her Walls by Erin Zak. Could a love worth staying for be the key to breaking down Julia Finch's walls? (978-1-63555-369-7)

Exit Plans for Teenage Freaks by 'Nathan Burgoine. Cole always has a plan—especially for escaping his small-town reputation as "that kid who was kidnapped when he was four"—but when he teleports to a museum, it's time to face facts: it's possible he's a total freak after all. (978-1-63555-098-6)

Friends Without Benefits by Dena Blake. When Dex Putman gets the woman she thought she always wanted, she soon wonders if it's really love after all. (978-1-63555-349-9)

Invalid Evidence by Stevie Mikayne. Private Investigator Jil Kidd is called away to investigate a possible killer whale, just when her partner Jess needs her most. (978-1-63555-307-9)

Pursuit of Happiness by Carsen Taite. When attorney Stevie Palmer's client reveals a scandal that could derail Senator Meredith Mitchell's presidential bid, their chance at love may be collateral damage. (978-1-63555-044-3)

Seascape by Karis Walsh. Marine biologist Tess Hansen returns to Washington's isolated northern coast where she struggles to adjust to small-town living while courting an endowment for her orca research center from Brittany James. (978-1-63555-079-5)

Second in Command by VK Powell. Jazz Perry's life is disrupted and her career jeopardized when she becomes personally involved with the case of an abandoned child and the child's competent but strict social worker, Emory Blake. (978-1-63555-185-3)

Taking Chances by Erin McKenzie. When Valerie Cruz and Paige Wellington clash over what's in the best interest of the children in Valerie's care, the children may be the ones who teach them it's worth taking chances for love. (978-1-63555-209-6)

All of Me by Emily Smith. When chief surgical resident Galen Burgess meets her new intern, Rowan Duncan, she may finally discover that doing what you've always done will only give you what you've always had. (978-1-63555-321-5)

As the Crow Flies by Karen F. Williams. Romance seems to be blooming all around, but problems arise when a restless ghost emerges from the ether to roam the dark corners of this haunting tale. (978-1-63555-285-0)

Both Ways by Ileandra Young. SPEAR agent Danika Karson races to protect the city from a supernatural threat and must rely on the woman she's trained to despise: Rayne, an achingly beautiful vampire. (978-1-63555-298-0)

Calendar Girl by Georgia Beers. Forced to work together, Addison Fairchild and Kate Cooper discover that opposites really do attract. (978-1-63555-333-8)

Lovebirds by Lisa Moreau. Two women from different worlds collide in a small California mountain town, each with a mission that doesn't include falling in love. (978-1-63555-213-3)

Media Darling by Fiona Riley. Can Hollywood bad girl Emerson and reluctant celebrity gossip reporter Hayley work together to make each other's dreams come true? Or will Emerson's secrets ruin not one career, but two? (978-1-63555-278-2)

Stroke of Fate by Renee Roman. Can Sean Moore live up to her reputation and save Jade Rivers from the stalker determined to end Jade's career and, ultimately, her life? (978-1-63555-62-4)

The Rise of the Resistance by Jackie D. The soul of America has been lost for almost a century. A few people may be the difference between a phoenix rising to save the masses or permanent destruction. (978-1-63555-259-1)

The Sex Therapist Next Door by Meghan O'Brien. At the intersection of sex and intimacy, anything is possible. Even love. (978-1-63555-296-6)

Unforgettable by Elle Spencer. When one night changes a lifetime… Two romance novellas from best-selling author Elle Spencer. (978-1-63555-429-8)

CPSIA information can be obtained
at www.ICGtesting.com
Printed in the USA
LVHW090111200420
654092LV00005B/1122